PETER TURNBULL

THE MAN WITH NO FACE

HarperCollinsPublishers

HarperCollins*Publishers*
77–85 Fulham Palace Road,
Hammersmith, London W6 8JB

The HarperCollins website address is:
www.**fire**and**water**.com

This paperback edition 1999
1 3 5 7 9 8 6 4 2

First published in Great Britain by
HarperCollins*Publishers* 1998

Copyright © Peter Turnbull 1998

Peter Turnbull asserts the moral right to
be identified as the author of this work

ISBN 0 00 651128 7

Set in Meridien and Bodoni

Printed and bound in Great Britain by
Caledonian International Book Manufacturing Ltd, Glasgow

MONDAY

1

___

Spring forward, fall back.

It was that time of year. The time of daylight saving. For many years he couldn't remember whether the clocks went back one hour or forwards one hour each autumn and whether they went back one hour or forwards one hour each spring. He never could remember which, and was often insufficiently alert to be receptive to publicity about the matter which was in his opinion, modest and discreet in the extreme. So that looking back over his life, he could recall times when he had strolled into his place of work anticipating the first leisurely cup of tea, only to be told icily that he was an hour late. Equally, on other occasions he had travelled to work, startled by the lack of traffic on the road and wondering if the rest of Glasgow and Scotland and the United Kingdom of Great Britain and Northern Ireland knew something that he didn't: which in a sense it did. Then one March, close to the spring change, he was in the company of a woman he didn't care for but had to work with and they, for want of conversation, talked about the clocks changing twice a year, and he volunteered that he often forgot about the change and had to catch up or slow down to get back in step with the rest of the population on the right little, tight little island, and also couldn't remember which way they went when. The woman then offered that should he steel himself and accept the Americanism of 'fall' for 'autumn', he could perhaps then employ the mnemonic of 'spring forward, fall back' to assist him, at least, to remember which way they went. It had been, he had to concede, a useful aid to his memory, except that this autumn he didn't need it. This blustery October on the cusp of the millennium it had been his great misfortune to have

3

been on the night shift, which began at 22.00 hours, and then, two hours later at midnight, a fresh-faced constable dutifully went round the building at midnight or thereabouts, turning all clocks back to 23.00, or thereabouts. It was not having to work the additional hour that the man begrudged, because in fairness he had in preceding years worked the night shift in the spring when the clocks had 'sprung forwards' and he had been able to get home one hour early. What piqued him about this particular 'fall back' was that he was at his desk, feet up, hat pulled over his eyes, sliding gently towards 06.00 hours, and 'lowsing time' which was really, his body was telling him, 07.00 hours, when at 05.15, which was really 06.15, the phone on his desk rang. He hesitated a moment, vainly attempting to dream the sound away and then reluctantly picked up the phone. 'CID,' he yawned, 'DS Sussock.'

'Control, sir.' The female voice was to Sussock's mind astoundingly crisp even at this ungodly hour.

'Yes?'

'Papa Tango Foxtrot request CID attendance, code four-one.'

'Murder?'

'Code four-one, sir.'

Sussock glanced at his watch. He hadn't adjusted it. It read 06.15. The morning shift should be here, he thought, bustling about with first editions of the *Glasgow Herald* and the *Scotsman* and the *Daily Record*, full of energy and beans, ready to do the handover, but they're not, because the clock on the wall, a silent digital thing with glowing green figures on a black background, said 05.15 because the junior constable had changed it five and a quarter hours ago. No, he hadn't, he'd changed it six and a quarter hours ago, and he'd made this call come in on this shift, not on the next shift, because . . . Sussock groped for his ballpoint and notepad . . . and anyway, outside it was dark and it was raining and the rule of the game is like the TV quiz show . . . you start, so you finish . . . and he wanted to say, but it's really 06.15 and he should be climbing into his car to drive home, not climbing into his car to drive to a locus someplace . . . but . . . He suddenly wondered if people had been executed on the morning after the clocks had gone back or forwards? Had the gaolers on death watch in the condemned cell ever stopped playing monopoly with the condemned man or woman for a few seconds while they put their watches back to 23.00? Or forwards to 01.00? He pulled the top of his ballpoint off with his teeth and, trapping the phone between his head and shoulder, said 'OK . . . go ahead.'

'Locus is Winton Drive, sir. Glasgow twelve. One male deceased . . . apparent cause of death is gunshot wound to the head. Papa Tango Foxtrot in attendance. Police surgeon also requested to attend.'

'Very good. I'm on my way.'

'Thank you, sir.'

Sussock replaced the phone with a gentleness which surprised him because his urge was to slam the thing down so hard that it might break.

He stood and reached for his coat and as he did so he caught sight of his reflection in the glass, mirrored by the lights of Charing Cross and Sauchiehall Street beyond. He saw a lean, angular face, lantern-jawed, deeply creased with age and worry. He turned from the reflection and slid his coat on. It was a battered cream-coloured raincoat, grimy and streaked. It hung from his shoulders like a sack. It was too light for the coming winter and sufficiently old to warrant it being offered to one of the charity shops in Byres Road, along with his trousers which shone with age. His shoes too were low-cut summer shoes, scuffed and scratched. Soon, soon, he would have to take a trip out to Rutherglen, something to prepare himself for, to play the scene in his head and then act it, frame by frame, line by line, as if on automatic pilot. He tugged on his misshaped felt trilby and grabbed his notepad and mobile phone. He left his office and entered the CID corridor, descended the stairs to the ground floor of the building and noted with a certain envy and resentment that the early, and keen, arrivals of the uniformed offices were beginning to trickle into the building to commence their day shift. He signed 'out' at the uniform bar and left the building by the rear 'staff only' exit. The sudden blast of cold air pressed his lungs with a stabbing pain, being, he had found, the legacy of a lifetime as a cigarette smoker; inhaling, high tar, no filter. The drizzle and the fresh air did, however, invigorate him, waking him up and he sensed himself clutching his second wind. He clambered into his ancient Ford which had a reputation of being a poor starter in the wet. On that morning it started on the button. Sussock thought that it just *had* to. On this day, this one occasion when he found himself clutching at unclutchable straws, this one day when just forty-five minutes separated him from being able to hand over the call to DC Abernethy on the day shift, an unstartable car might just swing it . . . less than forty-five minutes now . . . a code four-one, a murder . . . the body's not going anywhere . . . and dawn's coming up . . . and he felt there to be a thin line across his eyes from pupil to pupil . . . damp points, a flat battery . . . anything . . . but all he was greeted with was a healthy roar at the turn of a silver key. All he needed to complete the image was the gold-capped smile of the second-hand car salesman saying, 'Lovely, sir, does that every time . . . hadn't had a better motor in all year . . .' Sussock left the car park at the rear of P Division Police Station at Charing Cross and turned left, up to St George's Cross, noting the lights in the tenements in the distant high-rises burning in great numbers as the city awoke, and noting the increased volume of traffic on the M8 below him. He couldn't see the traffic from St George's Road but he read the reflection of the headlights and the concrete bridges and read the frequency of the hiss of tyre on wet tarmac and the roar of diesel and noted the onset of rush hour. He turned left at St George's and on to the Great Western Road which drove arrow-straight westwards out of the city, driving between a canyon of red sandstone tenements, early buses, postmen, milk floats, a few cars nosing towards the city. Only his car driving westwards, away from Glasgow. And this, he reflected, was the fabled 'road to the Isles', at least the beginning of it. Start at St George's Cross, G20, and walk westwards and you'll end up in the Hebrides, after catching a ferry or two, by Oban way. Not a bad road to travel to a murder.

Sussock drove over the hump from Kelvinbridge and down the far side towards the traffic lights at Byres Road. He halted at the red light and cast his eye over the curved windows of the hothouses of the botanical gardens to his right, and then to the graceful lines of the Grosvenor Hotel to his left, the concourse-facing bricks of which had been moulded from casts taken from the eighteenth-century terrace which it adjoined so as to continue the Regency style of the terrace, and was in all, at that moment, still floodlit, most pleasing to Sussock's eye. He drove along Great Western Road, edging into the crown of the four-lane carriageway and turned right at the next set of lights by the twee green garden hut post office that had, in his observation, become as much of a landmark in the cityscape as George Square or the Finneston Crane. A left turn by a suburban area of stone-built villas with generous gardens, and he followed the road round, with the tall angular University Halls of Residence to his left, turned up the hill and saw ahead of him, work, gainful employment – two blue, silently lapping lights atop a white car: a beacon he did not want to go towards.

Sussock pulled up behind the area car, got out of his car and gathered his coat collar about his neck against the drizzle. A uniformed constable approached him. Beyond the area car Sussock noted a second car, and beyond that a black, windowless van.

'What have we got?' Sussock glanced at the locus. On one side of the gradient that was Winton Drive was a row of low-rise maisonettes, giving way at the crest of the hill to more large, stone-built villas. To his left, opposite the maisonettes, was a large expanse of grass, plunged in darkness, two blue-and-white tapes on poles parallel to each other and at ninety degrees to the road.

'Deceased male,' PC Hamilton replied crisply, nodding in the direction of the tapes and the darkness. 'Anonymous caller.'

'Deceased?'

'Deceased. Dr Chan's at the body now, sir. But pronunciation of death is a formality in this case, I'd say.'

'Oh?'

'Well, his face has been blown off.'

'Blown off?'

'Gunshot injury.'

'Dr Chan said that?' Sussock glanced at the maisonettes, many faces appeared at the windows, discreetly, not bothered about being seen, standing about one foot from the pane of glass, not prying, not eager to ogle, just understandably curious. This was G12: professional, middle-class Glasgow, people here behaved with a certain restraint, so observed DS Raymond Sussock.

'Not exactly.'

'You mean you said it?'

'Well, yes, sir. I just did an in-service firearms course – that is, injuries and emergency treatment thereof rather than using the things.'

'Hence your expert assessment . . .' Sussock glanced towards the tape and the darkness and made out a figure approaching him in the cracking dawn light. 'Well, we'll see if you're right. Good morning, Dr Chan.'

The figure revealed itself to be a slightly built man of Oriental extraction, with dark hair, spectacles, white coat and black bag. He smiled and nodded. 'Good morning, Mr . . . ?'

'Sussock. Detective Sergeant, P Division.'

'Chan, police surgeon.'

'We have met.'

'I'm sure . . . but so many police officers . . .'

'Of course.'

'Well, he is deceased, life extinct, pronunciation of same being a formality in this case. I'd say death was instantaneous. He was shot in the back of the head, there's a small hole at the base of the skull and not much left of his face. I'd say that that probably had something to do with his death.'

'It sounds like it ought to.'

'No, I'm quite serious, Sergeant. He may already have been deceased when he sustained the injury, but I don't think so. I am the police surgeon, he is dead, and the time is six-forty a.m. . . .'

'No, five-forty,' Sussock replied icily, scribbling in his notepad. 'Thanks, Doctor.'

'I'd like to stay to speak with the pathologist, but I have another call to make, another suspicious death, this time in Partick, Mansfield Street. Do you know where that is?'

'I don't, I confess.' Sussock's eyes became adjusted to the gloom and he began to make out a mound on the grass.

'No matter, I have a street atlas.' Dr Chan walked away and got into the car which was parked between the dark, windowless van and the area car. He drove away, to Partick, Mansfield Street, G11. Sussock walked between the lines of tape and stopped short of the deceased, who lay, his head on one side, about thirty feet from the roadway.

So far as Sussock could tell, the body had in life been a dark-haired male of slight build. Very slight build. Sussock's eyes were drawn irresistibly to the injury: the small hole at the back of the skull was barely discernible; easily discernible was the crater where the man's face had been. Sussock, standing over the corpse, could see both the entrance and the exit wounds, the head of the deceased being turned to one side. Frankly, it came as a surprise to him that a bullet could make such a mess, and he found himself understanding the argument that far from being too violent, television is not violent enough. Television portrays people who have been shot as laying as still and unruffled as if they were sleeping, but it's not like that, it's like this, ordinary people – small, frail looking, who wouldn't pass a screen test, and they don't lay as if sleeping, no one lays on damp autumnal grass and goes to sleep, and they are not unruffled, it's like this – all the bits that made up the man in life are still there, except the brain. That bit was blown out, forced out of a big hole caused when his face exploded outwards with the bullet sucking the brain out after it. That's what it's like. Bang, you're dead. Not like on television, no one's going to yell at this guy and say, 'One more time with feeling, luvvie.' Not this guy, he's out of time and out of feeling. Bang, you're dead. OK, that's a wrap. And the smell, the smell of death, even out here in the crisp autumnal morning air, the man smelled of death, a musty smell a little like rotting leaves, it's pernicious, insidious. It gets in your clothing and stays in your nostrils, right at the bridge of your nose.

Bang, you're dead. But not the way the children play the game.

Bang, you're dead. Four hundred miles an hour; in and out again in one-tenth of a second.

That's a wrap. Pray for us now and at the hour of our death.

Sussock drew his eyes from the man's head and pondered the clothing. He was, thought Sussock, poorly clad for the time of year: a grey jacket, grey trousers, white ankle socks and black shoes. A prison discharge suit if ever Sussock saw one. So this guy, just out of the slammer after a fair stretch,

9

at least five years to get a discharge suit like that, out for only a matter of hours because everybody but everybody knows what *that* suit means and so the lags get shot of it within a day or two of being released. A few borrowed pounds will get you top to toe in old denim, a few second-hand shirts in red or blue, a pair of worn Nikes, and then only a cop will figure you for a lag, and only then if he knows you.

So dead man is breathing free air for a day or two and then he has his brains blown out.

Sussock turned and walked back towards where Hamilton and Wanless waited. He looked at Hamilton and nodded. 'I see what you mean, but the police surgeon's point is valid, you know. You heard him, I think?'

'He could have been dead before he was shot?'

'Yes, this is one for the pathologist. Wanless . . .'

'Sarge?'

'Erect a screen around the deceased, the view will distress the citizenry once the dawn breaks, it's almost dawn now. Hamilton . . .'

'Sarge?'

'Get on the radio, please, we need more uniformed officers here. We'll have to sweep this expanse of grass at first light. And request further CID assistance. Abernethy will be coming on duty about now – I'd like his presence here, help me with the door-to-door. That'll take me up until lunchtime, I should think. Oh, and the pathologist as well. If you please.'

'Very good, Sarge.'

Sussock surveyed the maisonettes, lights burning at most, faces in the window of many. He shook his head to attempt to invigorate himself and walked across the street.

It was as if she was awake before she knew that she was moving, but feigned stirring in her sleep rather than betray the jolt into wakefulness that the first ring of the muffled bell of the phone at her husband's bedside had caused. She kept her eyes closed but listened intently as her husband said, 'Yes . . . yes . . . Winton Drive, G12 . . . I know it . . . One adult male . . . Right, I'm on my way.' He slid the phone gently on to the rest and slipped out of the bedroom, gathering clothing as he went, in order to dress in the bathroom so as not to disturb his wife. Once he was out of the room and had closed the door behind him with a gentle click, Janet Reynolds rolled on to her back, stretched and yawned, and only then did she glance at the luminous dial of the radio alarm clock and saw with no small measure of disappointment that it was already six a.m. or thereabouts, the clocks in the house having been reset the previous night, and that the curtain left open at the extreme left-hand pane of the bay window revealed the cold, grey cracking of dawn.

She felt cheated.

Once she used to feel cheated of sleep: now she felt cheated of consciousness.

Once she was so upset by her insomnia that she used to knock herself out with alcohol, or pills. Or both. Just so she could be in a state of sleep for eight hours every twenty-four, just like the rest of the world's population, just like 'normal' people. Then when a young adult, possibly still a teenager, she couldn't remember exactly when, it occurred to her that if she didn't need eight hours' sleep, she didn't need it. She realized that her insomnia was in a sense extending her life, not by years lived, but by measurably increasing the hours of a consciousness available to her to use, or abuse, as she thought fit. She had chosen to use them, she had stopped drinking to excess and had thrown herself into her studies while having the time and energy left to enjoy a full social life. She had entered university where she had met her wonderful, wonderful husband. She had had children and often felt she could not have got through the early years of noise and night-time feeds and demands for attention if she had not had the two or three hours of peace and tranquillity to herself in the wee small hours. In short, she had seen herself not as being cursed by insomnia, but as being privileged to be an insomniac. Now the children were older she had used her extra time to consume novels and to learn languages, and often it was her husband's receipt of a phone call to summon him to a dreadful incident that woke her. No matter, it seemed, what time the call was received, she would require no more sleep once she was awake, one a.m., two, three . . . it didn't matter, and now she had come to enjoy an earlier rather than later call, though she felt deeply for her husband having to leave home in the dead of night, because an earlier call meant more time to herself before the

11

children had to be up. This morning she was not disturbed until six a.m. Or thereabouts. How odd, she thought, how odd, that now she felt cheated of consciousness. She lay in bed and listened to the trickle of running water as her husband washed. Then she listened to his footfall on the stair and the rattle of plate and pans and the clunk of the bolt on the kitchen door being drawn back so that Gustav, the St Bernard, could romp in the garden. Her husband, man of the house, was in charge, but laid down few rules. The day-to-day running of the house was left in her hands, but one rule he did lay down was that no one, family and visitor alike, shall leave the house with an empty stomach, without breaking their fast. The rattle of the pan on the plate, and the chink of mug placed on a working surface, the gushing of water into kettle, meant that Dr Reynolds observed the rule that he set. Janet Reynolds imagined him leaning against the sink sipping coffee as the bacon sizzled; a sandwich, doubtless, she often suspected, shared with the slobbering St Bernard, if in fact he didn't have one all to himself, and then the house was once more secured with dog inside. Then she listened as his feet crunched the gravel – something else he had insisted upon as being the world's best-known burglar deterrent – and followed by the engine starting, the whine of reverse gear as wide tyres supporting two tons of steel carried the vehicle over the gravel with further, louder, crunching to the road. The car accelerated away, climbing through the gears. Only then, when the sound of the Volvo had died completely, did she switch on the light and turn out of bed, reaching for her housecoat and slippers. She went downstairs and smiled at the remnants of a bacon sandwich both on the place by the sink and in Gustav's bowl. She glanced at the clock on the wall above the door. Six-ten. No time to settle to anything before the children had to be up. Just a huge mug of coffee and breakfast television. Dangerous habit, she thought, breakfast telly. Very dangerous. In fact, she thought it was so dangerous she then opted for a darkened room with the curtains shutting out the world, and Radio Four for company.

Reynolds drove away from his home in well-set Pollokshaws and pondered the dawn cracking about the villa rooftops and thought that each part of each day and each type of weather has its own particular type of beauty, should one care to look for it. Even wet grey dawns in October, in the west of Scotland. He crossed the M8 at Cardonald and drove past the Southern General Hospital, lights burning on every floor, as the wards were wakened for the day. He emerged from the Clyde tunnel into prosperous Broomhill at the time of bread and milk deliveries, of shutters being pushed up the front of shop windows, of the early starters shuffling in loosely packed queues at the bus stops. He drove down the curving descent of Clarence Drive into the prestigious tenemented development at Hyndland, left down Hyndland Road, across Great Western Road and then fourth right into Winton Drive, driving downhill to the locus, whereas earlier Sussock had approached uphill. He halted his silver Volvo Estate in front of the dark, windowless mortuary van and was irritated to see the driver and his mate sitting in the cab smoking cigarettes and leafing through that morning's edition of the *Daily Record*. But, he reflected, it was a job to them, not a profession, not a vocation, but a job, and this was just one more shift. He walked past the van towards where PCs Hamilton and Wanless stood, both youthful, tall, conventionally handsome men who turned smartly at his approach. Hamilton's hand went to the peak of his cap in a half doffing, half salute. Reynolds smiled in recognition of the acknowledgement. He looked at the tape, and the screen. 'Adult male, I believe?'

'Yes, sir.' Hamilton's response was snappy, alert.

'And the senior CID officer?'

'Just here, sir.' Hamilton nodded to his right; Reynolds turned and saw the baggy, bustling form of Raymond Sussock striding across the pebbled surface of Winton Drive, moving as fast as he could without actually breaking into a run. 'Sergeant Sussock.'

'Sergeant?' Reynolds smiled. 'We meet again.'

'Thank you for coming. I saw you arrive . . . I was doing the door-to-door . . .' Sussock panted, wincing in the thin air 'No luck so far . . . would you like to . . . I'll show you . . . what . . .'

'Just lead on, Sergeant.' Reynolds spoke calmly. 'I'll pick up the gist of it as I go along.'

Reynolds followed Sussock between the white-and-blue

tapes to where the screen had been erected, noticing as he did so a line of constables forming up to sweep the area of green from top to bottom. Reynolds stopped at the screen and peered over the top. 'Ah . . .'

'Sir?'

'Well, I can see why Dr Chan was able to pronounce this gentleman as being life extinct. I won't detain the removal of the body a great deal. All I'll need to do is take air- and ground-temperature readings and a rectal temperature, that'll tell me how long he's been deceased. What time do you have now?'

'Little after six-thirty, sir.'

Reynolds glanced at Sussock and grimaced.

'Six . . .' Sussock glanced at his watch. 'Six-thirty-four, sir.'

'Six-thirty-four.' Reynolds scribbled on his pad. 'Thank you, Sergeant. I'll take these three temperatures now and then you can put upon the mortuary van driver and his mate to dog their fags and place our friend here in a body bag and take him to the mortuary of the GRI. I'll conduct the PM later this morning.'

'Can you give us anything to go on, sir?'

'Just the obvious. Death occurred a few hours ago, so you're in the important few hours after the event, the trail will still be hot . . .' Reynolds paused as an Aer Lingus Boeing flew low overhead, flaps and wheels down on its approach to Glasgow Airport, and mused that no one would be talking on the plane at that moment, all conversation would have died a minute or two earlier as the captain announced the commencement of the final approach, and as the stewardesses scurried up the aisle ensuring all cigarettes were extinguished and all seat belts fastened and all seats in the upright position. 'I can tell you that he wasn't shot here . . .'

'He wasn't?'

'No . . . the rest of him would be on the grass about him, sort of sprayed in an arc over a twenty-foot radius from the head. But, as you see, nothing, and also I would guess that the people hereabouts would have heard something. The sharp crack of a gunshot is not so common in Glasgow, not yet anyway, and if the gun had a silencer, the victim here is not gagged, one could expect him to shout in panic just before he was shot.'

'If he knew he was going to be shot.'

'Good point,' Reynolds conceded. 'The entry wound is at the back of the skull, he could have been kept ignorant of his fate. He'd have been easier to handle but again, if indeed that was his fate, he could very well have been life extinct before being shot. As you see, being shot in the back of the head as he has been, with a high-velocity bullet, has had the effect of exploding his face. It's hindered your job, being the determination of his identity.'

'Of course . . . that hadn't occurred to me . . .'

'Well, I'll just take a temperature reading or two and then we can remove the body. How do you get into this thing . . . ?'

'Round the side, sir, there's a sort of a door . . . a flap . . .'

Sussock waited until the body had been removed, the screen dismantled and the tape taken down. He left the sweep of the greensward by the line of constables in the hands of Sergeant Piper and returned to the common stair of the newly built maisonettes. He was working down the hill, Abernethy worked up. They would meet a little more than halfway from Abernethy's point of view, given the time Sussock had spent with Dr Reynolds. Sussock pushed open the glass-fronted street door of the common stair he had left upon Reynolds's arrival, and his nostrils were once again assaulted by the acrid, pungent smell of a carbolic-based cleaning fluid clearly used to clean the stair. It was a smell he would have found particularly difficult to live with if he had to, but he had to concede it was better than the odour of stale urine and fresh vomit he remembered so vividly from the Gorbals of his childhood, and still met in closes and common stairs in parts of the city, such as the lift shaft of the high-rises in Royston, or the stairs in the East End schemes, once the security door had been kicked in. He went back up to the first floor. He was working down the stairs, knocking on the doors of the top floor, then down the second floor, down to the first, and finally he called on the flats on the ground floor. The door on the first floor had the homely and inviting name of Neighbourly on a tartan background. Sussock rang the bell.

The door was flung open. A small but stocky man stood on the threshold. He glared at Sussock and bristled with cleanliness, smelling of soap and toothpaste and aftershave. Silver-grey hair slicked to his scalp, not one that Sussock could see was out of place.

'Mr Neighbourly?' Sussock said.

'Aye,' Neighbourly snarled in an unneighbourly manner.

'It's about the incident on the green opposite, we're making general enquiries.'

'So you've come to arrest me?'

'No,' said Sussock, not being able to tell whether or not Mr Neighbourly was being sincere or sarcastic. 'Should we?'

'What?'

'Arrest you.'

'You've done it once before, why not now?'

'We have?'

'You have. Ruined my life, the Glasgow police did.'

'Oh yes?'

'Yes. So why should I help you?'

'Did you see anything?'

'Might have. Might not have.'

'So, did you?'

Silence.

'There is such a crime as wasting police time.' Sussock stared at the man. Small, muscular, embittered. Cold blue eyes. Behind him his flat was precise, neat, just-so, nothing out of place.

Another silence.

'I lost my British Rail apprenticeship because of you.'

'Not because of me.' It was odd, Sussock pondered, how often people can't see the individual behind the uniform, but he had come across this attitude so often: a grudge against the police because of the actions of one officer is directed against the force as a whole. Give this man a gun and he'll look for any uniform to shoot at. It doesn't happen in professions where there is no uniform: a grudge against a probation officer will be held against that man or woman specifically, not against any PO because of the actions of one. Same for teachers, same for doctors. But a cop can get it in the neck because of the actions of another cop, years, even decades, earlier. 'Sorry to hear that, anyway,

16

but we're investigating a murder. Do you have information or don't you?'

'Murder?'

'Aye.'

'That's serious.'

'Doesn't get much more serious. It means that any obstruction on your part is also serious.'

'You'd better come in.' The man stepped aside with an angular, clockwork movement. He was not fluid of limb.

The inside of the man's flat was, as Sussock had expected it to be given the nature of the hall, exact. Everything in its place, the books, annoyingly in Sussock's view, having been arranged on the shelf so that the ones with the tallest spines were in the centre of the shelf and then fell away at either side, so that the small stubby volumes were at the end. Even more annoying were the clocks in the house. All shared the correct time: Sussock felt this man would have put them back an hour at midnight. Not waking up and sorting them in the morning after a coffee or two for this guy. If they went back at midnight, they went back at midnight. Not eight hours later. Mr Neighbourly took Sussock into his living room, which afforded a view of the green over which a line of constables were walking, eyes looking just ahead of their boot toecaps. Occasionally one would pause and stoop and pick something up and drop it in a plastic bag.

'I saw it.' Said matter-of-factly.

'You saw it?'

'That's what I said.'

'Would you like to tell me what you saw?'

'Would you like to give me the apology you owe me?'

'I don't owe you an apology. I don't owe you anything.'

A woman glided into the room. She, like Neighbourly, was in her fifties. She was slender, dressed in a housecoat. She sat in the corner by a table, watching, but away from the action. This was man territory, she was the little woman. She didn't seem to show respect to her husband, if indeed they were married. Fear, Sussock thought, here was fear, whispering, walking on glass on tiptoe. The man glanced at her and then turned again to Sussock. He could have done without her presence in the room: it meant that her husband had to be seen to win, and Sussock, the cop, could not be seen to lose.

She pulled the fluffy pink collar of her housecoat around her and shrank further into the corner.

'I spent my years as a bus driver.'

'Did you?'

'I could have been an engineer. I lost my apprentice-ship because some cop wanted a cheap and easy conviction.'

'I could call back.'

'What!'

'I could call back,' Sussock repeated.

'No . . .'

'You want me to stay?'

A look of confusion flashed across Neighbourly's eyes.

'Do you want me to stay?'

Silence.

'Then I suggest you tell me what you saw.'

'I was jostled by a group of louts, neds. They were being watched by the police, causing trouble up Byres Road, I was knocked into a shop doorway, the police pulled me for breach. *Me*!'

'Last night. What did you see last night?'

'The Sheriff wouldn't listen. I was admonished, but it was a conviction. I lost my apprenticeship. I spent my days on the buses.'

'You seem to have done all right.' And having said that, Sussock instantly regretted it. It was a concession. He'd given up ground.

'This. It wasn't always like this, was it?' Neighbourly half turned his head and the cringing woman in pink shook her head vigorously.

'Mostly it was a ground floor in Queenslie. I drove out of Queenslie depot. Know Queenslie?'

'Aye.'

'Aye. Glue-sniffers, smackheads, bandits, that's where me and her lived, thirty years, because of the Glasgow polis. This, this, notice anything?'

'Last night?' Sussock spoke firmly.

'All new. It's all new. This is a lottery win. Not a big one, but enough.'

'Turned out all right then, didn't it?' Sussock said icily. 'You know, there are ways of appealing against a conviction, there are ways of renegotiating an apprenticeship, especially with an organization like British Rail as it was in those days. The union would have helped you. But maybe you needed the injustice, maybe you had to have something to complain about to keep you going. There are folks like that out there, find them a solution and they'll change the problem. I come across them from time to time.'

The woman shrank even deeper into the corner. Neighbourly's eyes glared with anger.

'May I also remind you of the offence of obstruction. That's one conviction you won't overturn lightly.'

'You threatening me?'

'No. I'm giving advice. Last night?'

Neighbourly glared at Sussock. 'I saw it.'

'It?'

'I was putting the clocks back.'

'When did you put them back?'

'Midnight. When else?'

'About midnight.'

'Exactly at midnight. I've got three clocks and two wristwatches in the house. It doesn't take me any more than sixty seconds to do all three. Does it?'

'No, dear.' The woman spoke in a whisper.

'Wasn't talking to you!'

'So what did you see? Exactly? At midnight?'

Neighbourly sniffed. He was going to do this on his terms. 'Car.'

'Car?'

'A car. A black car.'

'Yes?'

'Pulled up opposite the house. One man. Two women. Dragged the body out, dumped it on the grass. Drove off. In no hurry.'

'Descriptions?'

'Guy, he was tall, rangy sort of walk. Women were . . . well, you know, women.'

'I don't know.'

'Women, just ordinary women . . . see . . . like her . . . ordinary . . . not young, but not old, but big, not small. I went back to fixing the clocks. Keep them right. Not a second out . . .'

19

'You didn't report it?'

'Why should I. You ever help me?'

'You ever needed it? Did you know that more police time is spent protecting than prosecuting? You ever needed protecting?'

'Even so, Jim. If people kept their houses like I keep mine, we just wouldn't need a police force, aye.'

'One man, two women and a black car. At midnight?'

'That's it.'

On Winton Drive, Sussock met Abernethy, who he thought looked pleased with himself. Sussock said so.

'Just had a pleasant visit.'

'Is that coffee on your breath?'

'Yes.' Abernethy smiled. 'Called on a lady whose grandson has just joined the Lothian and Borders force, pictures of him everywhere, gold-framed, of course. I mean everywhere. She couldn't be more helpful, pressed coffee and cakes on me. How could I refuse?'

'Can't think.'

'She mentioned a car, a black car. Heard car doors slamming, got out of bed to look and saw three figures walk off the grass back to the car and then drive away, up the hill, Clevedon Road direction. She didn't see anything or anybody being taken from the car. Just three people walk out of the gloom and get into the car and offskie.'

'Two women and a man?'

'Aye, she . . . oh, you got the same information?'

'Seems like. I didn't get the coffee, though – mind I could use one. Black and very strong.'

'Well, I'll take it from here, Sarge, for now.'

'For now.' Sussock squeezed his eyes. 'Did you get a description?'

'Guy was tall, aged about fifty.' Abernethy consulted his notes and as he did so Sussock found himself, as on previous occasions, struck by the relative youth of his colleague. Abernethy was in his twenties but looked younger at times, at times he looked to Sussock like a gangly schoolboy. 'One of the women she couldn't say much about . . . but the other . . . she made observations that it seemed to me that only one woman could make about another.'

'Being, in this case . . .'

'That one of the women carried herself with an attitude, a movement . . .'

'A body language . . .'

'That's the expression.'

'A body language that said, "I'm right, I'm right, I'm right," and also a sort of confidence which said, "I'm beautiful . . . I'm beautiful . . ." with long mane-like hair swept back. But apparently short legs and a large waist so that others might not exactly see her as quite so attractive. She said there was sufficient streetlighting to see all that.'

'I see. It's something.'

'The lady couldn't be sure of the time . . . she thought about midnight, summertime midnight, that is.'

'It was,' Sussock snarled. 'If I got anything at all from my only successful call on this house-to-house, it was the time of the dumping of the body. Midnight, exactly, by three clocks and two wristwatches.'

'Sarge?'

'Doesn't matter. Right, we'll leave Sergeant Piper to finish the sweep. Doubt if they'll find anything if they were dumping a corpse and nothing else. I'll go back to the station.' He glanced at his watch. 'Seven-fifteen. Be an hour and fifteen minutes before Fabian gets here. He'll be having an extra hour in bed this morning. As in fact you did, Abernethy.'

'Luck of the rota, Sarge.'

'That's the way of it, right enough. Me, I'm too old for this. Right, off to the GRI, represent the police at the postmortem. Pump Dr Reynolds for anything you can, anything he'll venture off the record. I'll send Bothwell to you.'

'Bothwell?'

'Bothwell. The deceased hasn't a face, but he still has his fingerprints, and if I'm right and he was wearing a prison discharge suit, that means he's known to us. His prints will be on the computer file. It'll be a start. We can start to have wee chats with his associates: known, criminal.'

'Very good, Sarge.'

Sussock returned, wearily, to P Division at Charing Cross. He half hoped, half prayed that the parking bay marked 'Reserved DI Donoghue' would be occupied by a highly polished maroon Rover by the time he reached the police station. It wasn't. Sussock parked his car in a vacant bay and entered the building by the rear 'staff only' door. He went to the uniform bar and signed in. He was elated, despite his fatigue, to notice Elka Willems standing there: crisp white blouse, black-and-white checked cravat of the police-woman. She smiled at him, a white beaming smile beneath high cheekbones, blue eyes and blonde hair. 'Welcome, Old Sussock.'

Sussock smiled as he signed in.

'I gather you've been busy?' Willems took the time sheet from Sussock and hung it up.

'Just a routine murder.' He managed a smile. 'Got to fill myself with coffee, got to keep going, the slave driver will want to "kick it around", as he is fond of saying.'

'He'll be late.'

Sussock's heart sank. 'Oh . . .'

'Sorry, he said he'd be late, just now, he phoned in. Only half an hour, he said.'

'Elka' – Sussock leaned forward – 'half an hour in my condition is a geological age. I'm finished, bushed, dead on my feet.'

Elka Willems stole a quick glance to either side of her and then laid her palm on the back of his hand. 'Look, Ray,' she said softly, 'it's quiet, I can leave the bar . . . you go upstairs. I'll fix you a coffee. Just as you like it.'

'Strong and black?'

'The strongest and blackest yet. I tell you, Old Sussock, the world will not have seen a stronger and blacker mug of coffee.'

Sussock smiled and pulled his hand away. He went up the stairs to his room on the CID corridor, peeled off his coat and slung it on the back of a vacant chair. He sat at his desk and took a new file from the drawer and added blank recording sheets. He picked up the phone on his desk and tapped out a four-figure internal number. He relaxed back in his chair as the phone rang.

'Collator,' a fresh-sounding voice replied.

'DS Sussock. I need a file ref number.'

Sussock heard the tapping of a computer keyboard, and then wrote the file reference number on the case file, boldly in blue felt-tip pen, as it was slowly read out to him. This done, he opened the file, causing the new cardboard to creak and began the longhand recording of the events of that morning. Early on in the recording he was, pleasantly to his mind, interrupted by Elka Willems, slender and smiling, who walked into the office holding a mug of coffee in one hand and a copy of the *Glasgow Herald* in the other. 'I don't imagine you'll be writing up until nine when Fabian comes in, so I brought you the *Herald*. Don't know whose it is, but if you're foolish enough to leave your paper lying around . . .'

'Nothing's sacred, not even in a police station. For this relief, much thanks.'

'Got to go, can't leave the bar unattended for long.'

Sussock nodded and smiled and sipped his coffee as he surveyed his office, grey steel Scottish Office-issue filing cabinets, his steel desk, with drawers to the right, but not to the left. A cabinet with old copies of *Police News* and dusty, weighty criminal law tomes, rarely opened but the visual effect was impressive. A Police Mutual calendar hanging on the wall. Any softening of the working area by posters and prints was frowned upon by the police authority. His office, like all other CID offices, was spartan and businesslike. Once he had occasion to visit the premises of the Social Work Department in Maryhill and had been pleasantly surprised by the colour that burst from every direction, caused by the staff putting up posters depicting far-off places basked in sunshine, or politically correct messages in angry red or black. But whatever, he left the premises impressed by the visual stimulation therein compared to the drabness of the interior of a police station. He put the mug down on the side of his desk and continued to write, sipping the coffee at intervals. At eight-thirty a.m. he had finished. He sat back and picked up the *Herald*, an early edition, could even have been left behind by an outgoing member of the night shift. It contained no mention of the corpse found on the green at Winton Drive G12, but by now the newspapers would have phoned the police headquarters at Pitt Street, as the media did each hour, and by then the press officer would have given all known information and the story would make the fillers in the margins of the later editions of the *Herald* and doubtless a leader in the *Evening Times* and the local radio and television news bulletins. Ray Sussock folded the paper flat and began to attack the crossword puzzle when his phone rang. 'Sussock,' he said slowly.

'He's in and on his way up.' Elka Willems spoke softly. 'Just thought you'd like to know.'

'I owe you one.'

'You owe me more than that.' She replaced her phone before he replaced his.

Sussock stood and collected the file, swallowed the remnants of the coffee, drew on the remains of his strength and alertness and left his office. He walked the length of the CID corridor and tapped on Donoghue's office door.

'Come,' called out, but only after a pause of imperious length.

Sussock stepped into Donoghue's office, glancing to his right up the length of Sauchiehall Street towards Queen Street at the brow. Dawn had given way to a grey morning.

'Ray!' Donoghue beamed, clean-shaven, early-morning start of the day fresh in a dark-blue three-piece suit, a gold hunter's chain looped across his chest. At that moment Donoghue's office was still, blessedly in the opinion of Ray Sussock, free of smoke. By the end of Donoghue's working day it would, if Sussock knew his senior officer, be a blue fog of stale tobacco smoke. 'Take a pew.'

Sussock sat in front of Donoghue's desk and opened the file. Then he closed it. He could remember the little that was in it. He patted the file. 'We have a code four-one, sir.' Donoghue, much younger in years than Sussock, and senior in rank, remained silent but held eye contact with him. He remained steadfastly interested as Sussock related the story of the man found on the grass in G12 with his face blown out by a bullet fired at the rear of his skull, moving only to plunder his tobacco pouch and pipe from his jacket pocket, and placing the latter in a huge glass ashtray which lay on his desk top. The ashtray was sufficiently large for one junior constable, in a Bateman-cartoon-like comment of crushing impropriety which entered the lore of P Division Police Station, to offer that all the detective inspector now needed was some water and a couple of fish. That particular junior constable was, for his sins, in receipt of an equally crushing glare from said DI. Not an experience to be forgotten. So it was said.

Sussock reached the conclusion of his delivery and was saddened to see Donoghue reach forward and pick up his pipe, near lovingly, from the glass ashtray and, using only one hand to hold it and the tobacco pouch, begin to finger tobacco into the bowl.

'So.' Donoghue placed the pipe in his mouth. 'Something for us to kick about, Ray.'

Sussock's heart sank. A 'kicking about' with DI Donoghue had been known to last for an hour at times. Neither did he want a 'kicking about' in the atmosphere of pipe tobacco smoke already seeping into his lungs. 'Yes, sir,' he said.

'I like your observation about the clothing, prison issue upon discharge. So he'll be known to us?'

'Yes, sir. In fact, I still have to ask Bothwell to attend the GRI to lift the prints of the deceased.'

'I'll do that.' Donoghue flicked his gold-plated lighter and rekindled the tobacco in his pipe bowl. 'First pipe of the day, Ray, always the most enjoyable.'

'Yes, sir, I remember that about the first cigarette of the day.'

'I imagine you do, Ray . . . You don't mind if I . . . ?'

'Not at all, sir. Doesn't bother me at all.'

'Good. Let me know if it does.'

'Certainly will, sir.'

'Gunshot?'

'Sir?'

'The method of murder. If indeed that was the cause of death; I take the point that the deceased may already have been deceased when his face was blown out, that being done to hinder ID. What I'm saying is that this speaks of gangland, does it not? Ex-cons, shooters . . . I mean, this isn't your rammy during a bender, this is planned, perhaps opportunist, but whatever, it's got the mark of cold blood about it. Follow?'

'Yes, sir.' The pain of tiredness rose between Sussock's eyes again, the invisible line that linked pupil to pupil. Sounds swam, distant then near, then distant again.

'So, we have Abernethy down at the postmortem; Dr Reynolds is addressing that quickly. I'll ask Bothwell to join him – if he can get at the fingerprints we should have a positive identification before lunch. One stage at a time and we'll see what we shall see.'

'Yes, sir.'

'If you'd leave the file with me.'

Sussock handed him the file.

'So, you're on nights this week, Abernethy on day shift. King and Montgomerie will be on the back shift?'

'Yes, sir.'

'Montgomerie's snout, what's his name again?'

'Tuesday Noon.'

'That's it. Sorry, Ray, I'm just making a mental shopping list out, Bothwell to the GRI, Montgomerie to Tuesday Noon. You see, if this is gangland, Tuesday Noon will likely have heard a whisper. All right, Ray, that's it. I'll carry it from here. Thanks for staying on.'

Sussock nodded and rose from the seat. He didn't call back to his office, but went directly downstairs to the uniform bar where Elka Willems was busy giving directions to an out-of-towner, a Hebridean, Sussock thought by his accent, who had difficulty with Willems's slight Dutch lilt: '. . . no . . . Ballater Street . . . B-a-l-l-a . . . here, I'll show you the map . . .' He signed out and drove home to the West End and his flat, overconcentrating, fighting fatigue as he did so. But he made it, listening to the ten a.m. news on Radio Scotland. '. . . the body of an unknown man was found early this morning in the Kelvinside district of Glasgow. Police are treating the death as suspicious and are appealing for witnesses. No further details are being released until relatives have been notified. Now the other headlines . . .' Sussock switched the radio off as he parked his car. He left the vehicle, entered the big house, checked the table in the hall for post, sifting through the envelopes, many for others, none for him. He climbed wearily up the stone staircase and let himself into his room on the first floor. The clock on the mantelpiece read 11.05. That *was* the time. Sussock sat on his bed. His body said eleven and eleven it was, not ten. That's five hours of overtime at the end of a night shift. Five hours at the end of a day shift or at the end of an evening shift is survivable, but at the end of a night shift. He managed to peel off his coat and tug off his shoes before blackness swept over him.

It was Monday. 10.05 hours.

2

Reynolds snapped on the latex gloves and felt into the pocket
of his white coat for the on button of the tape recorder. He
pressed the button and said, 'Testing . . . one . . . two . . .
just to use up the leader tape, but don't type this, Noreen.'
He pressed the pause button. He surveyed the body which
lay face up on the stainless-steel table with a starched towel
draped carefully over the coyly termed 'private parts'. The
table had a lip of one inch running round the edge and stood
on a single hollow pedestal which also served as a conduit to
drain any blood which might be drawn by the pathologist's
knife during the course of a postmortem. At the foot of the
table stood a wheeled trolley containing sharpened sterilized
silver instruments. At the head of the table stood a second
man with slicked-back hair who seemed, to the third man in
the room, to be eyeing the corpse with a sinister, unhealthy
gleam in his eye. The floor of the room, so far as the third
man could see, was covered in industrial-grade linoleum,
heavily sealed with disinfectant. The walls were of white
tile, gleamingly clean, except one wall given over to a large
pane of glass behind which was a banked row of seats, all at
that moment vacant. The room was brilliantly, if not harshly
in the mind of the third man, illuminated by filament lamps,
the bulbs concealed behind perspex covers to eliminate the
potentially epileptic-fit-inducing flicker.

'The deceased' – Reynolds spoke softly, knowing the micro-
phone of the cassette tape recorder was attached to his lapel
– 'is an adult male, white European whose identity . . .'
Reynolds turned to the third man in the room and raised
a questioning eyebrow.

'Not known,' replied Abernethy.

'Not known at present,' Reynolds continued. 'Present in the room with myself are Everard Millard, mortuary assistant and . . . ?'

'DC Abernethy. P Division.'

'DC Abernethy of P Division. That's Charing Cross, isn't it? DI Donoghue's team?'

'Yes, sir.'

'Yes, I know Donoghue, good man. We haven't met before, I don't think?'

'No, sir.'

'Over the years I've gotten to know officers of the various divisions . . . P Division . . . you have Sergeant Sussock. I saw him this morning, of course, and I've run into him several times over the years . . . Who's the young bearded fellow?'

'King,' said Abernethy. 'DC King.'

'Dare say he's heard jokes about King Richard . . . ?'

'He had plenty of that at school, he once told me.'

'But, yes, I remember his name. He has a tall and handsome sidekick?' Reynolds continued the conversation but Abernethy noted his concentration was fixed on the death-white corpse on the stainless-steel table.

'Montgomerie,' Abernethy offered, standing reverentially against the wall, close to the door.

'Is that his name? Ladies' man, methinks. I find his attitude somewhat flippant, I'm bound to say.'

'Yes, sir.'

'But good enough. Good enough. Now, in terms of the identification, I dare say you'll want to take the fingerprints of our late friend here?'

'DS Sussock indicated that he'd ask our forensic chemist to attend to do that, sir.'

'Of course. He'll have to wait, only room for one round the table at a time and I was here first. And anyway, it's my table.' Reynolds grinned. 'The deceased has a tattoo which may help you, an old tattoo, certainly not new, of a blue bird at the top of the thumb on the right hand, in the joint between finger and thumb. If you flex your thumb the wings of the bird move as if in flight. It's not an uncommon tattoo.'

'I'll note it,' Abernethy nodded.

'No other . . . oh, the date – sorry, Noreen, put this at the – well, you know the place – is October twenty-fifth and the time is ten-zero-five hours. No other marks of an identifying nature. The deceased has a small frame even by the west of Scotland measure, where we are not noted for our height. This chap was in life a 'tottie wee guy', as is said. He measured . . . Can you pass the tape, please, Mr Millard?' Reynolds and Millard held the tape from head to toe '. . . he measured five feet three inches in his stocking feet . . . five-three in the appropriate box, Noreen, please. He has a frail frame . . . I mean, he's all here but there is a visual impression of a certain awkwardness and imbalance in the skeleton. Such people are often the product of late pregnancies compounded by alcohol abuse on the part of the mother during pregnancy. Doesn't have, didn't have, foetal alcohol syndrome, but may have been lucky to escape it. You see, Mr Abernethy, it is a medical fact, a scientific fact, that a heavily drinking woman who becomes pregnant when in her forties will give birth to a small, sickly infant who will have a sickly childhood and grow into a small, awkwardly moving sickly adult. And here we have a man who in life was small, sickly and probably very awkward in his ambulation. In fact, the most appropriate age for a woman to give birth is around her seventeenth year.'

'Really?' Abernethy became acutely aware of his own 'late baby' status. That he had clearly been fit and healthy enough to pass the police entrance medical meant that he too must have had a lucky escape. It was something he had never before considered.

'Really, though, only from a purely scientific perspective. In the real world there is emotional maturity to achieve, universities to attend, career foundations to be laid, life to be explored, miles to be travelled complete with backpack and all the rest of it which means that in the wider perspective, pregnancy before the mid to late teens is often a bit of a disaster. But from a purely medical point of view, seventeen or thereabouts is the optimum age for child-bearing. And this fella's mum probably missed it, in his respect, anyway.

'So in terms of ID you have stature, ethnic group, and a single tattoo. No other marks that I can detect which may point to his identity. He has short, curly black hair, I mention this for the report, grey at the edges and I would put his age at thirty-five to forty-five. I can't be more accurate at the moment but I could take a tooth and cross-section it, which will give his age to within one year of his actual age. I'll do that for you and I'll also send his lower jaw to the School of Dentistry so that they can attempt to match his teeth with their dental records, always a useful source of information, your teeth are. If he had dental treatment in the city of Glasgow, his records will have been copied to the School of Dentistry archives, but I'll only do that if you can't determine his identification from his fingerprints . . . which . . . are intact . . . not surgically removed or lost by accident that I can see. I don't mind getting to the bottom of things, but I could never see the point of work without a purpose . . . so if I chance my arm and assume that the fingerprints will provide the answer to the question of his ID, I'll confine my efforts to the determination of the cause of his death. Keep it efficient, DC Abernethy, keep it efficient.'

'Of course, sir.'

'So, we'll consider that now and also the approximate time of death, which will be a matter of hours ago . . . no decomposition, rigor just beginning to establish itself. This man was alive and walking and talking this time yesterday, possibly even alive and well and walking and talking this time yesterday evening, weren't you, my friend?' Reynolds laid his hands on the arm of the body. 'It feels cold and stiff. So we are looking at death occurring between ten a.m. yesterday, and two a.m. this morning. We'll narrow it down yet, though, don't worry.'

'Appreciate it, sir,' said Abernethy, for want of something to say.

'By far the best way to determine time of death in this instance, I would suggest, is by examining postmortem cooling. This is not as straightforward as it might seem, no Newtonian single exponential curve for we poor pathologists, too many other factors to consider. Humans are as complicated in death as they are in life.'

'Indeed, sir,' Abernethy said, having not the faintest idea what a Newtonian single exponential curve was, and who was in any event still preoccupied by the implications of his mother's age when she gave birth.

'Can't assume that the living temperature was normal at ninety-eight point four degrees fahrenheit or thirty-seven degrees centigrade and cannot be measured retrospectively anyway. I mean, of course, how can it? Can't heat up a corpse. Did you know that there is a difference in temperature in different parts of the living body?'

'Didn't, sir.'

'Did you, Mr Millard?'

'I had heard something along those lines, in fact, yes.' The mortuary assistant's eyes still gleamed as he surveyed the corpse, particularly the wound, the gaping crater where the face used to be.

'They vary according to health as well. We've all run temperatures, but terminally ill folk have a cooler than normal body temperature. Day temperature is higher than night time temperature by as much as one degree centigrade. In scientific terms that's a significant margin.

'But, to the matter in hand. We have a thin body which will cool more quickly than average. He was lying face down, arms by his side, which is a rapidly cooling posture. That is to say, a posture which will permit rapid heat loss. If he was curled up in a foetal position, for example, that would lessen the rate of heat loss.

'Clothing . . . ?'

'At the Forensic Science Laboratory, sir, Pitt Street.' Abernethy was quick to respond.

'Comprised' – Reynolds consulted his notes – 'suit, ankle socks, shoes, shirt, undergarments . . . insufficient clothing for the time of year really . . . but . . . well, more your province than mine, but I would have thought that that would indicate the murder having taken place indoors . . . something perhaps for you to think about?'

'Yes, sir, I'll pass it up.'

'But from my point of view, the scarcity of clothing means that the clothing would not have inhibited heat loss, so heat loss is looking ever more rapid in this case. The clothing was dampened by rain and that would assist heat loss . . . and so I err on the side of a rapid heat loss. These are rule-of-thumb measurements, DC Abernethy . . . I'll do more accurate calculations after I've performed the PM . . . this is offered as something for you to work on.'

'Understand, sir.'

'The air temperature when I viewed the scene was two degrees centigrade and the ground temperature was one degree centigrade. Again, this would cause a rapid heat loss. The rectal temperature of the deceased was recorded as thirty-two degrees centigrade. There is a fairly complicated model . . . Henssge's nomogram method which I favour above other methods. It has been found to have been accurate in the past when it's been able to be checked against police findings and confessions, for example. I'll phone DI Donoghue with the results of that method later today. It'll be this afternoon, won't be able to get it to him before lunch. But with a rectal temperature of thirty-two degrees centigrade, and factors which indicate a rapid heat loss, then without committing myself I'd say this chap had his face blown out from behind at about midnight, plus or minus an hour, maybe two hours to keep me safe.' Reynolds smiled. 'He was cooled between ten o'clock last night and two o'clock this morning.'

'Between ten and two,' Abernethy repeated. 'I presume that means the gunshot did kill him. I mean, he wasn't already deceased when he was shot?'

'Most probably . . . but at the moment all we can say is that if the gunshot didn't kill him then it followed hard upon the heels of whatever it was that did. But let's remain with the issue of time of death . . . Mr Millard, can I have the scalpel, please?' Millard handed Reynolds the scalpel, placing its handle firmly in Reynolds's palm. Reynolds placed the scalpel at the thorax of the corpse and drew the blade down to the groin. As he did so he said for the benefit of the tape, 'Standard midline incision made.' He peeled the skin back from each side of the incision. 'Small stomach . . .'

'Sir?' Abernethy leaned forward.

'I just mention that he has a small stomach. Odd organ, the stomach, can vary greatly from person to person, but there's no obvious outward sign of the size of it. Some people can drink a pint of beer in one go and can pack away a huge meal with minimal effort, such is often the only way of determining the size of the person's stomach without actually opening him up. But Mr Case No. whatever here had, still has, a small stomach. Has he perchance been a guest of Her Majesty's of late?'

'Sergeant Sussock's contention is that he has, sir. The clothing appears to be prison discharge issue.'

'It would fit. And it probably means that we can be assured that the fingerprints will be able to prove his identity. I confess the only stomachs I have seen which are as small as this are of those who were teetotal in life, or of those who have been a recent long-term guest of Her Majesty and whose stomachs have for said long term been denied the stomach-expanding properties of alcohol-induced carbohydrates. You get lean and fit quick in the nick, or so 'tis my ever so humble observation.'

'Indeed, sir.'

'So let's see what he had for his last meal.' Reynolds slid the scalpel blade across the stomach and it opened effortlessly with a minimum escape of gas. 'Quite healthy, quite a muscular stomach. Again, that would fit if he has spent time in the prison gym pushing weights. Over all, in fact, he is quite muscular. Oh . . . he was hungry when he died. Digestion can continue after death, like facial hair can grow after death. The corpse's whiskers are well documented, and in fact the deceased here has a stubble on his chin which is markedly increased over the stubble I noted when I first saw him at the locus. There appears to be the remnants of meat, thin meat, bacon perhaps, and bread. A very late-taken breakfast, perhaps. But nothing, I'd say, for, well, eight, ten, twelve hours before he died.'

'Hungry, as you say, sir.'

'But his last meal was, as I said, perhaps bacon and bread. A bacon roll, perhaps. It may be important. I mean if you do get a positive identity and then someone says that they had a chicken curry with him at an Indian restaurant just before midnight last night, you'll know that that person is giving false information, if not telling a downright porkpie. You know, I think this chap slept late yesterday, like a lot of ex-lags do, had a bacon roll at lunchtime and then had nothing else to eat. Ever. But for our purposes I'm afraid that the content of the stomach can't help determine the time of death. Stomach contents have helped in the past. If, for example, they have a recently ingested and identifiable meal which he was seen eating, and no other food, then it would confirm that meal he was seen eating was his last meal, and thereby indicate the time of death.'

'But in this case . . . ?'

33

'In this case it tells us nothing. His stomach, like his face, is a cavity. But you know your DI, Mr Donoghue, he has a phrase that he employs from time to time: "a stone worth turning over", I think it is. Opening his stomach was a stone worth turning over. There was nothing underneath it, as it happened, but it was worth a keek in a keyhole, to mix my metaphors.'

'Yes, sir.'

'In other circumstances we could attempt to gauge the time of death by examining vitreous humour taken from the eye and testing the potassium concentration, there being a significant and graded increase in the level of potassium in the eye fluid after death. The greater the potassium level, the longer the time since death occurred. But as we have been denied access to both eyes courtesy of a high-velocity, large-calibre bullet, it seems that is not an option we can explore.'

'No, sir.'

'The only other method of determining approximate time since death is by examination of the postmortem chemical changes, which are extremely useful in a corpse of some years of age, by which I mean when death occurred some years hence, bodies found in shallow graves, for example, but in respect of such a recent corpse, the messages given out by chemical changes are rapid and confused and not a reliable indicator. Which brings us back to determining time of death by considering body cooling. I'll do a careful calculation, but I'll say now, off the record, he died about midnight last night.' Then, clearly for the tape, Reynolds said in a more authoritative voice, 'Stomach was small and healthy, covered by muscular tissue. It contained what appeared to be meat and bread, remnants of a snack taken approximately twelve hours before death. Early indications are that death occurred at midnight on the twenty-fourth/twenty-fifth October. Clocks went back last night, didn't they?'

'Yes, sir. At oh-hundred hours, to be exact. Oh-hundred became eleven p.m. Bad luck for the night-shift boys.'

'Could complicate your enquiry. But possibly not. Well now, we turn to the second question, being the cause of death. Death by gunshot or death by other means. We shall see.' Reynolds pondered the corpse, pinching his nose

between thumb and forefinger in an unselfconscious, involuntary manner as he did so. 'Well, immediately obvious as
a probable cause of death is massive trauma to the head.
It appears to be an injury caused by a bullet fired from a
weapon with a high-muzzle velocity. It impacted at the base
of the skull and it appears that the kinetic energy has in effect,
caused the head to explode. No trace of the face, apart from
the jaw, is recognizable. It is in the manner of a cavity. There
has been complete disintegration of the skull and a traumatic
removal of all cerebral tissue.' Reynolds paused. 'I confess it is
as near a case of brains being blown out as I have ever come
across – you could get a haggis in there.

'Mr Millard?'

'Sir?'

'I'd like to rotate the body . . . if you grab the ankles, I'll
handle the shoulders . . . this way round, clockwise from my
perspective, anti from yours . . . three, two, now . . .'

Abernethy watched as the corpse was flipped over on to its
front in a manner clearly practised by Reynolds and Millard.
Millard grabbed the white towel and placed it neatly over
the corpse's small buttocks.

'Thank you,' Reynolds said automatically. 'The entrance
wound is clearly visible . . . the muzzle of the gun was not
held against the skin. I would expect to see the so-called
"muzzle imprint" were that the case . . . neither does there
appear to be any evidence of muzzle gases entering the
subcutaneous skin. It was close though. That is to say, the
muzzle was close to the point of entry, a few inches away.
The wound is circular and there is a distinct abrasion collar.
The perimeter of the wound is everted, or raggedy, due to
the skin being torn by the bullet. The hairs at the back of the
neck, his scalp hair, that is, is clubbed or singed, caused by
heat melting the keratin. There is a small amount of bruising
which may increase with the postmortem interval. That, Mr
Abernethy, is another indication that this gentleman was shot
just a matter of hours before he was found. In twelve hours'
time this bruising will have become more evident. Bruising
does not occur after death, it can't, but bruising sustained at
the time of death becomes more marked as the time period
after death increases.'

'I see, sir.'

'So, barely evident bruising is a further indication of recent death . . . I find the tattooing round the wound of interest . . . a circular pattern around the wound . . . but distinctly of powder grain, not soot. Soot, if I am not mistaken, but will check my references, does not travel much above six inches from the muzzle of the gun, but powder grains travel up to eighteen inches. From this you can say that the muzzle of the gun was more than six inches from the victim when it was fired, but not more than eighteen inches . . . now . . . here . . . here . . . I can help you . . . I can assist you greatly.'

'Oh?' Abernethy stepped forward.

'Blue . . . blue bits of explosive . . . this is unburned explosive . . . minute, barely discernible to the naked eye . . . but I'll collect it for you. It will help to determine the manufacturer of the ammunition . . . you could perhaps trace that to a user . . . but only perhaps . . . because my inclination is that this is the work of someone who has an illegally held weapon . . . designed for military use . . . not target-practice use. I can't determine the exact distance between the muzzle and the entrance wound without data from test firing of the weapon itself or a similar weapon, but, as I said, given the tattooing, the fouling, the presence of unburned explosive . . . between six and eighteen inches is a reasonable estimate.'

'That's close enough, I should think, sir.' Abernethy smiled his thanks.

'Certainly means it's unlikely to be accidental.' Reynolds looked at his assistant. 'Could we flip him over, please . . . same direction as before . . . three, two . . . now.'

Again Abernethy watched the practised procedure and the deft grabbing and replacing of the towel by Millard.

'Often' – Reynolds spoke as if to the room, as if to a lecture hall full of students, as if to himself, but did not speak directly to either Abernethy or Millard – 'often a high-velocity bullet comes out the other side . . . it has a through-and-through characteristic . . . so much so that not only does the bullet pass straight through the body, but the exit wound can look . . . well, not dissimilar to the entrance wound. So what has happened here?' Reynolds tapped the side of the table with his fingertips. 'What has caused his face to explode and pull his brains out after it? My guess is two things, that is, one of two things or a combination of both. In the first place, the bullet has struck the upper vertebrae, that has shattered the bone and may well have also shattered the bullet causing a dumdum effect. You know what a dumdum bullet is, DC Abernethy?'

Abernethy said, yes . . . he did know.

'They were first used near the town of Dum Dum just to the north of Calcutta during the Indian Mutiny. Hence the name. Quite true. If ever you're looking for quiz questions for the division's Christmas party, that's a good one to use.'

'I'll bear that in mind, sir.'

'So, either this was a dumdum bullet, or the bullet shattered upon impact and had a dumdum effect, or this is a good example of cavitation. I confess I think the latter.'

'Cavitation?'

'A comparatively recently understood phenomenon, DC Abernethy. Essentially, just as a speeding bullet pushes energy out in front of it, it also pushes energy out all around it as it travels at about one mile per second. And the higher the velocity, the greater the energy being pushed out all around it. If said bullet were then to enter an area of soft tissue such as brain, which is encased in a hard shell such as the human skull, then the energy waves are trapped, they have nowhere to escape to and so are transmitted back inside the skull, turning the grey matter to mush in the process until they have somewhere to escape to which is provided by the bullet, or many parts of same forcing an exit wound. In this case at the front of the head. The energy waves desperate for somewhere to escape to effectively follow the bullet out, bringing the brain with them. And all this happens in a nanosecond. In the twink of an eye.'

'I see,' said Abernethy, feeling a little weak.

'I think that's what explains this wound. Cavitation complicated by a fragmenting bullet. We came across the concept of cavitation when we examined flesh wounds, so called, non-fatal wounds where the bullet had been a clean through and through and found tissue damage extending for a considerable distance either side of the track of the bullet. It was caused by the bullet pulsating energy out to the sides as it went through the air, and through flesh. That helped explain a lot, such as why bullets which didn't strike vital organs have still proved fatal.'

'The shock wave got to the organ in question?'

'That's it. If the bullet is of sufficiently high velocity. Now, I cannot detect any other trauma, can you, Mr Millard?'

'I can't, sir.'

'No bruising, no maceration, rippling of the skin caused by immersion, clothing dampened by rain but not saturated . . . when found he was recently deceased going by the body temperature . . . I don't have to cut open his ribcage and look at his lungs to tell you that this person did not drown, Mr Abernethy.'

'No, sir.'

'So the only other causes of death could be suffocation or poisoning, for which I'll have to do tests on his blood. If he sustained a fatal head injury prior to being shot I'm afraid that that evidence has quite literally been blown away. So, I can't take it any further, Mr Abernethy. I'll take a sample of his blood and do tests right away. That will point to oxygen starvation or the presence of toxins, if either is present, but I have now finished my examination and your fingerprint chappie can come and do his stuff.'

'Thank you, sir.'

'You may convey my respects to Mr Donoghue. If it please him, my initial finding is that this adult male was most probably killed by being shot from close range, about one imperial foot separating the entrance wound from the muzzle of the firearm. He was shot by a high-velocity firearm. I can't now and won't later even guess at the calibre of the weapon because the elasticity of the skin makes such estimates unacceptable and unreliable.'

'I see, sir.'

Reynolds peeled off his gloves and dropped them into a stainless-steel bowl. 'He was not shot where he was found. But he was placed there within a few hours of being shot. Time of death . . . between four and eight hours of being found. I can't . . . I won't be drawn into being more specific . . . and you wouldn't want me to, it could do your investigation more harm than good. It could close doors that should stay open . . . you see, if he was shot in a warm room and laid next to a radiator which was turned up full and kept there, then the rate of heat loss would be less than if he was shot on a hillside and left there while they decided what to do with the body.'

'I understand, sir.'

'So I won't be drawn.' The tall, slender pathologist ran his long 'artist's' fingers through his silver hair. 'But I will do some calculations, and look at his blood and phone your Mr Donoghue later today. What time? Lunchtime now . . . be mid p.m. at the earliest.'

Abernethy left the pathology department. He walked down the narrow corridor with pipes running along the ceiling, with recessed doors on which were fastened signs warning of radioactivity within. Eventually, he found it to be a long corridor and experienced a feeling of 'at last' whenever he reached the end, no matter which direction he travelled, though he also found that travelling the outward leg of the corridor towards the central rotunda of the hospital, the feeling of reaching the end of the journey mingled with a sense of release. It was down this corridor, he pondered, that next of kin are escorted with reverential solemnity to identify the remains of a relative. Not in the pathology department where he had been, but to a room close by, and not viewing the body of a loved one in a drawer as is often depicted on film, but from the other side of a pane of glass, where the deceased, by ingenious use of light and shadow, appears as if floating, neatly and tightly tucked into blankets and at peace. In such cases the corridor is sensitively long, detached from the bustle of the hospital, a quiet and private place to be when hope fades. Abernethy climbed the circular staircase of the central rotunda, up to the ground floor, and then out into the car park at the front of the hospital between the main ward block and the Accident and Emergency building which fronts Castle Street.

Anthony 'Tony' Abernethy felt himself to be maturing, either that he thought, or he was growing jaded and cynical. When he had first joined the police as a uniformed cadet he was keen, eager, accounting for every minute, grateful and proud . . . then he had found that he slackened off, had found his 'drops' that every uniformed officer has, a place on his beat where he can drop in for a smoke and a coffee. During the day it's an elderly lady who is delighted to have company, especially of young police officers, smart and handsome and sexually thrilling in their uniforms, to say nothing of the sense of rock-solid-Aberdeen-granite security that visiting police officers bring to the vulnerable elderly. Then he had been awarded an earlier than normal transfer to the CID and had again been keen, eager, accounting for every minute . . . grateful and proud. He no longer had his drops but began to steal time like he'd noticed other CID officers doing, Malcolm Montgomerie, for example. Especially him. Dropping in on lady friends whilst en route back to P Division after a call and reporting that the visit had lasted longer than it had, eating out while on call then finishing early or claiming an hour's overtime at double time for having worked through a meal break, for example. Abernethy didn't want, ever, to reach the extreme of cynicism, but he did notice he felt the lack of energetic urgency that had once driven him. And that day was no exception. He should have returned to P Division to offer a verbal feedback to Donoghue, then grabbed a pie and peas in the staff canteen. But . . . but . . . but . . . he'd seen the way it was done . . . and no harm . . . it was his lunch-break time. He looked about him. The day had grown into a sharp, breezy, dry, autumn day, of sun and blue sky and white cloud at five-tenths, as pilots would say, at least according to the war comics he had read as a child growing up in Thornhill. Even many years after the Second World War had ended, comic strips about Spitfires and 'wizard prangs' had found a ready and sizeable market, as he noted, they still do. Behind him, the impressive edifice of the GRI, to his left and behind, the cathedral of St Mungo, the size of which is belied by its position, being a natural hollow in the lay of the land. The cathedral, he felt, was a bit like the city as a whole, more, much, much more than what it first seems. Even Glaswegians keep finding out things about their town, and incomers . . . well, incomers . . . they allegedly have that sense of being thrown in the deep end when they move to Glasgow, for it is a living thing, this town, this place of heavenly green, the fish that never swam and the tree that never grew and the ring never worn. Abernethy felt a surge of love for his city and wanted to walk its streets, he wanted to walk the grid system, laid out so confidently in the nineteenth century with buildings of stone, so strong, so confident, glowing in the sun under green copper roofs. Investment, faith in the future, those planners and masons would not have lived to see their vision of Scotland's premier city come to fruition, but like fallen soldiers, they had in a sense given their todays for the tomorrows of succeeding generations. Now, at the cusp of the millennium, Abernethy could choose, as he did, to leave his car in the car park of the GRI with a 'police' sign in the window to prevent it being clamped by a finely built zealot in a peaked cap, and walk Cathedral Street, towards the Concert Hall and the city centre, ostensibly taking his lunch-break, but really clearing the lingering scent of formaldehyde from his nostrils by seizing the opportunity to walk the streets of a city he was just growing to realize that he loved very, very much indeed.

It was not just, he thought, the architecture, the care gone into the masonry which made people say that if you want to know this city you have to walk around looking at the sky. Those carefully carved statues set high in the wall, the single pinnacle, no higher than a man but which must have taken years to assemble and carve, such is the complexity of the ornateness. Rather, it was the emotional chemistry, the spirit of the city, as is captured by the bold sweep of bronze in Buchanan Street which is Henry Moore's sculpture, his gift to the city. The art of giving a gift is understanding the personality of the recipient. Henry Moore, Abernethy thought, had got it just right and the city had honoured him by placing the sculpture in a place of pride so that it greets pedestrians as they turn into Buchanan Street, having perhaps alighted at Central Station, and having left the station by the low level exit.

. . . A woman . . . Abernethy pondered as he turned down the steepness of North Hanover Street towards George Square where crowds had thronged on VE Day, 1945. At that time Glasgow had scored heavily over Edinburgh, so Abernethy later learned, for Edinburgh is a city without a centre, without a focus. On VE Day in Edinburgh some people had gone to the castle, some had even gone to the forecourts of Waverley Station, some had climbed Calton Hill, many had gone to Rose Street, famous for its endless number of pubs, but most wandered the length of Princes Street searching for a point to congregate. But at the same time, the same day, with the same feeling of elation and sorrow for it all, forty-five miles away, Glaswegians had known where to gather.

... A red-haired Celtic ... definitely a woman ... the city feels like a woman feels, deep, driven, passionate, fierce, loyal, hating, loving ... committed ... these womanly things are also Glasgow things.

See London, Abernethy thought, well see her ... that's a mother. And see New York, see New York, well that yin's a shipyard bully, that yin's a gangster, that yin. And see Perth up by Dundee, see Perth, well, Perth's a twee lassie who says please and thank you and her prayers at night, and see Dundee, well, Dundee's a hard wee street Turk, so it is, and see Edinburgh, well, that yin's an old woman with a fur coat with rags beneath it and holes in her shoes. Paisley and Greenock are rare wee sojers tae, but see Glasgow. Oh see Glasgow, see her ... fine, fiery red-haired Celtic woman ... those long legs either side of the Clyde, the grid system where they meet ... her arms going up to Bearsden and Bishopbriggs, down the south side to Giffnock and Castlemilk. Her head's at Dennistoun and that mane of hair falling back to Rutherglen and Cambuslang and out to Bothwell. That's Glasgow ... and she never sleeps ... the nearest she gets is a half-sleep slumber in the dead hours, whisper who dares ... poke this bitch and she'll rise up snarling. Mess with her and you die. Glasgow. Abernethy wouldn't live anywhere else.

Elliot Bothwell blinked. The glare of the fluorescent lights went for his eyes. Even though they were shielded behind thick perspex, the light was too bright for his taste and comfort. He was, to an observer, an overweight man who moved in badly, barely coordinated movements, who could be seen from the side aspect, to blink involuntarily behind spectacles with extra-thick lenses. He placed his plastic work case at the foot of the corpse and began to cut the fingerprint forms as he always did when fingerprinting a corpse. A living person is not at all difficult to fingerprint; they often, most often, cooperate, just seem to fall into step once the procedure starts, offering each finger as requested, keeping the others bent back and well out of the way. A corpse, especially one stiffened by rigor and the chill of the postmortem theatre, presents difficulties in that the other fingers will not, or cannot, be moved out of the way and will tend to smudge the paper strip which is divided into five squares, one square for each finger. The recommended way to fingerprint a corpse, Bothwell had been taught, was to cut the strip into five sections and lift prints from each fingertip by placing them on individual squares, then pasting the squares on to a blank strip, thus making the single strip of five squares as required by the Criminal Records Section. One strip for each hand.

Bothwell worked methodically, lifting the prints from each hand, faltering only on the left thumb when his grip of the bony, icy, clammy-to-the-touch digit slipped and he was obliged to repeat the operation. He noted that the fingerprints of the man without a face appeared to fall into the 'Arches' category. That he could tell quite easily with the naked eye and that, he felt, ought to make things easy for CRS, given that only five per cent of the population have fingerprints of the 'Arches' type. Five per cent. That would make things very easy indeed. Bothwell fumbled round the stainless-steel table to lift the prints from the other hand, and as he did so he couldn't help but stare in horrific fascination at the black, red, bloody hole where the man's face and brain had been.

'That's what guns do to you.'

'Aye.' Bothwell nodded and glanced at Mr Millard, with his gleaming eyes and slicked-back hair, observing the lifting of fingerprints as procedure dictated. He pondered that a man must be possessed of certain qualities to be drawn to the post of mortuary attendant. He pondered further that whatever those qualities were, Mr Millard clearly had them, such was the evident pleasure he drew from his employment.

'See they cowboy films and war films and gangster films, they don't show it.' And that, Bothwell heard with a kick-like jolt to his stomach, was said with an unmistakable note of disappointment, of frustration. Films are made for the likes of Millard, he thought, so he had heard, smuggled in, he had heard, mostly from Latin America, and distributed on the underground network. Or so he had heard. He certainly wouldn't get what he wanted on the BBC. 'See, you'd think they decided to roll over and go to sleep the way it's shown on the telly. That's not right, they're blown apart, man. I was talking to this guy one time – he'd served in Malaya during the emergency – he said he saw a terrorist, a young lad of about fifteen, he reckoned, saw this terrorist take a short burst from a Bren gun right in the chest at a distance of about two hundred feet, four little holes in his ribcage but his back was blown open, lungs, liver, heart, kidneys, you name it, splattered all over the jungle. That's what guns do to you, and this guy here without a face. One bullet did that. Just one. All you need, really, just one in the right place.'

'So I see.' Bothwell worked on, trying not to be upset by the gleaming-eyed man in the white coat.

'See some sights in here though, see some sights right enough.'

Bothwell didn't reply.

'Bet you see some too in your job, aye? Same as mine really, we get paid peanuts, you and me, but we see life. You and me, aye?'

'Aye,' Bothwell conceded. Now he was in a hurry to finish. But he thought the man was right in a sense, about seeing life. He had been working as a chemistry assistant in a riot-ridden inner-city comprehensive school, he had spent years mixing dull and harmless chemicals for pupils to use in experiments which were not really experiments because everybody knew what the result was going to be, or was supposed to be if the said experiment survived the sabotage of equipment; exploding test tubes in the Bunsen burner flame being a particular favourite, or so Bothwell had noticed. And all the while he watched the hair of the chemistry teacher turn grey, he saw the lines appear in his face, he saw the man begin to walk with a stoop and he thought, 'Whatever they pay you, Jim, it's just not enough.' Then, sitting in the staff room one lunchtime on a rainy day, he recalled, he was browsing through the vacancies bulletin distributed weekly by the local authority and he saw the post of Forensic Assistant with the Strathclyde Police being advertised. He applied for it, was accepted and just did not look back. No two jobs were ever the same, the pay wasn't any better but like the man had just said, he began to see life. As at present, in fact, lifting fingerprints from a man on a stainless-steel table who had no face. 'Aye,' he said again, and thought pityingly of the grey-haired teacher with the stooped walk and recalled the man arriving at the school straight from university full of

44

vigour and zest, radiating enthusiasm, wanting only to teach but encountering only pupils who didn't want to learn.

He lifted the tenth and final latent and placed it safely with the others and snapped the case shut and locked. 'That's me,' he said, turning to the assistant.

'Aye. I'll get him put back in a safe place, ready for the box.' He advanced with a trolley and wheeled it against the dissecting table.

'Lifting it yourself?' Bothwell was surprised.

'No, I'll get a mate to help me, swab down the table for the next one. This is a never-ending story this, Jim, never-ending. Find a job you like and it's one long holiday, so it is.'

Elliot Bothwell said he'd see himself out.

Fabian Donoghue glanced at the face of his gold hunter and replaced it in his waistcoat pocket. Midday. There was a lull in the traffic coming to his desk or down his phone. Abernethy was still to feed back, as was Dr Kay, who had notified him of her receipt of the clothing the deceased had been wearing, and would be giving it, she said, her immediate attention. Elliot Bothwell would probably at the moment be lifting the latents from the deceased so it was too early to expect him to feed back. No further witnesses had come forward. The file was still very, very thin. He had, in fact, devoted that morning to catching up on paperwork in respect of other outstanding cases, deciding which requests for leave over Hogmanay to approve and which to refuse. He had decided to pursue a policy of awarding Hogmanay leave to those who didn't get it last year. Which meant that Montgomerie and Sussock had lucked out and King and Abernethy had lucked in. He further felt that this meant that Ray Sussock would soldier through Hogmanay alone because Montgomerie would doubtless phone in sick. Malcolm Montgomerie's attitude being, in Donoghue's view, that if he couldn't have leave he'd take it anyway. Mild food poisoning was, Donoghue had noticed, an ailment that Montgomerie was prone to suffer from time to time, very rapid in onset and having the benefit of a full and speedy recovery, usually necessitating only twenty-four hours off work, occasionally twice that. But only occasionally and only about three or four times in the last year. Not enough to warrant a compulsory medical, nothing to worry about if it was genuine but something Donoghue found infuriating when he knew fine well the detective constable was lying through his teeth. It wasn't so much the lack of CID cover on such occasions, other officers were easily tempted by an extra shift at double time because of the less than twenty-four hours' notice, rather it was what it said about the man's attitude and commitment to a job which was after all supposed to be a vocation. A police officer subordinates more of his life to his job than the majority of the workforce. He, and she, is expected to. Yet occasionally there is a Malcolm Montgomerie with a flippant, cavalier, devil-may-care attitude, doing enough, more than enough, in fact, to keep his job, and not infrequently getting a good result, but . . . Donoghue stood and reached for his coat and homburg . . . it was the attitude of the man that Donoghue found irritating. He found that getting hold of Montgomerie was like . . . well, like soap on a rope, like trying to nail jelly to a wall . . . he'd tell Montgomerie that he'd be working over the New Year, but knew that Montgomerie would probably be up the West End, drunk and womanizing, at somebody's party. And there was not a thing he could do about it. But that was a couple of months hence. Today, the first day of the working week, Donoghue felt anxious to get back into his routine. Although he relished his wife's cooking, there was, he felt, nothing to beat a plate of chilli and rice and pitta bread at Malone's Bar on Sauchiehall Street; good-size portions, a reasonable price, leather seats, deep carpets, coloured glass to filter any harsh sunlight, a place where he was a patron, felt valued and wanted and was happy to return day after day. He left his office a little earlier than he would have liked, but felt that it was an appropriate use of his time. And he really wanted a plate of chilli, so much so that he felt his mouth watering in anticipation.

He walked along the CID corridor, down the stairs to the uniformed bar, where he signed out and told Elka Willems that he was going out to lunch.

'Very good, sir.' Elka Willems smiled, high cheekbones, blonde hair done in a tight bun, a flash of blue eyes, crisp, starched white blouse, black-and-white cravat fastened at the nape of her neck with a strip of Velcro. Should she get into a confrontation, it couldn't be grabbed by an assailant so as to

46

throttle her. It would, as designed to do, come off in his, or more likely her, hands.

Donoghue dropped the pencil back on the time-sheet pad and left the building. The air was fresh and cool, a pleasant change to his office where he conceded he didn't help matters by smoking. He walked up Sauchiehall Street and entered Malone's.

'The usual?' The young man in a red shirt and black tie smiled as he appeared.

'If you don't mind.' Donoghue returned the smile. He liked that young man whose name he didn't know. His manner, he found, was quite genuinely warm and cheerful. It was a manner that would carry him far in life, especially since he had yet to display, to Donoghue's observation, even a trace of arrogance, though he was clearly handsome enough to flaunt it. Later, after a second cup of coffee and a glance at Malone's copy of the *Glasgow Herald*, Donoghue decided upon a turn to George Square and back, exercising his legs, his lungs, getting out of the office for an hour. Taking in the city, the architecture, the bustle, the traffic . . . He reached George Square and stood on the corner of Queen Street, looking out over the expanse, the statues, to the City Chambers at the far end of the square, just standing, looking, like police officers do, and he saw Tony Abernethy emerge from North Hanover Street, jog across George Street and resume a leisurely pace across the square, tending, so far as Fabian Donoghue could detect, to walk looking upwards as if at the skyline.

'I just can't believe I did it.'

'Well, I suggest you start believing it.' The second woman too was shaking. She was more composed than the first but she too was shaking.

'I woke up this morning—'

'You mean you slept!'

'I woke up hoping it was a dream . . .'

'Well, it wasn't . . . look at your carpet . . . look at the wall . . . this is him . . . what did you? . . . oh . . .'

'I wish we'd hidden the body . . . I wish I hadn't . . . there would have been other ways . . . we panicked . . . they'll have found the body by now . . .'

'They have. I heard the lunchtime news. But what did you expect? Did you expect him to get up and walk away and conceal himself, or is . . . ?'

'We should have . . . that would have given us a few more days . . . it's only a matter of time before they link him with me . . . me . . . with you . . .'

'Don't bring me into this. I didn't pull the trigger. I didn't even know that you had that blunderbuss in the house . . . the noise. I'm surprised half the street didn't come round chappin' on the door.'

'All right, all right.' The man spoke and the two women fell silent. 'What's done is done . . . we have to decide how to recover from this . . . if we can. But Mary's right, this could be the end for us. Now we really are going to have to cover our tracks. You're going to have to cover your tracks.'

'Me?'

'You. Well, I wasn't here . . . and if you threaten to take me down if you go down . . . well, look at what happened to boy Ron. What's sauce for the goose . . .'

The woman's face paled.

'Get everything out of this room.'

'Everything?'

'Everything.'

'You'll have to help me.'

'I won't have to do anything. Clean up the mess, wipe it off the wall, clean it up as best you can.'

The woman nodded.

'Hang a painting over the worst mess, it shows up too much. Then call the charity shops, ask them to come and take the furniture away, it's good stuff . . . they'll jump at it.'

'It's new!'

'Say you've had a burglary and that you feel violated so you're chucking it out. They'll buy that. You've got to get shot of everything in this room, strip it down to the bare plaster and the bare floorboards. Then lift the carpet and take it up to the dump at Dawsholm and chuck it in a skip.'

'That I'll need help with.'

'I'll help you,' said the second woman, lighting a long cigarette with trembling fingers.

'Then strip the wallpaper, dig the bullet out of the plaster, then repaper, and paper over the bullet hole first. When the police come you say you're redecorating. OK?'

'OK,' the first woman nodded.

'It's got to be like this, see the thing that'll link this room to Ron's death is . . . something you probably can't see with your naked eye . . . a speck of blood . . . one of the hairs from his head . . . The word is sanitize . . . this is a crime scene . . . a locus of the offence . . . so sanitize it.'

'If I just started a fire . . .'

'No.'

'The whole lot would burn.'

'It's an idea . . .' the second woman said.

'It is. It's a bad idea too. We haven't got enough time to do it properly so it looks like a genuine accident. An old building with dodgy wiring, full of furniture, well, that was one thing . . . but a bungalow in Kelvinside . . . no way . . . the only way is to clean it, this room, as if you're redecorating.'

'The whole room?'

'Well, it's your room, you pulled the trigger . . . your life sentence, hen. I mean, you're no chicken, Mary Carberrie, no chicken at all. You'll be old and shot with Alzheimer's when you get out. If all the dykes don't get you first . . . the things they can do with a chair leg. So they'll find out who he is today. How long till they link him with you?'

'Day. Two days. His mother doesn't know my address.'

'Just your name, that's enough . . . your prints are on the police files . . . you visited him . . . they'll link you together, it won't take them long to find you. Are you in the phone book?'

'No.'

'Well, that's something.' The man stood. 'I'm going. I'm sorry I came here now. I won't be back until this is over. If it ever will be, stupid female. Why didn't you give him the money?'

'I spent it.'

'You spent it?'

'I spent it. I spent it. I spent it. All right! Anyway, you're the one who said what's done is done. I can't unspend it any more than I can bring him back to life.'

'Jesus . . . what a mess . . . we'd done it. We'd pulled it off, things were quietening down . . . we were rich . . . and you spent his cut. Now we're all looking at life sentences . . . Thanks a bunch. So what did you do with the gun?'

'It's in the Kelvin.'

'Off the bridge at the top of Belmont Street,' offered the second woman.

'That could be recovered. You know that? It could be linked to the bullet . . . Is that . . . ? God in heaven, is that more than one hole in the wall?'

'Aye . . . there were a lot . . . bits . . . fragments.'

'You'd better dig out every bit of metal you can find in the wall . . . start now.' He picked up the phone and put it down again. 'Get rid of the furniture . . . any charity shop, any second-hand dealer . . . the first one that will collect it all this afternoon . . . then lift the carpet, strip the wallpaper . . . work through the night . . . don't burn anything in the night . . . it'll make the neighbours suspicious, they must be deaf as it is, it'll be too much to hope they're blind as well. Go out and buy one of those steam strippers, that'll make short work of it, and it will get shot of a lot of evidence as it destroys the paper . . .'

'I'll go and buy one for you,' the second woman offered. 'I mean while you're phoning round the furniture places . . .'

'Put the paper in liners and take it up to Dawsholm . . . get the carpet up there today . . . if you work well into the night you'll have the room stripped before dawn. Get the stripped paper up to the dump as soon as you can. Redecorating the room isn't so important as destroying the evidence . . . but redecorate as soon as you can.'

'You could help . . . if the police put two and two . . .'

'Look, Carberrie. Listen. Just listen . . . I don't know you . . . I don't know your name . . . I've never met you . . . all right. What happened to Ron could easily happen to you. Keep it zipped or we're going to have a massacre here. I shouldn't be here. I've got a distinctive car . . . so I'm off . . . if the police trace you, cough to murder.'

'Cough to murder?'

'Cough to culpable homicide, involuntary manslaughter . . . don't tell them . . . I mean . . . at least that way when you come out you'll still come out to money. If they get

to know about the rest, we'll all go down and we'll come
out to zip. Ron took a rap . . . it may be time for you to do
the same.'

'I'm not going to prison.'

'I hope you're right. I hope to God you're right . . . but I'm
going . . . start phoning . . . my God . . .'

'What?'

'Is that one of his teeth?'

'Yes.' Mary Carberrie nodded. 'I got the worst up but
there's still some bits about here and there.'

'Start phoning.' The man turned, and then turned back to
face the two women. 'You do not know, you can't believe
the handstands we are going to have to do to get out of
this. It was sorted, Carberrie, well sorted, dusted and done,
signed and sealed. We have enough dosh to see us out, but
you, Carberrie, you had to be greedy. Should have known
really, Mary Carberrie, greed is your middle name. Start
phoning. Oh, and your car . . . you'd better burn it. That
you *can* burn.'

Fabian Donoghue returned to P Division Police Station. He
signed in and checked his pigeonhole. There were two circulars: one about being cost effective whenever possible – using
both sides of a sheet of paper, phoning after two p.m., using
second-class postage – and one notifying of the retirement
of one Chief Inspector Gill of X Division. Those wishing
to contribute should contact Detective Sergeant Virgin at X
Division. Donoghue knew Virgin, he bore his unfortunate
surname with soldierly stoicism, but had once drunkenly
confided that his schooldays had been, 'sheer hell, Fabian,
you've no idea'. There was also a message to the effect
that Dr Jean Kay of the Forensic Science Laboratory had
phoned him.

Donoghue skipped up the stairs to the CID corridor two
at a time, strode confidently down the hard-wearing brown
carpet, along the corridor to his room, placed coat and hat on
the hat stand and slid into his chair. He placed the circulars
and the note in his in-tray. Then he reached for the telephone
with one hand and his pipe and tobacco pouch with the other.
He punched a nine for an outside line and momentarily
longed for an old-fashioned rotary phone. He had noticed

that as his forties had dawned so had the harbingers of nostalgia for strange things: buses with diesel engines that growled rather than whirred and fast food meaning a ham sandwich on the Flying Scotsman, being but two. His longing for rotary phones had stemmed from the days that he had caught his ankle in the phone cord and had brought his newly installed pushbutton phone crashing to the floor. He had been dismayed not only by the ease with which the thing had disintegrated after falling from such a modest height, but also by the flimsy, fragile appearance of the electrics inside the phone. But the march of progress couldn't be halted and he tapped the numbers on the keyboard of the phone while filling his pipe with the other hand. He was just able to ignite his gold-plated lighter and play the flame across the contents of the bowl of his pipe before a voice in his ear said, 'Dr Kay.'

'Ah . . . DI Donoghue. P Division.' Then he drew the smoke up the stem of his pipe and relished the taste of the tobacco on his tongue.

'DI Donoghue, you received my message?'

'Just that you phoned, Dr Kay.' He reached for his pad and ballpoint.

'I thought you may be interested in the preliminary findings about the clothing that was brought in this a.m.'

'This is quick. It's rapid.' Donoghue allowed his smile to be 'heard' down the phone as he held the phone clasped between his head and left shoulder, being obliged to use his hands to hold the notepad and his ballpoint.

'It's a quiet period. Make hay while you can.'

'Indeed. But it's still good of you to put yourself out like this.' Donoghue was more than aware that Dr Kay's expertise was sought after by the neighbouring forces of Central, Lothian and Borders, and Dumfries and Galloway. That she had attended to this particular referral with such alacrity was a favour indeed.

'It's not preferential treatment, Mr Donoghue, the policy is that if something has obviously waited before coming here it can continue to wait, if something is fresh it gets as rapid attention as possible.'

'I see.'

'It's a response to the observation that the first twenty-four hours of a murder investigation are the most crucial. We don't want to be responsible for any hold-ups.'

'Still, I'm very impressed.'

'Well, you may not be so impressed with the content. The clothing was newly issued.'

'Issued?'

'Scottish Office prison discharge suit, grey, white ankle socks, white shirt, boxer-type underpants. It even smelled new. No name tag, no wallet, some loose change amounting to about two pounds. One pound and eighty-six pence, so my notes tell me . . .'

'We thought that.' Donoghue scribbled on his pad. 'We recognized the suit . . .'

'As you would.'

'As we would.'

'The inference being that he was recently discharged from prison after serving a sentence of . . .'

'Five years or more . . . or unless he hadn't any clothing anyway for whatever reason . . . a down-and-out might be kitted out after a short "drying-out" spell but that's not official policy.'

'I see, but that's more for you rather than me.'

'There were traces of soil and grass on his anterior aspect clothing, shirt front was muddy. In other words . . . we found only one item which may be of use.'

'Oh . . . ?'

'A fibre, three, in fact, which is very useful.' She had a soft voice. 'Of a carpet, a synthetic polymer, trapped between the sole and uppers of his shoe. Red in colour . . .'

'New meaning of the red carpet treatment.'

'Indeed . . . at least I believe it to be carpet. Could be something else, but what I can't think. They're synthetic, and uniform in length, hence the usefulness of having these fibres, and they appear to have been cut at each end. They haven't been torn or uprooted or hacked, but cut cleanly. I've come across this before . . . I believe it's associated with a process known not surprisingly as "flocking".'

'Flocking?' Donoghue wrote the word in his pad.

'Flocking is the process whereby nylon is drawn into long strands which are then cut into smaller strands with a machine known as a guillotine. The small or shorter strands of nylon are electrically charged and then fired with some velocity at a base material covered with adhesive. The fact that they are electrically charged means, for some reason that I don't fully understand, that the short bits of nylon impact with the expanse of base material end on, rather than lengthways. It's a manufacturing process which has various uses, one of them being carpet manufacture.'

'I see.'

'The uniformity of the length of the nylon strands put me on to the flocking process, and their length indicates a carpet, their length being about a quarter of an inch.'

'A red carpet.'

'Or a carpet with a red pattern. I should also add that their thickness is carpet-strand thickness.'

'So a house, or similar, with a red carpet. Shouldn't be more than a few hundred thousand.'

'Hence I may be able to help you, Inspector.'

'Oh . . . ?'

'Yes . . . it's for you to make the decision. The option is that I melt the fibre, just one. If I note at what temperature it melts at, that may, and only may, indicate which particular type of nylon the fibre is made of. That could isolate the source. But it would destroy the evidence. But like I said, I may be able to do it with one fibre only, that would preserve two for evidential purposes.'

Donoghue asked her to proceed.

He replaced the receiver and the phone rang immediately. There was also at the same instant a knock on his door.

'DI Donoghue . . . come in.'

Abernethy opened the door and entered Donoghue's office and smelled the sweet-smelling tobacco he favoured. Donoghue beckoned him to sit in either of the two chairs in front of his desk. Abernethy did so and listened reverentially whilst Donoghue responded to information clearly being provided by the telephone.

'I see . . . yes . . . yes . . . got that . . . Well, as soon as is convenient, Dr Reynolds. Yes, many thanks . . . good day.' He replaced the receiver and let his hand rest on it while he looked at Abernethy and said, 'That, as you may guess, was Dr Reynolds . . . he's tested for poison and indication of suffocation, both tests being negative. No toxins in the body apart from a wee drop of alcohol, which I can accept if our man has just been released from the pokey, and plenty of oxygen in the blood; he was breathing when he was shot. So death is due to gunshot wound to the head.'

'As we suspected, sir.'

'But now we know. Saw you in George Square.'

'Sir?'

'This lunchtime, I saw you in George Square.'

'Well, yes, sir . . . my refreshment break . . . as entitled . . .'

'About an hour ago.'

'Well, yes.'

'Sir.'

'Yes, sir.'

'The issue, you see, Abernethy, is not that you had lunch outside the office. I did that, in fact. Nor is it that you may have hoped to have lunch discreetly somewhere and then come back to the station, claiming to have worked through lunch and either got off an hour early or claim one hour's overtime at double time, because I know all the dodges. I have been a detective constable, you have yet to become a detective inspector. I know all the angles.'

'Yes, sir.'

'The issue is that you chose to keep information to yourself. For an hour you sat on the preliminary results of the PM, hoping possibly for an hour's overtime or free time, to which you were not entitled, when you know fine well the importance of the first twenty-four hours in any murder investigation. I wanted that information as soon as you had it.'

'Yes, sir.'

'Consider yourself reprimanded. We'll leave it unofficial. Next time you do that it'll be reported.'

'Thank you, sir.'

'There are two cultures in this police station, Abernethy. As in all police stations, in fact.'

'Sir?'

'There is a culture of cynicism, of grabbing what you can get for minimum effort. I have noticed that the greatest overtime claims are put in by officers who put little else in. There is also a culture of professionalism and dedication. I am gratified to observe that of the two the former is significantly less of a force than the latter, but the former exists and when morale is low its size swells. You've won relatively early promotion into the CID, that means that faith has been invested in you. It's up to you to betray that faith or not.'

'I understand, sir.' Abernethy shifted uncomfortably in his chair.

'Of those two cultures that I mentioned, try to keep yourself in the latter. People who show professionalism and dedication tend to go further anyway in the long run. Such has been my observation.'

'Yes, sir.'

'Right, we'll leave the matter there. So let's kick this about.' Donoghue placed his pipe in the huge glass ashtray. 'We have a male victim, ID unknown. Definitely a murder. Not even an attempt to make it look like suicide. What do we know?'

'Well . . .' Abernethy felt uncomfortable. He had been reached by Donoghue's rebuke. 'He appears to have been recently discharged from HM prisons. Going by his clothing.'

'Yes . . . that's been confirmed. Incidentally, Dr Kay phoned just before you knocked on my door. She also said that the deceased may have been standing on a red carpet just before he died, or that part of a patterned carpet which was red. She isolated three strands, each crucial evidence, but we've decided to sacrifice one of the strands to attempt to determine it's manufacturer. Apparently that can be done, but it involves destroying the individual strand.'

'A risk worth taking, sir.'

'I am of that opinion. So he's released, he has a beer, he goes to a house or similar and gets his head blown open, all within a few hours.

'Tell me about the dumping of the body?'

'Sir . . . well, it was dumped on a piece of ground in the West End . . . an area of grassland . . .'

'Significance?'

'Panic?' Abernethy thought quickly.

'That's my opinion also. If the murder had been planned then so would the disposal of the body. I would think it's fair to assume that the deceased arrived unwanted, or unexpected, rattled a cage or two for some reason and provoked what my father, with his fondness for Westerns, would have called gunplay.

'He had a score to settle, perhaps; somebody grassed him up and he ate a lot of porridge, immediately on discharge he went looking for revenge? Could very well be. But that's not so important as the messages given to us by the disposal of the body. Firstly, as you say, it's dumped, so it's probably not a premeditated murder. And the location of the body . . . no attempt to hide it, not even waste ground, or in the river . . . on a piece of grassland opposite houses . . . in a quiet residential area, and it is no surprise that there was a witness who tells us of a black car, one man with a, what was it?' – Donoghue consulted his file – 'a tall man, rangy walk.' He closed the file. 'Two women and a tall man with a rangy walk.'

'Rangy?'

'All arms and legs, flying out as he walks, that's what I take it to mean.'

'Arrogant,' Abernethy offered.

'Arrogant?'

'Mm, yes, sir. I mean, if I had dumped a body on a stretch of open ground opposite a row of flats, I'd be scurrying about like a squirrel that had just found out about winter. I'd be in a state of panic to be sure, but this fella can saunter back to his car with his "rangy walk".'

'Good point. Worth noting.' Donoghue placed his pipe in the ashtray. 'What do you think about the locus of the shooting as indicated by the location where the body was found?'

'It's close. It's a get-it-out-of-the-house, anywhere-but-do-it-quick sort of response, a pushing away. No thought had gone into it, the disposal of the body, no thought at all, which reinforces my, our, belief that it's a non-premeditated murder. If you plan a murder you most always plan to dispose of the body, so our man took them by surprise.'

'Possibly. Possibly.' Donoghue rattled the stem of his pipe against his teeth. As he did so Abernethy saw a glint of gold in the upper left gum. It sat easily with Donoghue's image, but Abernethy didn't like him for that. He just never had liked people who had fillings capped with gold. 'The murder weapon?'

'A firearm, high velocity, large calibre.'

'A military weapon. Fired execution style at point-blank range. Comments.'

'Not a legally held weapon.'

'No.'

'Not gangland?'

'Are you suggesting that or asking, Abernethy?'

Abernethy paused. 'I think I'm suggesting it, sir.'

'In that case I won't argue. I don't think it's gangland either.' Donoghue glanced out of the window. He noted that it was beginning to cloud over. 'Gangland have these weapons but they don't like to use them. If they did, when they do, we rarely find out.'

'Brings us back to the dumping of the body, sir. That's not gangland.'

'As you say.'

'So he was shot late last night, when standing on a red carpet, or the red bit of a patterned carpet. He was shot by an illegally held weapon but not by a gangland member. So he was shot indoors, in a building, not too far from the place where the body was found. He must have known something, sir.'

'He was in a position to do some damage to someone, certainly. Someone was so frightened of the damage he could do that they blew his brains out before thinking through the consequences.'

'Fortunately for us in a sense . . . I mean it makes our job a wee bit easier.'

'I won't argue, Abernethy. All help, whether by accident or design is gratefully received. The truth is that most people are victims of crime in some way at some time in their lives and most crimes are never solved. So all help . . .' He tapped out the remnants of the tobacco into the glass ashtray, by this time, mid afternoon, it was a container of a potage of grey and black and the room was a box full of layers of blue smoke. 'I'll see the Chief Super this afternoon, apprise him of all that has transpired to date. I'll wait until Bothwell—' The phone on his desk rang. 'Speak of the devil, I hope.' Donoghue lifted the receiver to his ear. 'Donoghue . . . yes . . .' – Donoghue smiled and nodded at Abernethy – '. . . yes . . .' He scribbled on his notepad. 'Got that . . . yes, send it up for the file which is with me. Many thanks.' He replaced the phone and opened the file and, glancing at his watch, he added a small item of recording. He then reached for a felt-tip pen from a drawer in his desk and wrote something on the front of the file. 'We've got a name, Abernethy.'

'We have, sir?'

'We have, sir.' Donoghue's enthusiasm at receiving the information seemed to Abernethy to fade and to become replaced by a manner of perplexity. 'We have . . . he's one Ronald Grenn.'

'Ronald Grenn,' Abernethy repeated, committing the name to memory. 'It doesn't mean anything to me.'

'It doesn't to me, but it does ring bells . . . you know yon way . . . something, something, something . . . something . . . something is meant by that name. Anyway, Bothwell did the trick, or at least Criminal Records did the trick once Elliot Bothwell had passed the latents to them. They're sending the file up now. So . . . a job for the back shift. Who . . . ?'

'Montgomerie, sir.'

'Ah.' Donoghue glanced at his watch. 'Ask him to come and see me when you hand over. He's got some work to do today.'

'Yes, sir.' Abernethy stood. 'Will that be all, sir?'

'Yes . . . yes.' Donoghue reached for his tobacco pouch. 'Grenn . . .'

It was 13.55 hours.

3

13.30–18.52 hrs

He had never been there before. He had heard of it. But circumstances had never before taken him there. He turned in at the gatehouse and gave his name to the uniformed man and was directed to proceed up the drive to the main house.

He had slept late that day, even allowing for a back shift start at 14.00 hours, he had slept late. She had left earlier. That, he thought, that had probably accounted for his later than usual rise. They had probably lain in each other's arms all night, awoke together at about six or six-thirty he judged by the amount of light in the morning sky and the amount of traffic on Highburgh Road, heard not seen. Buses in the main, moving speedily along near-empty roads. Sometime between the dawn and the rush hour this time of year, six, six-thirty. They had gripped each other tighter, fondled, stroked, mouth-to-mouthed, had slumped back to sleep as she, invigorated, had slid from under the duvet and hummed as she showered and scented. He was unaware of her eating breakfast and drinking coffee and closing the door behind her with a loud clunk, breezing, light-stepping down the close to the street door, smiling, beaming; a woman fulfilled. When he opened his eyes again the inexpensive but faultlessly accurate clock on his bedside cabinet showed he had just less than three hours before he had to sign in for the back shift. He levered himself out of the double bed and clawed his way groggily into a full-length, large-size, blue towelling bathrobe and padded into the bathroom and drew a long bath, savouring his muscular image in the mirror before the condensation covered the surface. He had an angular face of chiselled features, blue eyes above a black, down-turned moustache and rich black hair, expensively cut. He checked the mail box behind the door. A gas bill told him that that morning's post had been delivered. The bill itself was blue. He tore it up without opening it and contemptuously tossed it into the wastebin in the kitchen. He did not pay bills unless they were red. He made himself a coffee and poured it into a huge round mug which he found he could hold in one fist, but was more comfortable if held in both palms to drink from as if it were a bowl, biblical style. He carried the mug into the bathroom and slid into the bath. A shower he held was for getting clean quickly and efficiently, but a bath, a bath was a sybaritic experience to be savoured. It calms the soul, it relaxes utterly, it allows one to start one's day on one's own terms. Anybody, he thought, anybody who adopts the quick dip attitude is just plain missing the point. He lay back, sipping the coffee, holding the large round mug in both hands, and adjusted the hot-water tap with his big toe. Yes, he thought, just plain missing the point.

He lunched in his pine-clad kitchen overlooking the swing park between Highburgh Road and Havelock Street, a safe railinged place for the weans to play, surrounded on three sides by caring, watchful tenements and a main road on the fourth side. As he ate he listened to the lunchtime news. Little nationally or internationally held his interest but he groaned when he heard the regional news, the item about the body found in open ground in suspicious circumstances. He knew what he was going in to do, there'd be something to be addressed on that one. He glanced at his watch. If the news was correct and if the information hadn't been massaged by the press officer to assist the police enquiry, then they were still well within the first twenty-four hours, the 'drop everything and look at this one' twenty-four hours.

At 13.30 he left his flat and went down the clean, scrubbed stone stairs of the tenement, the gleaming porcelain tiles from floor to waist height of cream mainly, but red and dark blue here and there proclaiming his stair to be a much prized 'wally' close. The West Enders, the G12 dwellers, love their tiles. Not for them the plain plaster walls of the closes in the East End. Here be 'wally' closes. The afternoon, he noted, was fresh, dry, a heavy cloud cover. But not bad, he thought, not at all bad for October. He drove his ageing VW into the town, along the narrow, dark canyon that is Argyle Street, feeling fully rested, and then realized the reason, the clocks last night on the back shift, he'd put his watch back when the clocks in the police station were put back and all the back shift officers had stopped what they were doing and with only restrained complaint, had changed 00.00 to 23.00 and had then recommenced work. What that explained to him is why he should feel so rested. His watch may well read 13.30, but his body was saying 14.30. He had not just fallen back to sleep when Claire had left for her work, he had in effect slept for another hour on top of that.

He turned into the car park at the rear of P Division. He entered the low two-storey, interwar concrete-and-glass building by the rear 'staff only' entrance and signed in as PC Elka Willems was handing over the uniform bar to the back-shift officer. He went up the stairs to the CID corridor and went to the detective constables' room. Abernethy stood at his desk, cream-coloured padded rally jacket on his shoulders, ready to get off, anxiously, it seemed.

'Fabian wants to see you,' Abernethy said. 'Soon as you get in.'

'About the body that was found? Has to be. I heard it on the news. Can't be anything else given that I'm rejoicing with a clear conscience at the moment. Unusual state of affairs but quite enjoyable.'

'Lucky you.' Abernethy zipped up his jacket. 'But yes, it's about that.' He picked up his copy of the *Glasgow Herald*.

'Cream's the wrong colour for a jacket like that,' said he of down-turned moustache. 'Shows up the dirt.' He peeled off his own darker-coloured waterproof jacket and went back into the corridor and walked to the office of DI Donoghue and tapped reverently on the door.

'Come.' The command was clear, imperious and given as usual only after a pause.

He had opened the door and stepped into the office. Donoghue looked at him, remained stone-faced and had indicated a chair. 'Yes, Montgomerie, I've a job for you. Take a seat, I'll put you in the picture.'

And Malcolm Montgomerie had taken a seat and had listened politely, attentively, as Donoghue, pulling and blowing lovingly on his pipe and consulting a still fairly thin file and also consulting a thicker, older file, had put him in the picture. He listened as he was told about the body found on the expanse of grass at Winton Drive, of the gunshot wound to the head, of the supposition that the crime was committed at about the time the clocks were going back, not gangland, and close to where the body was discovered. The deceased subsequently identified as one Ronald Grenn, aged forty-five. 'Some track,' he said to Montgomerie putting down Ronald Grenn's file. 'Petty ned, went down for seven years for burglary and wilful fire-raising.'

'Seven years?'

Donoghue had nodded. 'Yes, I thought it was a short stretch but it was the Cernach Antique's job . . .'

'That one!'

'That one. Never did feel right. A lot of expensive gems, none traced, he had to have had accomplices. He wouldn't cooperate, kept his lips sealed and took his secrets to the slammer with him. Upon release he was at liberty for forty-eight hours, less in fact, before he gets his brains blown out somewhere in the West End.'

'Came out wanting his share, got told he couldn't have it, threatened to cough and was filled in?'

'It's happened before. At the moment he's our only lead. We have a house address in Easterhouse and his last prison . . .' Donoghue had paused. 'Don't know which to go to first. Just you and King on the CID back shift?'

'For our sins, sir.'

'Yes . . .' Donoghue took his pipe from his mouth and held it like a pen, by the stem with his fingers. 'The question is, which one to go to first? We informed Mrs Grenn of the identity of the deceased only an hour or two ago . . . We have to be sensitive . . . all right, we'll allow the lady her grief before we start firing questions at her . . . so, off to his last slammer if you will, Montgomerie.'

'Which was, sir?'

'Traquair Brae. Nice drive out for you. It's down by Selkirk way. Glance at his file before you go. Talk to the staff, talk to any of the cons who'll talk to you. See what you can dig up. Anything he might have said, contacts outside, any visitors, you know the sort of thing.'

Montgomerie had said, yes, he knew the sort of thing, and after a glance at the file of Grenn, Ronald, which told a tale of endless convictions for petty theft and motoring offences, and which contained a photograph of a thin-faced, weak-chinned individual with a long crooked nose and wiry black hair. Leaving Glasgow by the A74, he took the A72 to Lanark, to Biggar, to Peebles and eventually to quiet Innerleithen, nestling in the hills, the nearest town to Traquair Brae Open Prison. He enjoyed the drive, he didn't often get to turn a wheel of this nature at the company's expense, just he, and he alone, save for Paul Simon or Nancy Griffiths on the hi-fi. And once beyond Lanark he was in strange country, flat, rolling hills, forests, buses of the Lowland Scots Bus Company serving rural routes, a castle by a river of clear water surrounded by Douglas fir, under a wide sky; two horses, one larger than the other, galloping together in a field with a bronzed autumnal backdrop, large houses set back from the road, the occasional other motorist, the wide, quiet central street of Innerleithen where he stopped and asked directions for Traquair Brae at the hotel. He noted the directions given clearly in a distinct Borders accent by a man in a yellow cardigan and a not-to-be-trifled-with manner. The directions took him to a pair of stone gates, a gatehouse and man in a uniform who asked him to enquire at the main house.

Montgomerie drove up the narrow drive, his progress slowed by frequent speed ramps, and the remoteness of location continually reinforced by the large numbers of rabbits which darted out of the rhododendron bushes across his path. The road went on, Montgomerie found himself mustering faith that the main house would appear. He found himself wishing he had noted the mileage his odometer showed when he stopped at the gatehouse. Then, through a gap in the rhododendrons, at a lower level than the road, he caught a glimpse of a football match, a team in red and a team in blue. Houses appeared, set back from the road, of a bungalow type, nestling in the foliage, leaves on the small front lawn and eventually, the road opened out into a courtyard in front of a large mansion, grey stone, beneath a grey and darkening sky. Self-effacingly, he parked his VW beside a gleaming Mercedes Benz and pondered that salaries in the prison service had clearly improved of late.

'Ronald Grenn.' The man, Assistant Governor Laing by

the nameplate on his desk, leaned back in his leather chair, causing the fabric to squeak. 'So that was him. I heard the news at lunchtime . . . well, well, well. The lads will be upset . . . I presume you're releasing the name?'

Montgomerie pursed his lips. 'I presume so . . . frankly, I can't see any reason not to . . .'

'Well, I'll keep it to myself just to be on the safe side . . . but if it's released the boys will hear it on the evening news.'

'I wasn't told not to release the name to the cons. In fact, if I'm going to be able to chat to any who knew him, I'll have to tell them he's no longer with us.'

'You don't *have* to, but if you want cooperation you'd be better doing so, especially here in an open prison.' Laing's office was wood panelled, a large window made up of smaller glass panes looked out over the car park, and to the sun sinking beneath a distant skyline, giving the impression that a wood was burning. Laing himself was a young man, about late twenties – ex-services, judging by a photograph of a submarine on the wall behind his desk. And could that, Montgomerie wondered, be an even younger Laing, white peaked cap, bearded, on the conning tower of said submarine? 'So how can I help you?'

'By telling us what you know about Ronald Grenn. We're a bit short of background at the moment. We know little about him, not enough to explain who – or why – would want to shoot him stone dead, just a day or two after he was released.'

'Ron . . . Ronnie to his pals . . . he was just an inoffensive wee guy . . . tended to be a follower, but he was well suited to the open prison . . . joined in the haggis hunts we have from time to time . . . the warders hide haggises in the grounds . . .'

'Haggis hunts?'

'They're popular, as I said, warders hide haggises in the grounds and the inmates root around hunting for them, once found they're cooked up and scoffed. Have to be quick though, you've no idea how quick the foxes are round here. The "hunts" are done at night, you see.'

'Ah . . .'

'Not all the inmates take part, those who've been convicted of white-collar crimes, people with some education, turn up

65

their noses at such antics, dare say I would if I were in here, against my wishes, that is . . . but many enjoy them. It may seem an emotionally immature pastime for grown men, but remember that these grown men have, for the greater part, the emotional maturity of the average ten-year-old and so haggis hunts have their appeal.'

'I see. And Ronnie enjoyed them?'

'Aye . . . he was what you'd call a wee softie, not a lot of bottle about Ron Grenn, allowed himself to be led around . . . being inside didn't bother him . . . that's probably why he enjoyed the haggis hunts. We have guys in here who've been in the professions, thrown it all away, embezzled money, for example . . . men like that go into a deep depression upon conviction, and while they've recovered by and large by the time they get here, they still think that such childish games are beneath them. So they lock themselves in their cubicle and listen to classical music on their hi-fi equipment. Others don't join in the merry-making because they have an all-consuming sense of guilt and don't believe they should be allowed any form of enjoyment.'

'Ron Grenn was neither.'

'No. He gave us the impression that he was happy to be in prison, many people are. They've got their cot and three and that's all they want. That's not so common in an open prison where escape is easy . . . if people can't cope with the responsibility asked of them in here, all they have to do is walk down the drive and stand on the road. It happens. We go after them and find them just standing there and we'll say, are you coming back or do you want to be reported as an escapee? Most of those who've got that far will ask to be reported and then they'll run just for the hell of it, just to see how far they can get. People like that are asking to be put back where they're locked up and escape is difficult, they feel safer, they don't like being given responsibility, even for themselves. It frightens them.'

'But Ron Grenn cooperated?'

'Fully. He came to us from Peterhead, before that he was in Barlinnie.' Laing opened a file. 'He got seven years. He was out in four and a bit . . . So he was arrested, six months in the Barlinnie prior to trial, sentenced to seven years, spends another six, twelve months in there, transferred to Peterhead to break rocks for a period of ... two and a half years and spent the remainder of his sentence with us doing pin drawings and haggis hunting. Not bad really. Half a million quid for being a kept man for four and a half years, half of which is spent in an open prison which has been likened to an extended stay at a health farm ... balanced diet, sports equipment, grounds to run in ...'

'I saw a soccer match.'

'Oh, we have tennis courts for the summer ... plenty of good reading material in our library ... limited access to tobacco and no access to alcohol, people can leave here physically and emotionally refreshed. I can understand the sentence of seven years. It seems lenient, in fact.'

'He never talked about his crime?'

'Not to the staff. He might have spoken to one or two of the inmates ... one guy in particular, "Weasel" Iveson, seemed to latch on to Ronnie Grenn. If I know "Weasel" it would have been because he could smell money ... I didn't know if our Ronnie said anything ... I may have been a bit dismissive of Ronnie and his enthusiasm for childlike games, because if his sentence tells us one thing, it tells us that he can keep his mouth shut and that he plays his cards close to his chest.'

'Good point.' Montgomerie nodded.

'But "Weasel" Iveson's your man if anybody is. You'd like to talk to him?'

'If that's possible.'

'I'm sure it could be arranged.' Laing smiled and picked up the phone on his desk and tapped two numbers. When his call was answered Montgomerie heard him ask. 'Yes, AG Laing ... can you find, er ... I can't remember ... oh yes, Sandy Iveson ... a.k.a. "Weasel" and bring him to the agent's room, please. Thanks.' He replaced the phone gently, sensitively, almost sliding the handset on to the rest. 'Left me for a moment.'

'Sorry?'

'His name ... so used to referring to him as "Weasel".'

'But it's Sandy.'

'Alexander, invariably shortened to "Sandy" in Scotland and "Alex" in England.'

'I didn't know that.'

'Oh yes. I served in the navy with a guy called Alex, Alex

Lutyens. The English have strange ways, believe me. I served in a navy full of them.'

Montgomerie grinned. He found himself liking Assistant Governor Laing. He asked if Ron Grenn had had any significant visitors during his time at Traquair Brae.

'Hall officer would be the best man to put that question to. All visits are logged, the prisoners have to send visitor's passes to their relatives and friends and we keep a record of all passes issued . . . his mother visited once or twice, but she's elderly as you'd imagine, mind like a tack but her bones were chalk. She was brought by a charity, some people organized themselves into an escort service for elderly people, they'll take elderly people anywhere within half a day's drive . . . that is half a day out, half a day back, for the price of the petrol only and with two weeks' notice.'

'So as long as the return journey can be completed in one day?'

'Is another, neater way of putting it' – Laing nodded – 'but she was brought by them on two occasions . . . I imagine that she found the journey tiring and didn't have a great deal of dosh and so two visits in two years was all that she could manage one way or the other.'

'Interesting.'

'Yes. I mention it because it didn't speak of a wide family network. I mean, if he had been blackballed from the family, I'm sure a relative would still drive his mum to visit him.'

'It's interesting from another point of view as well.' Montgomerie glanced out of the window at a now scarlet sunset. 'It means that Ron Grenn didn't have access to any money while inside, and he wouldn't be able to get credit from gangland for anything he went down for, otherwise his old mum wouldn't be in poverty like that . . . he stole gems worth . . . half a million . . . he'd reset the lot by the time he was arrested, which was only a day or two after the raid . . . he'd left his fingerprints everywhere . . . that's what happened . . . he'd no time to collect hard cash for the gems so he served his time, ate his porridge, went to collect upon discharge and got his head blown off. Simple.'

'So all you have to do is find who he was into for half a million quid? No wonder he got offed. I mean, what would you do if some inoffensive wee guy comes knocking on your door asking for a considerable wedge with no means of enforcing his claim except a threat to go to the polis? He was soft in the head for even trying if you ask me.'

'Aye . . . he was asking for it right enough.'

'I can't . . .'

There was a tap on Laing's door.

'Yes?'

The door opened. A uniformed man in his fifties stood in the doorway. He nodded to Montgomerie and then addressed Laing. 'That's Iveson in the agent's room now, sir.'

'Thanks. Mr Minford . . .'

'Sir?'

'Could you please cut along to records and bring me the file on Ronald Grenn? He was discharged a couple of days ago. The file won't have gone off to the Scottish Office yet.'

'Records. File on Ronald Grenn. Right away, sir.'

'We knew each other in the navy.' Laing nodded at the closing door. 'Ex-Chief Petty Officer Minford, good man, helped me find my feet. He was the sort of father figure who looms over gawky young officers and says things like, "That is not a good idea – sir". The British armed services depend on men like Mr Minford. But, as I was saying before he came in, I can't think off hand of other visitors, but his record will tell us and lo, who should walk in but the stalwart Mr Minford, who obliges us by fetching said record. Something for you to glance at when you've had a chat with "Weasel" Iveson. Don't let him get hold of you.'

'Oh?'

'I don't mean physically, but it might be a good idea to have someone in with you . . .'

'He might not talk so easily.'

'I'll make sure someone's outside the door. Iveson . . . I can only warn you about him. He's dangerous. Manipulative is the wrong word, he'll try to control you . . . he can play mind games . . .'

'Ah.'

'You might know the type. He's been eating porridge now for ten years and he's ruined a lot of people . . . other prisoners have lost their remission for good behaviour because they found themselves doing what Iveson wanted them to do . . . and one prison officer with twenty years' service is now

serving time himself . . . lost everything because he helped
Iveson to escape. The story follows Iveson from slammer to
slammer . . . the prison officers never allow themselves to
be alone with him because he can control one person if he
can, but not two, can't control two . . . the story is that the
prison officer who helped Iveson escape said, "I went along
with him, he controlled me. I knew it was wrong. I knew I
shouldn't be doing it, but I went along with it. He controlled
me . . ." or words like that.'

'A dangerous man.'

'Very.'

'What's he in for?'

'Schedule One offender, specifically sex with a minor,
many acts of the same with many minors. We know about
his daughters but rumours apparently persist about many
other children, of both sexes, whose lives were ruined by
him . . . anyway, he's in the only place for him.'

'An open prison?'

'He's nearing his release date . . . dare say you'll be notified
if he moves to Glasgow but he's a Dundee man, and I
think the Scottish Office will be notifying Tayside Police of
a Schedule One offender in their community, especially since
in one of his rare unguarded moments he was overheard
drooling with anticipation about what he referred to as
"Tayside fairies".'

Montgomerie grimaced and put his hand to his stomach.

'Gets you like that, doesn't it? But he's served his sentence,
we can't keep him in.'

'The Yanks can. Did you know that? So I heard, of the
likes of the "Weasel" Iveson. They say all right, you've served
your sentence but we think you still represent a danger so
you won't get out. Last I heard, the legality of it was being
challenged.'

'I should think it is!'

'But I can see the argument for it, and I can see the
argument against it.'

'But thankfully this is Scotland. We don't have that issue
to deal with.'

'So, Iveson . . . all I can say is thanks for the warning.'

'I'll take you along there. Come and see me when you're
finished.' The two men stood. 'I'll be interested to know how

you got on. And Ron Grenn's file will be here for your perusal by then.'

Ray Sussock sat in his room. It was, he found, cramped. It had long ago failed to appeal to him because of its cosiness. He had escaped here during the bitter entrenched winter of the Glasgow Knife Murders case, the case in which Elka Willems had been stabbed. Then it had been as a haven, a small room, a single bed, a wardrobe, a small writing table and chair and an armchair. He had a small hi-fi system under the writing table and an old portable black-and-white TV which he kept on top of the hi-fi set. When he wanted to watch TV he would move the upright chair from in front of the writing table and sit looking at the TV, at a wide angle to the screen. His room had a small sash window which looked out into an elevated lawn at the rear of the house. When he had moved into the room, escaping Rutherglen, he had found sanctuary here. But now it was small, so, so, small – a cell, warm and dry but a cell, and now the walls seemed to close in on him. The room itself was in a large house in the West End of the city which had once been a family home of a merchant banker or a shipping magnate or some such, but now was divided up into a warren of bedsitters. Now, in the mid afternoon, midweek, the old house was silent. In the mornings from seven-thirty onwards for an hour there is a rustle and hubbub of noise as people leave for their work. At five p.m. or thereabouts they begin to drift back, some early, just wanting to get home, others later, having had an after-work drink. Then the noise begins. The couple upstairs from Sussock will scream at each other, threatening murder, and one day, Sussock fully anticipated, one will plunge a knife deep into the chest of the other and then collapse over the corpse making distraught protestations of abiding and everlasting love. And the two men who share the room next to Sussock's room and share the bed in that room which they insist upon pushing up close to the dividing wall will come home. Sussock never knew which he found more insensitive: the grunts of their coupling, whenever, like passionate lovers would, they could couple: before leaving for work, as soon as they got home, each weekend afternoon, or their hi-fi equipment, which would boom, boom, boom, through his

71

wall. Sometimes the two sounds would be mingled, boom, boom, grunt, gasp, grunt, boom, boom. There was the man in the room across the hall, a young man who seemed to change his name with the phases of the moon, a new name is a new identity, a new identity is a new hope. Last time Sussock had met him in the hallway he was sifting through the mail on the table between the door and the mirror, tearfully looking for a letter for 'Billy'. Sussock had said, 'Hi, Tom,' and the young man had said, 'No, no, it's Billy . . . there's no mail for Billy.' On occasions the young man would be found sitting on the edge of his bed with his door open, a water pistol in his hand, fighting off sleep, waiting for the Martians that were coming to abduct him. Eventually he would collapse, exhausted, and he would not be seen for some months, though a lady from the Social Work Department ensured that his rent was paid. He would return, calling himself Fred, he was always Fred when he returned, calm, he no longer became tearful when there was no mail for 'Billy' or 'Tom' or 'Cy' or 'Angus', and many weeks would elapse before he sat up all night awaiting the Martians, calmer certainly, easier to live with certainly, but away somewhere. Sussock was happier for the young man when he was distressed, not out of malice, but because it was only when he was distressed that he seemed to be alive and thinking and feeling, and part of the world.

Sussock stood and walked across the room the short distance to his window. A blackened stone wall surrounded the lawn, beyond was the upper floor and rooftops of a villa and above the rooftop of the villa was a blood-crimson sunset. He gazed at it. Sunsets had always reached him. He left his room, locking the door behind him. He had little worth stealing; the gesture was rather to preserve the sanctity of his living space. The small room, probably no more than a broom cupboard when the house was new built and first occupied, was his personal space. It wasn't much, but it was his. So he kept the door locked. He went down the inside stone stairway, clambering into his coat as he did so, holding his battered trilby in one hand as he struggled with the buttons of his coat with the other. He turned left at the foot of the stairs and entered the kitchen. He kept little food in the kitchen, knowing such a policy was fatal in bedsit land. Keep only what you're going to eat in the next hour or two, you can't stand guard over it. It was no surprise to him that the last of his teabags had gone, as had the can of beans he always kept as an emergency source of food. And that was something else he had found out about bedsit living; if a can of food remains unconsumed for long enough, it moves into a state of ownerlessness, upon which it vanishes. Fast. He had resisted keeping a cardboard box of foodstuff in his room, it had seemed like a defeat in some way to do so, but he felt his resolve on that issue slackening. It was either that or have his food pilfered.

Beside the kitchen door was a second door. It led to the cellar of the house where the Polish landlord lived with his wife. Sussock had had one occasion to go there, to request a replacement light bulb, only to be rebuffed with a 'buy your own', but he had thus been able to see how they lived. They too lived in cramped accommodation, just upright chairs round a dining table next to a sink with an ancient black-and-white TV sitting drunkenly on the draining board and a double bed pushed into a recess beyond the cooker. After that insight into their lives he didn't like them any more but gave them grudging respect. They were not absentee landlords who lived in luxury while their tenants shivered and starved; they lived frugally and expected their tenants to do the same. Sussock could respect that.

He left the house and turned right and walked down Victoria Crescent Road, he enjoyed the walk, he always did; the graceful sweep of the terrace curving downhill he found uplifting. Like the house he lived in, these terrace houses were now split into multiple occupancy dwellings but unlike the house he lived in, the houses on Victoria Crescent Road were divided into owner-occupier flats favoured by the yuppies of the city. Those people in the basement flats benefitted from massive iron bars over windows to keep the burglars from getting in, though Sussock had learned they were an original feature designed to stop the servants from sneaking out.

He turned left at the bottom of the crescent and walked the short distance to Byres Road, the axis of the West End of the city. The long road, another of Glasgow's canyons, reaching south from G12 to G11 was the Sauchiehall Street of the West End, it was the Princes Street of the West End, the Oxford Street of the West End, it was the Avenue of the Americas of the West End; without it, and its bustle, Sussock held, the West End just wouldn't exist. It was an artery, pumping the life blood of this part of Scotland's first city. He stepped from the quietness of Dowanside Road into the crowded pavement of Byres Road, and weaved his way to the McDonald's and a quarterpounder with cheese and a plastic beaker of orange juice. On his way to the fast-feeder he saw Christmas cards being aggressively displayed in shop windows. And it was still only October.

Feeling put on by the quarterpounder and refreshed by the orange juice, he walked back to the large house. He hadn't slept since coming off shift, by this time, now four p.m., tiredness still ran like a sharp pain from pupil to pupil, from eyeball to eyeball. It was his policy to sleep immediately upon returning home after a night shift, to wake at about three p.m. and have the afternoon and evening to himself before reporting for duty again at 22.00. But he hadn't done so that day. He hadn't felt tired when he had returned to his room and had sat in the armchair, his thoughts dwelling depressingly on the state of his life, where he had fetched up, aged sixty, after thirty-five years of service. It had all seemed to him to be very unfair, especially when he couldn't put his finger on where *he* had gone wrong, what terrible crime he had committed to bring down such a judgement upon himself. And by now it was too late to sleep, he had let the precious hours of silence slip through his fingers. To return home now would be to try to sleep when the boys in the next room would be gasping and grunting, with or without the accompaniment of their hi-fi, and when the couple upstairs, fuelled after work with alcohol, would be screaming at each other. He walked to where he had parked his car, and fighting sleep and the numbing of his senses, he drove to Langside. To Baker Street.

Richard King cleared his throat. He looked down at the file open on his lap and said, 'Out of his depth.'

Donoghue pulled on his pipe and nodded. He noticed that King was wearing a sports jacket of uncharacteristically loud check; grey with yellow stripes. He had often noted with approval King's modest, sober, professional dress style and so his sudden taste in grey-yellow check for a sports jacket was, he found, head-turning. 'Go on.'

'Well, sir.' King shuffled on his chair. 'The first thing that strikes me about this is how out of character it is for him.'

'He is a thief.'

'But not in this league, not in this class.' King turned the pages of the file. 'It's all petty stuff, he's a petty ned, a light-fingered recidivist. Look at his track, probation, fines of a few quid, six months here, three months there, twelve months suspended, community service . . . and the offences. Breach, going equipped, theft by OLP, and then he leaps from that and opens the lockfast premises of them all and pilfers a quarter of—'

'Half.'

'Half a million pounds' worth of gems.'

'Which have not been recovered. Where do half a million pounds' worth of gems go to, Richard?' Donoghue liked King, he had time for him, he found the chubby, bearded cop dedicated, professional in his attitude and good at his job. He had the benefit of a calm and settled home life, wife and one child, so far, but Donoghue saw in King a man who took to fatherhood and he fully anticipated the announcement of another King on the way. Ray Sussock would be retiring soon, and if Donoghue were to be asked to nominate a successor he knew he would nominate Richard King. A detective constable well in the frame for detective sergeant.

'Beats me, sir.'

'No, it doesn't, Richard.' Donoghue lit his pipe.

'Sir?'

'It doesn't beat you. Do you remember the theft in question?'

'Certainly do, the building's still a burnt-out shell.'

'It never did satisfy me, I mean the outcome of that case. We drew a blank and went to the Fiscal with what we had and he ran with it and Ronald Grenn collected his seven years. It's an image that stays with me, you know, little Ronnie Grenn who'd never been in a higher court than the Glasgow Sheriff and he suddenly finds himself in the High Court with all its majesty and gravitas, standing there, a wee guy peering over the top of the dock looking lost and frightened, like a little boy having his first day at the big school. I confess I felt embarrassed for the police force, Richard, I really did. Half a million pounds' worth of gems vanish, then the building they're taken from goes up in smoke and a further half a million pounds' worth of antique furniture, paintings, artefacts of a general nature are destroyed and the only culprit we can find is wee Ronnie Grenn whom we make stand blinking in fear and anticipation and wonder in the dock of the High Court.'

'A patsy?'

'Has to be. I thought at the time that he was fed to us as a fall guy, but he wouldn't trade and so someone clearly made it worth his while to keep quiet. We pulled him soon after the fire and theft, about forty-eight hours, as I recall . . . this is over four years ago, time for him to hand the gems to someone else . . . a bit like bringing someone down with a rugby tackle after he's passed the ball.'

King smiled. He enjoyed the image that Donoghue had employed.

'We had his prints on the strongbox inside the lockable fire-proof cabinet, the gems having been kept in the strongbox. He didn't explain where he'd put the gems, who he'd given them to, he lived a hand-to-mouth existence in Easterhouse, no gems in his gaff, no bank account in his name that we could find, nothing to tie him to the fire, nothing at all. All we had was his latents on an empty jewellery box. He wouldn't tell us how he got past the alarm, wouldn't tell us anything.'

'He pleaded guilty, though.'

'He pleaded not guilty. That was clever of him, or it was clever of whoever it was that was putting him up to it. You see, if he coughed to a plea bargain, he'd have to tell us how he got into the building and he'd have to tell us to whom he gave the gems. But if he went with an NG to OLP, despite overwhelming evidence to the contrary, he could take those secrets to the slammer with him. The judge knew what was going on and sent him down for seven years which was quite lenient. Wee Ronnie set about working his ticket, volunteering to clean the toilets and ingratiating himself with the chaplain and he came out in four, half of which was spent in an open prison. Montgomerie is down there now, even as we speak, digging and sniffing around.' Donoghue paused and rekindled his pipe. 'So, Ronnie is happy to collect seven years, probably told to think in terms of four or five if he remembers his p's and q's and generally minds his manners, and to remember a wee nest egg that awaits him upon release.'

'Being conjecture?'

'Oh yes, of course, but if we start with a supposition we can at least look for something to prove it. So he minds his manners, gets released and forty-eight hours later he's on a slab. My guess is that he went for his pay-off and his pay-off turned out to be a bullet in the head.'

'It's happened before.'

'And it'll happen again. It's the old Pied Piper of Hamelin number, you see, reneging on a deal, but, unlike the Pied Piper, Ronnie hadn't got anything to hold over whoever had not fulfilled the promise made.'

'Except perhaps to turn queen's evidence, and so he was filled in to keep him quiet.'

'That would be my guess, Richard.'

'Where now, sir?'

'I know what I want to do, but I'd be interested in your thoughts?'

'Well . . . Malcolm's down at . . .'

'Traquair Brae.'

'Oh yes . . . a home visit to Ronnie Grenn's next of kin or known associates . . . they may well know something . . .'

'Montgomerie will do that . . . I was thinking of another approach.'

'Oh?'

'Come on, Richard. You disappoint me.'

King remained silent. 'I'm sorry . . .'

'We're going back into the case, Richard. Not the murder of Ronnie Grenn, but the theft he was gaoled for; there, we're going back there.'

'We are?'

'We are.' Donoghue placed his pipe in the glass ashtray and leaned forward, his forearm resting on his desk, and folded his hands together, interlocking his fingers. 'You see, it's my guess that an insurance fraud went down in this town around four years ago. Look at the figures, half a million pounds' worth of gems, say worth half that when reset. So that's three-quarters of a million pounds already, then the antique furniture and oil paintings and sundry nick-nacks, all of high value, worth another half a million with a resale value of half that, so we have a potential criminal profit there of one and a half million.'

'What was left in the fire, sir?'

'A lot of ash, but who's to say if the ash was from a beautifully kept Chippendale chair or a scratched and battered and worm-eaten bit of Victorian junk, so long as it's hardwood, not chipboard.'

'Of course, and the canvases . . . ?'

'Could have been bought from Barrows any weekend, framed paintings by enthusiastic amateurs from Victorian and Edwardian times, of no value at all.'

'The paintings would have been itemized, though, sir – always strikes me as a pointless theft, the theft of an art treasure, I mean who could you sell it to?'

'Good point, but I'm not letting go of my premise that this was an insurance fraud on a massive scale. Maybe they didn't claim for the paintings and sold them off before torching the building. We'll have to see what's on the insurance manifest.'

'Dare say we can expect a lot of help from the insurance company on this one, sir.'

'Dare say we can, because then there is the insurance on the building itself. Four floors of early Victorian stone-built commercial property, designed as offices, turned into a prestigious, high-value antiques shop, view strictly by appointment, on Bath Street. The development potential of that site would be worth more than the building itself; never get planning permission to knock it down, Glasgow valuing its Victorian heritage as it does. It's the most Victorian city in the UK. Did you know that?'

King confessed that he didn't.

'Take it from me, I have an abiding interest in the architecture of this city.'

'I didn't know that, sir.'

'Well, it is, but that's by the by. But one way round the planning permission is to destroy the structural integrity of the building and force its demolition.'

'And one way of doing that is by fire.'

'Exactly.' Donoghue smiled. 'So the site could be worth two million quid; in addition the value of the building would have to be paid for. The insurance company would be obliged to pay up the cost of a total rebuild but if a total rebuild was not possible because of the aforementioned structural integrity being compromised, then the owner of the building would pocket the cost of the total rebuild in hard cash and then sell the site as is. I mean, all in all, you could be talking about a fraud of four or five million pounds.'

'It wasn't seen at the time?'

'Apparently not. But sometimes you need distance to be able to realize things. At the time, I thought no more than that Ronnie Grenn must have had an accomplice who had persuaded him to take the rap and that they burnt the building to cover their tracks. I didn't see beyond that, none of us did – none of us being me and Ray Sussock. It's only after the usefulness of four years' time distance that's enabled me to see what I've just outlined to you as possibly being what happened. So someone pockets three, four or five million, they offer Ronald Grenn a hundred thousand to do a four-year stretch, hard cash. I mean, it's good money, and for Ronnie Grenn, who knows how to survive in the slammer, that sort of dosh is the end of the rainbow. Of course he'd jump at it.'

'But as you say, when he went to collect . . .' King shrugged his shoulders.

'Well, this is all conjecture. We won't know what happened until we start turning over a few stones. So, like I said, we're going back into the case and I want you to head it up.'

'Me, sir?'

'You, sir. With Montgomerie coming at it the other way, from the murder back in time, and you going from the theft of the gems to the present, you should, if I'm right, but only if I'm right, meet each other halfway.'

'Very good, sir.' King smiled, eager to start work. He stood and glanced at his watch. It was 17.00 hours. Exactly. Though his mind and body felt it to be 18.00 hours. Exactly.

It's the eyes. Montgomerie thought it was the eyes. Something sucked him into this man. He felt himself being sucked up by him. The man had no sense of presence, he wasn't a strong charismatic personality, at least so far as Montgomerie could discern. Yet somehow, he felt he was being pulled out of himself by this man, 'Weasel' Iveson, by name and nickname. He tried to analyse the technique. It was, so far as he could tell, a combination of facial expression and his eyes, but mostly his eyes. The facial expression was serious, no smile, no relaxation, concentrating fully on Montgomerie, holding eye contact, with expressionless eyes . . . no . . . no, they weren't expressionless, there was a depth to them, like looking into two dark tunnels and Montgomerie felt himself being pulled into the man's eyes. He felt himself losing contact with himself, as if being hypnotized. He glimpsed where this could lead. He knew, if he gave in, that this man could make him do things that he would otherwise have thought impossible. And he knew why the warders at Traquair Brae never allowed themselves to be alone with him. And he knew why the man was in prison: if he, a cop, sensed himself being manipulated by this man, what chance had his children, and friends of his children whose lives he had blighted? And when he thought how this small man with sharp features had been overheard 'drooling with anticipation' about the 'Tayside fairies' that await him upon his release, then Montgomerie knew why the Yanks do what they do. 'Sorry, we know you've served your time, but you're still not being released, it's too dangerous, too much of a risk. So here you stay.' It made sense. It was a massive infringement of civil liberty, but it made sense. There in the pleasant wood-panelled agent's room with a window which overlooked a darkening forest scene, it made sense. He looked away from the man, deliberately breaking eye contact and the instant that he did so he realized that the man was employing another technique: he was taking Montgomerie very seriously, at least he was giving out that message. This man would not be hostile, nor sneer, nor smirk, nor belittle, he would do nothing that might put up a barrier of resentment, but he appealed to the need of every person to be taken seriously, shown respect, being told by manner and body language that they matter and if the person to whom he is talking is needy, uncertain, insecure, as in the case of a 'Tayside fairy' then what a powerful seduction technique. Montgomerie realized that he was sitting in the presence of a very dangerous man. He also sensed a distinct annoyance from Iveson when he broke eye contact and decided not to allow the man any further such contact. He would look down at his notepad, or out of the window, but not into the two dark tunnels at either side of the bridge of Iveson's pointed nose.

'Ronnie.' Montgomerie wrote the name on his pad. 'Ronald Grenn.'

'Aye.' Iveson had a soft voice, sinister, with an attractive, easy-to-listen-to quality.

'I gather he was a friend of yours?'

'Aye.'

'You know he's dead?'

'Been shot. I heard the news, I heard the gossip in the hall here. News like that travels fast. Be in the paper tomorrow. Be in the paper this evening.'

'Spent a lot of time with him?'

'Not much really.'

'Did he ever express any fear of anyone?'

'No.'

Montgomerie doodled on his pad. He knew he was going to have to work hard at this interview. He pondered whether to allow Iveson a degree of eye contact. He felt he was able to play games so long as he retained ultimate control, he had to do that. Dangerous, this man is dangerous. But is he? The thoughts bounced inside Montgomerie's head. The man is in an open prison, a soft bed, no need for a Vulnerable Prisoners Unit, nobody here will be doing anything to rock their boat, attacking other inmates or escaping is not on their agenda, they'll all be working their ticket to an early release. So Iveson wouldn't present a danger. It would be a gamble. He glanced at Iveson and said, 'Tell me about him.'

Iveson's eyes slightly dilated. A signal of approval. Montgomerie again felt himself sliding into Iveson's influence.

'Just a wee guy.'

'No more than that?'

'He was pally with me, he chummed me about. See, I'm a beast, in any other pokey I'd been on the VPUs 'cos the lags would be out to fill me in, but here there's none of that, here they all want their porridge behind them so they make no waves. I get left alone, me and beasts like me, we don't get attention, nobody wants to know us, we don't get on the football team, they don't want us in the showers and we know that it's best not to join in the haggis hunts in the grounds, but Ronnie, wee man, he didn't seem to mind. So we palled up.'

'I see.' Montgomerie broke eye contact and glanced out of the window. It was now dark, the window acted like a mirror, he saw his reflection, he saw Iveson's reflection. The small room smelled of pine and creosote. 'What do you know about him?'

'He didn't belong here.'

'Innocent?'

'No, he was guilty all right, not quite sure what of, but he was guilty. What I mean is that he was a ned out of his depth . . . people that come here are big timers, wee Ronnie Grenn, see him, wee man that he was, he'd think getting away without paying your bus fare was big time and then he'd spend a week planning it. Here he was out of his depth. Which might be why he spent time with me, none of the others would have anything to do with him, just not in their class. So I suppose we found each other in here. The main crew wouldn't have anything to do with either of us. I reckon that was it, me I'm a beast and Ronald Grenn, well if they were tigers, he was a pussycat. I mean, if you put Ron Grenn in a room with two rabbits, the rabbits would attack him. He'd kind of glide up to you with a daft wee 'please-like-me' smile . . . ugh . . . I mean in other circumstances, he'd not be my choice of pal, but here . . . well, choice is limited and we all need human company. You know, when I was in the world, I used to subscribe to the notion that no company was better than the wrong company . . . but in here . . . after a while . . . I can spend time by myself but I found I changed my attitude . . . I found that loneliness is so vast that I came to think that any company is better than no company. Total inversion.'

Montgomerie realized that the man who spoke lovingly of 'Tayside fairies' was not without education. He asked Iveson what he was before being convicted.

'Besides being a paedophile, you mean?'

'Yes.'

'A teacher. Well, what else would attract a guy like me to teaching or social work with children? We don't have a "danger to children" stamped on our foreheads, they're desperate to fill the posts and if we present well at interview we'll get in, eventually. I mean, all those after school sports clubs and camping trips in the summer. Lovely. It's just the way it is; I mean, some people are sexually attracted to the elderly, they seek jobs in old people's homes or geriatric hospitals. That is what happens out there. If you want in, you hide that gleam in your eye. It's the first thing you learn how to do. I got caught. Eventually. Caught with my pants down. Literally.'

Montgomerie closed his eyes and then looked down at his pad. It's a further technique, he thought, another of Iveson's tricks – telling people what they want to hear. He said, 'You're going back to Dundee?'

'Aye,' Iveson nodded, 'I'll be back there by Easter.'

'You'll be watched.'

'Aye, like a hawk.'

'You'll be going back to your old ways?'

'If I can. There's no cure, no therapy . . . just long spells of porridge if you get caught . . . so don't get caught . . . I'll use videos and magazines more than I did. Safer that way. Safer for me and that means it's safer for the wee fairies.'

'Visitors?' Montgomerie looked away from Iveson.

'None. No one visits me.'

'I meant Ronald Grenn. Did he have any visitors?'

'His mum. Frail old dear. He clearly doted on her. She came in a car driven by a charity. Twice.'

'Just his mother?'

'No.'

'No?'

'No. He was visited by a woman.'

'Oh?'

'Aye . . . soon after he arrived here . . . she came to see him . . . couldn't forget really, he was over the moon about her visit . . . you ever seen a dog beside itself with joy, running round in circles in excitement . . . Ronnie Grenn was a bit like that. Bit pathetic, really. A large lady with black teeth not at all connected with the world.'

'You could tell that, could you? I mean from a distance, seeing her just the once?'

'It was an impression I had. I still have it. She was well, a bit big, her hair was swept back, a lot of it but it was greying and the fact that she wore it like a mane made it even greyer. If she had cropped it short and made it more suited to her middle years, it would have been more appealing, and those teeth . . . oh . . . they'd rotted until they were black. Yet she carried herself as if she was a fashion model. And not only that but she said something else by her body language, she said, "I'm right! I'm right! I'm right!" You've probably met the type. Not at all attractive and invariably wrong all the time, but convinced otherwise on both counts.'

'Name, perchance?' Montgomerie allowed Iveson eye contact. Here was something he wanted. He had to trade.

'Mary.' Iveson held Montgomerie's eye contact. And he held the pause. Then he said, 'Carberrie.'

Montgomerie wrote 'Carberry' and Iveson corrected the spelling. Montgomerie said thanks and crossed out 'Carberry' and wrote 'Carberrie' on his pad. It was a previously unknown name. A lead to be followed up. 'Did Ron Grenn say anything about their relationship? I mean, what was she to him, do you know? Did he say?'

'Hard to tell . . .' Iveson once again caught Montgomerie's eye. 'I mean, when you think of the hoops that Ronnie was jumping through when he knew Carberrie was to visit him, you'd think they were lovers. Mind you, the thought of wee Ronnie and big Mary getting it off together would make anybody puke.'

And that, thought Montgomerie, coming from you, Iveson, you and your 'Tayside fairies', is rich beyond richness. But he said nothing. He wanted information. He wanted Iveson's cooperation.

Iveson looked at Montgomerie. He wanted a smile, an approval of his humour. He got neither and his eyes narrowed slightly. He was used to getting what he wanted. He didn't like it when he didn't. Montgomerie suddenly saw that and he also felt the momentum of the interview failing. He said, 'Did she seem keen on him?'

'No. That's what I was going to say. She visited once. Once only. If there was something between them she'd be down here weekly. She wasn't short of doh-ray-me. She dripped with rocks and bangles and squeezed herself into designer clothes. Had a fancy car, too. I watched Ronnie walk her back to it, Sierra Cosworth, no less, alloy wheels, metallic blue, personalized numberplate.'

'Which you don't recollect?'

'Don't I?' Iveson smiled. 'ME 2.'

'Well . . .' Montgomerie wrote the numberplate on his pad. 'What can I say?'

'I remember it because if the woman was as self-orientated as her body language telegraphed, then her numberplate was . . . well, accurate is just not the word.'

'Me too.' Montgomerie nodded, 'sounds like a woman we ought to have a wee chat with. One visit only. Sounds like a business visit to me, and if that is the case then we want to know what it was about.'

'Really?'

'Yes, really.' He said nothing else but silently pondered the implications of a woman clad in designer clothes, dripping with rocks and bangles visiting, just once, a man eating porridge for the theft of half a million pounds' worth of gems. It stank like two-day-old fish. And the nice thing about the personalized numberplate was that she would still have it. The vehicle may well have been traded in and replaced, but the numberplate would be retained.

'Did Ron Grenn talk about her?'

'Aye, and that didn't add up and deliver. I was watching them when she left, you know, and she smiled at him and he turned away looking like the cat that got the cream, but as soon as he was with his back towards her, her expression changed. Scowl . . . she had a face like a jar of frogs. Jumped into her metallic-blue Sierra and roared off. He did talk about her, in the manner of someone to return to, someone waiting for him. He said that she wouldn't be visiting because she didn't like prisons, but that didn't mean that she wouldn't be waiting for him when he got on the outside. I didn't know what to make of it. I wondered whether he was trying to convince himself of a fantasy being a truth or whether he did believe it. He spoke like he believed it, but then he didn't see the jar of frogs once his back was turned.'

'I see.' Montgomerie nodded his thanks and then pulled his eyes away. He sensed Iveson's disappointment as he did so. 'I have the impression of a man looking forward to getting out, not merely to come to the end of a period of imprisonment, but getting out to do something, be with someone. Would that be accurate?'

'Of Ronald Grenn, yes . . . yes, I'd say that was accurate.'

'So . . . did he tell you of his plans?'

'Not in so many words . . . he said he was "finished with crooking" . . . said that a few times. Whether the issue of someone, Mary Carberrie or someone else, being there for him when he got out was a fantasy or a truth I couldn't tell, but I did have the impression that he had come to the end of a life of crime. That did seem sincere. He mentioned a guy called "Saffer".'

'Saffer?'

'Or Saffa, or Suffa, or Soffa . . . guy called Kit Saffer.'

'Kit?'

'A seventeenth-century nickname for Christopher. Today we say Chris, two hundred years ago the Christophers were known as Kit to their mates. As in the Island of St Kitts in the West Indies. It was named St Christopher by the Spanish and the English who had interests in the area always referred to it as St Kitts. They eventually relieved the Spanish of their property with a little help of a musket and shot and today, even as we speak, the island is still known as St Kitts. Sounds nicer than St Chris's, though.'

'I didn't know that.'

'So I've been of a little help?'

'More than a little.'

'You could perhaps put a word in for me? The close observation of the Tayside police is not something I look forward to. Been cooperative in a murder enquiry . . . reformed character . . . it's not unreasonable is it?' Said without expression, and Montgomerie could see why people flung themselves lemming-like to their own destruction following Iveson's influence. But he said yes and nodded. 'I'll make a phone call as soon as I get back to Glasgow.'

Iveson nodded and held eye contact. Montgomerie broke it to write 'Kit Saffa/Saffer, Soffa, etc.' on his pad.

'What—' Montgomerie doodled on his pad – 'did Ronald Grenn say about Kit Saffa, specifically?'

'Specifically nothing. He did indicate that this Kit guy had the right idea . . . he said, I'm going to look up Kit when I

get out . . . he's doing the right thing. Crookin's behind Kit
. . . I want to be like him. I'll follow him.'

Leaving the company of Iveson was difficult for Montgomerie.
Strangely so. Not simply a closing of the notepad and a,
'thanks, that'll be all for now', he felt anchored in some
way by Iveson's presence and he knew, he just knew,
that Iveson knew he was holding him, preventing him
from leaving. Montgomerie felt it was akin to a satellite
leaving the gravitational pull of a planet, he knew that once
he started moving he had to keep moving. He went through
the scene in his head and found himself pumping up his
muscles, mustering actual discernible strength as if about to
move furniture and then he stood, closed his notepad and
sensed disappointment on Iveson's behalf that he was not
able to hold Montgomerie. 'Back to Glasgow.' Montgomerie
avoided eye contact, as though talking to himself.

'You'll make the phone call?'

'Aye,' Montgomerie nodded, reaching for the door handle,
'I'll make it . . .'

Montgomerie stepped out of the hut which was one of a
line of similar huts and which comprised the agent's rooms
of Traquair Brae. He walked away up the pathway between
shrubs towards the main house. Behind him he heard Iveson
leave the hut and walk softly away in the other direction, and
he visualized the man melting into the shadows.

Back in AG Laing's office with the photograph of subma-
rines, Montgomerie received details of the visitors Ronald
Grenn had had whilst in Traquair Brae.

'Just two.' Laing looked at the file. 'His mother and a
woman called Carberrie. Mary.' He smiled. 'Interesting car
numberplate.'

'ME 2. Yes, I've heard about her. She sounds like an
interesting woman, from a police point of view, that is, very
uninteresting from every other point of view.'

'Well, she was his only other visitor, just a week after he
arrived here from Peterhead. Strange. Two visitors, comprising
three visits in over two years, yet Ronald never gave the
impression of being lonely or socially isolated. He always
carried himself as if there was someone with him in spirit,
as though he had someone on the outside waiting for him.
But the statistics of his visits just don't bear that out at all.

How did you find Mr Iveson? Mad, bad and dangerous to know, eh?'

'Couldn't sum it up better. He wants me to put a word in for him, make a phone call to the Tayside police on his behalf and tell them about the assistance he gave and how reformed he is.'

'Will you?'

'I'll phone them. Won't be saying what he wants me to say. Anything but, in fact. But he gave me two names, the one you've just mentioned and someone called Kit Saffa, or a name like that, who appears to be a criminal associate and who has gone straight. It's a question of asking Criminal Records to trace him . . . no numbers, but Kit is not a common name. It's apparently . . .'

'An old nickname for Christopher,' Laing said. 'Yes, I knew that.'

'As in . . .'

'Kit Marlowe . . . St Kitts in the Caribbean . . . knew that as well.'

'I didn't.' Montgomerie stood. 'I return to Glasgow a wiser man.'

'And with two names to follow up. Not a wasted trip.'

'Not at all.'

The two men shook hands. Warmly.

Returning to Glasgow, Montgomerie realized he'd met that use of intense eye contact and serious facial expression before. And before he'd encountered the way it induced him to do something he didn't want to do. Then he remembered, of course, of course, of course . . . salesmen use it, they had employed the same technique while sitting in his living room eager for him to buy that shower fitting 'that's installed in all the hospitals', or the insurance he didn't need.

He glanced at the clock on the dashboard. 18.52.

TUESDAY

4

10.05–17.32 hrs

Abernethy drove to Easterhouse. He drove out of Glasgow on the M8. He took the first exit to Easterhouse, left at the top of the ramp, in front of the grey angular Baptist church, left again after the fire station and first right opposite the health centre, left into Conisborough Road, a winding incline of four-storey tenements, as is the remainder of Easterhouse. Planted, attached to the extreme east of the city of Glasgow, Easterhouse has a population in excess of that of the city of Perth yet has only four pubs and one shopping centre. Abernethy drove to the brow of the hill, turned right into Balcurvie Street, and stopped outside 254. That stair, top left flat, being the discharge address of Ronald Grenn.

He left his car and walked up the short path to the close mouth. Overgrown gardens littered with plastic bags and empty lager cans stood either side of the uneven pathway. The close had been fitted with a security door but, as Abernethy had found is often the case, it had been vandalized into uselessness. He pushed the door open and he was met with the smell of stale urine which hung in the close. Paper bags, hardened with dried glue, had collected in mounds, one mound scattered at the bottom of the stair, another he found at the turn of the stair, halfway up to the first landing. Here, Abernethy glanced out of the window and saw that the back court of this stair had been allowed to become a collecting point for black plastic bin liners full of domestic refuse, many not tied at the top, many torn, doubtless, thought Abernethy, by animals both domestic and feral. Here, he thought, be rats. Many rats. Beyond the back court was farmland, pastoral, he noted, black-and-white cattle grazed on the green. Beyond the field was a woodland, and above the trees stood the twin towers of Gartloch Psychiatric Hospital, a relic of the days when such hospitals were built on the very edge of cities. Each major city in the United Kingdom has at least one such building, dark, brooding, Gothic, set in generous grounds but far away from civic pride. In nearly all cases, the expanding cities groping for living space have 'in filled' the open places as with the schemes of Garthamlock and Easterhouse G32 and G34. Now, Abernethy pondered, in the little over one and a half lifetimes since Gartloch Hospital was built in gently rolling countryside on the edge of Bishoploch, being as far removed from the City Chambers and Royal Exchange Square as possible, it has become possible, almost, to walk between the two sites through a continuous belt of urban and suburban development.

He continued up the stair, a simple plaster-covered close, painted maroon up to chest height then a solid black line above the maroon about two inches wide and then cream coloured above that. Both the cream and the maroon attracted graffiti, 'Fenian Drummie', 'Screw the Pope', as well as, Abernethy noted, the inevitable sexual obsessions, all written in black felt-tip. The doors on the close had two, three, occasionally four mortise locks and wired frosted glass set in the door. The names of the occupants were written on nameplates screwed to the door above the letter box – sometimes the name was written on paper and sellotaped to the door, sometimes it was written in pencil on the cream painted plaster beside the door and sometimes there was just no name at all. In Easterhouse, as in all schemes, there are stairs and there are stairs. Abernethy knew that. And he saw that 254, Balcurvie Street just was not a monied stair and he also sensed that the folk on this stair lived in a state of fear and siege behind their front doors. The Indian country, the shark-infested waters, the no man's land, stopped and started at the front doors of this stair, and Abernethy knew just what sort of flat he was calling on. He wasn't disappointed.

The door was splintered about the locks, though reassuringly, the splintered wood had faded with age. If someone had tried to kick this door in then they had done so some time ago. They hadn't done it the previous night and it was doubtful, thought Abernethy, that anyone would attempt to kick it in tonight. It was likely to be the battle scar of an old dispute. The fiery-tempered Scot may demonstrate a passion that can frighten an Englishman, but once disputes between Scots are over, it seemed to Abernethy, they remain over. Unlike the simmering grudges of Yorkshire people which can be passed from generation to generation, which Abernethy had once observed. Two men had fought in the main street of a pit village near Sheffield because the grandfather of one had supported the General Strike and the grandfather of the other had been a strike-breaker. Abernethy, passing through on his way back to Scotland, had witnessed the incident. The reason for the fight was explained to him by another onlooker in an accent Abernethy could barely understand and in a matter-of-fact manner which revealed no surprise at all in respect of the reason for the fight. This, Abernethy, as a Scot, had found to be as frightening in its way as was an Englishman's fear of a Scotsman's temper.

The door, of a modest two locks, the least number of locks of any door on the stair so far as Abernethy could tell, boasted a nameplate: 'Grenn' in gold letters on a tartan background. The nameplate had holes for screws at each corner but was held in place by only two screws in the upper holes. The sickly sweet smell of alcohol and alcohol-laden breath could be detected on the landing, seeping from the house of Grenn. Abernethy knocked on the door, tapping his knuckles on the frosted reinforced pane of glass set in the door at head height.

The door was opened. Eventually. It was opened slowly, apologetically, it seemed, without the often heard yell of, 'Who is it?' preceding it. The occupant of this house definitely had no enemies at present. The splintered door may even have been occasioned during the occupancy of the previous tenant. The face at the door was ghostly white, of a person who had been bled, veal-like, from the ankles. The hair was wild, straggly and white, the eyes were bloodshot. She wore only a thin nightdress which was transparent enough to reveal a skeleton-like body, and fully revealed stick-like legs bruised about the shin and bony, shoeless, slipperless feet with gnarled nails, cut or paired in a rough jagged fashion. 'Aye, son?' The woman peered at Abernethy as if trying to focus with bleary eyes. Her breath was searingly hot.

'Mrs Grenn?'

'Aye . . . I'm on a wee bender, son.'

'I can see that. I'm the police.' Abernethy flashed his ID but he fancied that for all the detail Mrs Grenn was able to observe, he may as well have flashed his library card.

'Polis . . . aye . . . you've come about my Ronald?'

'Aye.'

'You'd better come in.' The woman stepped aside and Abernethy entered the flat, the soles of his shoes sticking to the carpet as he walked down the corridor to the living room. Mrs Grenn shut the door and followed him unsteadily and paused to reach for a housecoat which was hanging on a coat rack on the wall, just inside the door. 'Sit down, son,' she called as she wound herself into the coat.

Abernethy walked into the sitting room. It was cold. It had a chill about it and an atmosphere of dampness which gripped at his chest. Dampness in the schemes, Abernethy had noticed, most often comes up from the ground with the ground-floor flats being most affected. But he had detected no smell of damp in the close as he entered and concluded that unusually, dampness in 245, Balcurvie Street was coming down through the roof. The fire grate seemed to have become a collection point for combustibles, cigarette packets in the main – a pile of ash and cigarette stubs had overflowed from an ashtray on the hearth – empty bottles of Buckfast Abbey, inexpensive blended whisky and the inevitable Irn-Bru lay strewn about the floor along with a copy of the *Daily Record*, that day's edition, with the headline 'Slaughter in Kelvinside' being the lead for the story of the murder of Ronald Grenn in whose mother's house Abernethy now stood, looking for the safest seat from a health point of view, in which to sit. He chose a plastic-covered armchair which swivelled and had wide arms. It proved to be tacky with spilled alcohol and he instantly felt itchy and wished he had remained standing. Mrs Grenn was in no condition, he reasoned, to worry about niceties. But he remained seated and noticed a portrait of the Royal Family propped up on the mantelpiece against the wall and he reflected how often he had visited households of the direst, meanest poverty and seen such a portrait prominently displayed. And above the framed photograph of the Royal Family was yet another icon beloved of poverty-racked East End families, a print of a painting, all in varying shades of brown, of an angelic looking boy of about five years of age with a single tear running down his cheek and with an expression of wide-eyed helplessness. It had been Abernethy's experience that families who had had to be visited in respect of Child Protection issues seemed to be overly fond of that particular print. It was as though the impact of real, noisy, demanding children not squaring with the silent, sentimental ideal, was often too much for immature parents who had many, many unmet needs of their own.

Mrs Grenn tottered into the room swathed in a dark-blue housecoat, sat in an armchair by the fire and lit a cigarette with trembling hands. 'Smoke, son?'

'I don't, thanks.'

'You'll take a wee drink?'

'Can't. But thanks.'

'On duty, aye?'

'That's it.'

'Aye . . . only . . . see me . . .' She put her hand in an upright position before her face with her palm at right angles to her eyes. 'See . . . I've been on a wee bender . . . since yesterday. Since they two polis called and told me my Ron's been killed. Murdered. But they wouldn't let me see his body . . . my Ronnie . . . see, who'd want to do that to my wee Ronnie?'

'That's why I'm here, Mrs Grenn, to find out who would.'

Mrs Grenn looked at a plastic container which stood on the mantelpiece. It was of a light-brown colour, almost bronze, with a screw top of darker brown and it sat easily, blending in with matching colour of the print of the naive painting above it. She raised her hand to the plastic container in a near-Nazi-style salute, and said, 'See me, I swear on my man's ashes that I don't know of anyone who'd harm my Ronnie.' Then she let her hand fall weakly to her lap.

Abernethy continued to read the room and saw nothing which said anything but poverty, compounded by alcoholism. He further observed Mrs Grenn and suddenly realized that she was not as old as he had imagined her, or been led to believe from Montgomerie's recording following his visit to Traquair Brae Open Prison. She was in fact a woman in her sixties, she would have been a young woman when she gave birth to

Ronnie, and Ronald Grenn's sickly appearance was not after all, he noted, the result of being born of too old a mother, but being born of a frail and most probably heavy-drinking, if not outright alcoholic, mother. But, he reasoned, she could be taken for an elderly woman, age is relative, if people can be bitten deep and ravaged with arthritis in their forties, then alcohol and smoking and stressful living doesn't help. And this is the East End, this is Easterhouse with its vast population and sparse services, here people age quickly and die sooner than in the well-set West End or in the smug suburban Glasgow south of the water.

'When did you last see Ronald, Mrs Grenn?'

'Yesterday, son.'

'Yesterday?'

'Aye . . . oh . . . couldn't have been . . .' Mrs Grenn closed her eyes and clenched her fists as if concentrating. Then, opening her eyes rapidly, she said, 'Day before yesterday.' She reached to the side of her and lifted a can of super lager from the floor, from a supply Abernethy had not realized was there, and tugged off the ring pull by hooking it underneath with a plastic bangle on her wrist. She raised the can to her lips and swallowed deeply. 'See today, today's Tuesday, it was yesterday that they two polis called and told me wee Ronnie was murdered . . . shot, they said . . . I said I wanted to see him for myself . . . they said I couldn't . . . I can't understand that . . . why'd they say that, son?'

Abernethy searched for an answer. He pictured Ronald Grenn's faceless exploded skull. He could only say that he didn't know why. It was a meek answer. He knew it was a meek answer. It made him feel meek after he had said it but it was the best he could do.

'But it was Ronnie, aye?'

Abernethy nodded. 'Yes. There's no doubt. The fingerprints confirmed it was Ronnie. I'm sorry.'

'Aye . . . I believe you are, son. They two polis that came yesterday didn't seem too upset. Just doing a job. But you seem . . . aye . . .'

'So you last saw him on Sunday?'

'Aye . . . that'd be right. Sunday right enough.'

Abernethy scribbled on his pad. 'He was discharged from prison on Friday last?'

'Aye. Came home on Friday and went out to the Centaur and came back with a good drink in him, so he did. But he'd never been inside the pokey for so long before so he needed a wee wet when he came out. Spent most of Saturday in his room, woke up with a rare sore head, so he did, just not used to it, see, and he'd taken a good bucket, so he had. Didn't go out on Saturday . . . needed to rest . . . but left on Sunday.'

'Sunday?'

'In the afternoon. Slept late. See, son, it's a way of saving on breakfast if you're on the broo and no reason to get up.'

'Did he say where he was going?'

'He did not, but he looked happy. Like he was looking forward to seeing someone, or doing something. Then he gets himself killed.' She took another deep slug of the lager. 'See first there was me . . . then there was me and my man, Jack . . . God rest him . . . then there was me, Jack and wee Ronald, then there was me and Ronald and now there's just me again.' She glanced up at the container of bronze plastic. 'See . . . I'll put Ron up by his dad . . .'

Abernethy felt deeply uncomfortable. Here, amid this grief in a life of limited horizons he had a job to do but wanted only to be far away . . . to leave Mrs Grenn to her emotions, to her memories. But he pressed on. 'What do you know about his pals?'

'Not a lot, son. I think he got involved with a bad crowd because he was never a bad lad. You know, he did do a few daft things but he was never that bad and I couldn't believe it when he went down for a jewellery robbery . . . that wasn't our Ronnie . . . I mean, it wasn't our Ronnie's way . . . I mean, a few breaches . . . a wee theft by OLP . . . all right, just till the wee man found a lassie and settled down, but jewellery . . . I just couldn't see it . . . it just didn't add up. See, wee Ronnie would take a jemmy and wrench off a padlock and hasp to open a shed or a lock-up, but breaking into an antique shop . . . a real posh one at that . . . getting past a burglar alarm . . . it just wasn't Ronnie . . . but he put his hand up to it . . . he never got a penny out of it but he went down for seven years. Came out in four, half of which was in an open prison . . . never seemed to have money.'

'Bit out of character for him, you'd say?'

'Aye, son . . . aye . . . that's a bonnie phrase . . . "out of character". I like that, so I do . . . "out of character".'

'But he had friends?'

'Only Kit Saffa.'

'Kit Saffa,' Abernethy repeated, that name he recalled had crept into Montgomerie's recording. 'That's a name we've heard before.'

'He's a mate . . . Kit . . . met him once . . . he's a nice lad, so he is, but he and Ronnie did daft things together but Kit stopped, so he did . . . stopped crookin' . . . Ronnie told me he was going to be like Kit. He said that when I visited him in prison, so he did. Said he was going to do what Kit's done when he gets out. Go straight. He might have been going off to see Kit on Sunday . . . but Kit lives in Garthamlock . . . and Ronnie was murdered in the West End so he couldn't . . .' Mrs Grenn drained the can and crushed it in her hand, revealing what Abernethy thought to be a surprising amount of strength for one of such frail appearance. She tossed the crushed can on to the floor where it joined other empty cans and empty bottles. 'Another dead marine,' she said, as it bounced on the carpet and came to rest against an Irn-Bru bottle.

'Mrs Grenn,' Abernethy asked, 'do you think I could have a look in Ronnie's room?'

'Aye, son. Through there. Back of the house.' She reached for another can from beside the chair. 'I'll stay here.'

Ronald Grenn's room in his mother's flat was small. It was little more than a boxroom. It had a divan bed, a wardrobe, it had bare floorboards. No curtains on the window, which looked out across the fields, the cattle, the woodland and the twin towers of Gartloch Hospital. The bed was unmade, the linen looked unclean. Abernethy thought it impossible for the linen to become so soiled in the few days that Ronald Grenn had been out of Traquair Brae, and could only surmise that Mrs Grenn had not changed the sheets when Ronnie was imprisoned four years ago, and Ronald, upon his release, had been quite happy to slump back into his old bedding. There were shoes under the bed and a few items of clothing in the wardrobe. This was Ronald Grenn's world, what he had amounted to, aged forty-something. Abernethy had noticed this before, when he had had occasion to visit the homes of various people in his professional capacity, and had felt the poignancy when he saw just how empty had been the lives of some people, Ronald Grenn being but one example.

In the wardrobe Abernethy found a shoebox.

He took it out and placed it on the narrow windowsill. He opened it. It contained newspaper cuttings about a kidnap. Abernethy recalled the case. It had received prominent press coverage, on an Edinburgh heiress called Ann Oakley, nineteen when she was abducted. That was eight years earlier. Abernethy was still in uniform at the time, but it was one of those cases. Everybody, everybody talked about it. The kidnap of Ann 'Annie' Oakley. She was not released by her kidnappers when the ransom was paid and her body was never found. Abernethy felt the hairs on the back of his neck stand on end. Many people collect press cuttings on a particular theme, but if anybody collects press cuttings about one news story and no other it means only one thing so far as Abernethy could see: that they had some connection with the story. And here in this shoebox in a spartan, threadbare bedroom in G34 were newspaper cuttings about one story and one story only. The kidnap of a young woman whose ransom demand of one million pounds had been paid and whose body had never been found. Also in the box was an Ordnance Survey map of the Kilsyth district. On the map an inch circle had been made in a remote-looking area.

Abernethy replaced the lid and carried the shoebox back to the living room. He had intended to tell Mrs Grenn that he wished to take the box and its contents away with him, but he found Mrs Grenn slumped in the chair, snoring softly. He let himself out of the flat taking the shoebox and its contents with him, having left a handwritten receipt for it on the windowsill of the bedroom.

It was 11.20 hours.

14.30 hrs

Against all expectations Richard King found that he liked the man. He had been fighting a prejudice against 'insurance smoothies' as he walked from P Division Police Station across Charing Cross to India Street where, surrounded by glass and concrete buildings of local government departments' headquarters, he located the modest frontage of the Glasgow and Trossachs Insurance Company. John Pulleyne was, King found, solid, businesslike, forthright, warm, good humoured; mid fifties, thought King, clean-shaven, keen, almost boyishly so, and the plum-coloured suit said liberal not staid. Somehow King could not see Mr Pulleyne in pinstripe. Behind Mr Pulleyne was a row of photographs of men in rugby strips posing for group photographs on a sports field. Insurance-law textbooks were relegated to the lower shelves beneath the sash window of Pulleyne's office.

'Confess I was relieved and excited to receive your call, Mr King.' Pulleyne patted the file. 'The Bath Street fire very nearly finished us.'

'Oh?'

'Claim for three million pounds. That kind of strike tends to be felt, the smaller you are, the more you feel it. As you may note, I used to play rugby and we used to say, "the bigger they are, the harder they fall", tended to work on the field but not in insurance. The bigger they are they don't fall at all, unless they finish themselves by criminal irregularities, of course.'

'There's been one or two of those in recent years. Taking the money but not paying out.'

'Because the money has gone into the pockets of the directors rather than into the company assets.' Pulleyne nodded. 'Yes, that has happened. But if you play the game you survive and you can make enough honest pennies in this game without being dishonest. As in most, if not all businesses. The problem is that small new companies don't survive being hit with a massive claim in the region of three million.'

'But you did. Clearly so.'

'Just. Just. Just. Just. Skin-of-the-teeth number. We had a directors' meeting which started at lunchtime and went on till midnight. We looked at the claim, we looked at the fire-service reports and we couldn't find a way through, all exits seemed blocked. It was a legitimate claim. Then we had to decide whether to meet the claim or fold and let the claimants have what assets we possessed as compensation. That was a sore point. In the end we decided to meet the claim, even though we hadn't the assets.'

'How?'

'The directors raised money, remortgaged their houses, sold possessions. We remortgaged this building we're in and somehow we covered the one-million-pound shortfall which we had to contend with. And we wrote a cheque for three million pounds. We continued to trade, but another claim, no matter how modest, just couldn't have been met if it had come in within six months. Talk about trusting to luck. But that's the way of it in this game, it's all down to reputation. We offer insurance to commercial ventures, we don't offer domestic policies, which is probably why you've never seen us advertised.'

'I haven't, I confess.' King shifted in his seat.

'We advertise in trade journals but that's about all. Well, to cut a long story short, we made our reputation by deciding to pay out rather than fold. People just flooded to our door with proposals for their business premises, their stock, their equipment, their fishing fleets, their aeroplanes . . . we built up our assets and we're now able to start paying the directors back the money they loaned the company. But at the time it was heart stopping.'

'I'll bet.'

'It's British insurance, Mr King. The reputation of this insurance industry was made after the San Francisco earthquake in nineteen-oh-six.'

'I didn't know that.'

'Oh, it's quite true. The American insurance industry was fledgling at the time and the buildings of San Fran were insured with British companies and after the city was flattened it wasn't expected that the insurers could pay out on such a huge scale. But they were wrong. Men in suits travelled from London and across the continent carrying claim forms with them, assessed said claims and paid out accordingly and San Fran was reborn using British money. Not a few people lost all their assets and went bankrupt, but that's the price you pay for being an underwriter or a name, as they are known. It takes at least a million pounds cash to buy into a syndicate which underwrites the loss of such things as oil rigs, in return you take a share of the insurance premium and your one million can become five million in as many years.'

'Not bad.'

'Well, you take a risk I personally wouldn't take and I'm an insurance man, I love this game, I really do, but the drawback of being a name is that if a legitimate claim is made against your syndicate, then you are liable for what amounts to an upmarket warrant sale, you lose not just your million pounds but all your assets, and I mean all, your house and contents therein, your capital, your valuables, you're left with the shirt on your back and are given directions to the nearest Salvation Army Hostel.'

'Blimey.'

'And you sign a contract accepting that risk. The reason being, to maintain the good name of British insurance. So a few names went under in nineteen-on-six, but because legitimate claims for the earthquake were met in full, and because the Titanic claim was settled in full and a few other similar claims were also settled in full, then throughout this century yens, dollars, francs, Deutschmarks, kronas, you name it, have flooded into the UK in their millions, and I mean millions. They are our so-called "invisible exports" and we don't want to lose business like that.'

'But you're not in that league, are you?'

'No, but we felt we had an obligation to uphold the good name of the British insurance industry and so we paid out, we put up our homes and sold sundry possessions and met the claim in full. And like our larger cousins in preceding years, the consequence of paying out has been that, as I have said, we have been rewarded with a continuous flood of proposals. Another eighteen months without a major claim and our assets will be very healthy and all the directors will have been repaid in full. Which is why I am surprised and excited by your interest in the Bath Street claim. Can I infer from that that it wasn't a legitimate claim after all?'

'No.' King smiled as he shook his head.

'I can't?' Pulleyne looked crestfallen. 'I had hoped that we might be able to claw some of that money back. It would be a pleasant compensation for the trauma it put us through.'

'Sorry, but you can't infer anything from my interest. Not just yet.'

Pulleyne smiled. 'How can I help you, Mr King?'

'By telling me all, everything about the claim, the identities of the people involved and any dark, lurking nagging suspicion you may have. At this stage we can toss all suspicions into the air and catch them as they come down and examine them until they no longer interest us. This isn't a court of law.'

Pulleyne pushed a file across his desk top towards King. 'Well, this is the file, you can access it but you can't take it from the office, not without a warrant anyway. I'll go and organize coffee for us.'

'Just milk for me, please.' King reached for the file.

'Oh, I'll get a pot and a tray of stuff.' He stood. 'It seems like we'll be on this all afternoon.'

It had been some years since circumstances had taken Malcolm Montgomerie to Garthamlock. He had not looked forward to returning to the scheme but when he got there he found it transformed. It was still Garthamlock. The streets were still the same, the same pattern, the same names. The houses were still Glasgow scheme housing, two, three, four apartments off a common stair, four storeys high, eight in a block. But gone were the neglected, overgrown gardens, to be replaced by neatly tended gardens, surrounded by wrought-iron fences which replaced the privet hedges of old and which had served only to conceal vandals and attract refuse. Gone were the roadways of old, replaced by roadways with speed-suppressing chicanes, sleeping policemen, existing through-roads had been closed off and designated 'play streets' for children – 'emergency vehicles only' read the signs. The dull fawn colour of the old Garthamlock blocks had been replaced by lighter-coloured facing and bright-coloured pebble dash. There was, Montgomerie found, a sense of optimism about the scheme, a sense of emotional uplift. The Glasgow Eastern Area Renewal Project could chalk up Garthamlock as a success, so Montgomerie felt as he turned his car off Tillycairn Road and into Craigneil Street. He did not, though, care for the satellite dishes which seemed to sprout from the outside walls of the houses like a vertical field of mushrooms. But that, he conceded, was the nature of Glasgow, nay Scottish housing schemes at the cusp of the century, at the millennium; the people in the schemes are the ones with the time to watch twenty-four-hour television, choice of forty-eight channels. The scheme may well have been beautified, but the job market has still shrunk. It was Montgomerie's assertion that the folk who live in the well-set and prestigious West End or in the more comfortable areas of the South Side, areas built and laid out by the late Victorians, care not for satellite dishes bolted to the side of their houses; finding them vulgar, finding they ruin the line of the building, but mostly because they advertise the occupants of the house as in possession of an unhealthy amount of free time. Middle-class homes do not wish to give out such signals. So Malcolm Montgomerie reasoned. He halted outside 233, Craigneil Street, entered the close, finding that the street security door had been carelessly left ajar, and climbed the stair until he came to the house of Saffa.

He rang the doorbell, which, to his relief, made only a conventional 'ding-dong' sound, echoing in the hallway. Montgomerie, try as he might, could only muster grimacing distaste for doorbells which played 'Flower of Scotland' or 'Auld Lang Syne'. Inside the house a large dog barked, a man's voice yelled, 'Quiet!' and then at the front door, 'Who is it?'

'Police,' said Montgomerie, as low as he could, but loud enough to carry through the door.

Again from inside the house he heard the man who had shouted at the dog groan, and then say to someone else, 'Put the dog in the kitchen.' There was some movement in the house, a bustle, footfall on carpet, a shadow on the other side of the frosted glass and the door of the house of Saffa was flung wide. 'What is it?'

'Don't worry.' Montgomerie smiled reassuringly. 'There's no trouble.'

'No trouble?'

'Nope.' He continued to smile. 'I wouldn't be here by myself if there was. Would I?'

'I was thinking you guys are a long way behind me . . . I haven't had the polis at my door for a good five years.'

'More!' yelled an indignant female voice from deep within the flat. A waft of air freshener seemed to follow the voice, arriving belatedly behind the man at the threshold.

'We're looking for information about a mate of yours. An ex-mate, really.'

'I've got a lot of ex-mates. Since I turned the corner and went straight I'm not too popular around here. I wouldn't grass anybody up but they don't know that. I know things but I'm not running with the wolves any more. Makes me unpopular.'

'No . . . this is a very ex-mate. Ronald Grenn, by name.'

'Ronnie . . . aye . . . oh . . . I read about him in the *Record*. You'd better come in.'

Montgomerie entered the flat. It was clean, well decorated, smelling of air freshener. The dog barked from inside the kitchen.

'Sharrup!' Saffa banged on the kitchen door with the palm of a meaty hand. The dog stopped barking but began to growl.

'What is it?' Montgomerie turned into the living room.

'Staffordshire pit bull.' Saffa followed Montgomerie into the room. 'We need him. The ex-mates I mentioned, they come to our door sometimes when they've had a wee bevvy, and it's not too safe for me to walk out in the scheme, not without my wee pal in there. We've been promised rehousing but the factors offered us Easterhouse or Drumchapel . . . I'm known there too . . . Sadie's from the 'Milk' . . . that'd be safer for us so we're waiting for an OK flat in Castlemilk. Five years now and we're still waiting, aye, Sadie? Five years.'

'Five years, so it is.' Sadie Saffa eyed Montgomerie coldly, suspiciously. She struck Montgomerie as still retaining hostility towards the police which her husband seemed to have lost. Kit Saffa twisted on muscular limbs and sank into an armchair. He indicated a vacant chair and Montgomerie lowered himself into it, reading the room as he did so. It spoke to him of self-respect. Furniture of a striped pattern on chrome-plated frames crowded round a fireplace and matched fawn-and-black curtains of broad diagonal stripes, both of which clashed loudly with a bright-blue carpet, so bright that it caused a dull ache in Montgomerie's eyes. A goldfish swam in a bowl of clean water which sat atop the television set. Montgomerie reflected that goldfish were not common pets in the East End. They just weren't. Kit Saffa sat leaning forwards, elbows on knees. He had bright ginger hair, piercing blue eyes, a neatly trimmed ginger beard. He had solid muscular legs which seemed to Montgomerie to be bursting out of his faded denim jeans, his feet were encased in scuffed Nike trainers. He was barrel chested, grey hairs protruded at the neck of his denim shirt and his arms were muscular and heavily tattooed with messy self-inflicted emotionally immature tattoos, gang slogans, girls' names. He was perhaps five feet tall. He smiled at Montgomerie. Mrs Saffa, by contrast, was tall and thin, she wore black with black spectacles and black leather sandals. Had she been younger, she could have found acceptance in the youthful 'Gothic' movement, but grey hair betrayed her age. In further contrast to her husband, she glared at Montgomerie, as if her husband had once suffered grave injustice at the hands of the police when running with the wolves, and while he could forgive the incident, she could not and never would. Montgomerie had found that that was often the way of it, a victim of injustice makes a better adjustment, reaches a state of forgiveness much more readily than his or her close relative who may have witnessed the injustice but did not actually suffer it themselves.

'So' – Montgomerie gave up trying to melt Mrs Saffa's ice-cold glare and turned to the more accommodating facial expression of Kit Saffa – 'Ronnie Grenn.'

'Aye, wee Ronnie, aye.' Saffa smiled.

'What can you tell me about him?'

'Probably not a lot. He and I used to run together in the old days, y'know . . . do daft wee things, get banged up together . . . but really stupid wee things, you know . . . we sort of drifted apart about eight years ago.'

'Oh?'

'Aye, then as not four years ago he was banged up for the Bath Street job.' Saffa shook his head. 'Let me tell you something, Mr Montgomerie, whoever did that, it wasn't wee Ronald Grenn. He had neither the nous nor the bottle.'

'You reckon?'

'More than reckon. Remember, I knew Ronnie, I knew him from way, way back . . . we were getting into bother with the police when we were at school and went before the Children's Panel. There is a few years age difference between us, but we were both part of the same gang in those days. Both got supervision orders, my social worker was a lassie straight from college. I remember a mixture of enthusiasm

106

and nervousness but she was all right, she cared and her heart was in the right place. Ronnie's social worker was an old guy with a grey beard and a wee baldie head. I remember him. He seemed, looking back, to be trying to care but just hadn't got it to give any more. A burnt-out case. You meet them in social work and teaching.'

'You do?'

'So I'm told, and so I'm meeting them myself.'

'You've a social worker for some reason? Probation Order in force? We've no record . . .'

'No. I want to be one.'

'Good luck to you. Confess it's not a job I'd fancy.'

'See, well, I've turned the corner, like I said, and I was looking for a job and it was a probation officer in my last nick . . . he says to me, you're not a bad lad . . . I was a man in my thirties by then . . . he thought I'd changed my tune . . . he said, look why not put all this to some use . . . stay out of trouble . . . use your time to study, do some work with a charity or a voluntary agency to show willing and get experience that you can talk about at a job interview and when your convictions are spent you could get a job as a youth worker maybe . . . So that's what I'm doing . . . I'm in the middle of a social studies course at Paisley College. S'a fair trek from here and back by public transport but I'm sticking it . . . I've got two years before my last conviction can be considered spent . . . then I want to do a course in youth work so I can reach some of these kids and straighten them out before they get too far down the wrong road. I can talk their language and I can reach them. I want to do it. I've got a purpose in life now. There's just no future in doing what I was doing. You end up with nothing . . . even if I get something like a half-meaningful job I'll still be finding it difficult to get insurance and that. Just look at Ronnie. Shot in the head, it said in the *Record*.'

'Less than forty-eight hours after coming out of the pokey. We wonder . . . I mean, this is just speculation . . . let me bounce it off you. You knew Ronnie, you're an intelligent guy . . . we think he went up the West End to meet someone as if to collect something. His mother could only name you as his friend . . . she didn't know of any other. Would you know who he was meeting?'

Kit Saffa remained silent but he was clearly mollified by Montgomerie's compliment.

'Yes? No?' Montgomerie pressed. 'Perhaps it's that you don't want to tell me?'

Saffa remained still, though he gave Montgomerie the clear impression of having a card up his sleeve.

'You see' – Montgomerie leaned forwards – 'you and I know that Ronnie couldn't have pulled the Bath Street jewellery robbery. Got past burglar alarms, opened a strongbox, took gems worth many pennies when he had no contacts who could reset them. I mean, he could break into a lock-up and steal tools, he'd know someone who'd reset tools for him. But gems, that's short league, he's not in the short league . . . and to set fire to the building after he allegedly robbed it to cover his tracks . . . so he's done for wilful fire-raising on top of major theft . . . but he's happy to put up his hands and get seven years.'

'Lenient sentence.'

'Very. He was lucky.'

'Or the judge just didn't believe him either.'

'So you really don't believe he did it?'

'Never did, Mr Montgomerie. I never did. He hadn't the skill, he hadn't the ability, he hadn't the bottle. He was an impetuous wee ned. Theft by finding was more Ronald Grenn, ask him to plan anything and you may as well be asking him to design the next generation of computers complete with artificial intelligence. He hadn't got it upstairs and even if he had, he hadn't got the bottle to carry it out.'

'So why did he put his hand up to it?'

'The oldest reason in the world, Mr Montgomerie.'

'Dosh?'

'Got it in one. Doh-ray-me. Has to be.'

'But you don't know?'

'See, Ronnie wanted to go straight but, and this is the big but, he had fallen into the old lag's way of thinking, one big job to see me out *then* I'll go straight. Never works like that. There's never one big job to give you enough dosh to retire on . . . you decide to go straight, realizing you'll be scratching pennies for the rest of your life. People go crookin' because there's the promise of a successful job just round the corner and that keeps you going. If you're not crookin' there's the promise of poverty until you're in the clay. See, that's what makes it difficult for guys like me and Ronnie to turn the corner, it's not just the peer pressure that keeps you in the wolf pack. Sorry about the jargon by the way, "peer pressure".'

'Paisley College?'

'Aye . . . you pick it up.'

'Well, that's what you're there for.'

'Aye, right enough, but it's the thought of going to a life of poverty that keeps guys crookin'. And there's another reason, it's exciting, it's thrilling, it's sexy . . . it has all those mixed together . . . so it seems . . . and life on the broo in the schemes has none of that.'

'But Ronnie?'

'Aye . . . one day he said that he really wanted to go straight but he needed cash to do it, so I said that it doesn't work like that. Going straight is not easy. It's hard, and the first thing you accept is that there's no money in it. Well, that bit didn't appeal to Ronnie . . . he came from poverty, both his parents were alkies, and both in a big way. The drink took his dad and last I heard, it was taking his mother. She's not a well woman, Mrs Grenn, not a well woman at all, and poor wee Ronnie, he was a weird-looking boy at school . . . small, odd, not put together right . . .'

'Foetal alcohol syndrome?'

'Possibly, maybe. Didn't know it existed till I was reading a book in Paisley College Library, and when I read it the one person I thought of was sickly wee Ronnie Grenn. A wee stick insect of a guy, but he was a pal of mine. Lopsided as well, left shoulder always higher than the right.'

'So you think he was lured into putting up his hand to the Bath Street job in return for cash?'

'I know so. I mean, without being told, without inside knowledge, knowing what Ronnie could do, knowing what he couldn't do, knowing what he wanted . . . a nice little stash of dosh to go straight with. He was offered money to put up his hand for the job. Has to be the script. Has to be. Someone who knew him as a petty ned says to him, "See you, Ronnie, will you just look at yourself, wee man, you're middle aged, no money, no prospects, you'll never amount to anything, you'll be bouncing in and out of Barlinnie like a ping-pong ball, you'll be collecting your sixty days twice a year until you drop and still have nothing to show for it. Now here's a wee proposition . . . we're going to do a job and it's a big job. We want you to put your hand up for it . . . and you might collect ten years . . ." And Ronnie would have said, "Ten years, in the name of . . ." but these guys, being serious about this matter, sayeth, "Listen up, wee man. If you get a ten-year stretch, don't panic, right? Join the Christian Union. Get in with the chaplain, volunteer for the dirty jobs . . . keep your nose squeaky clean, get a transfer to a lower-category prison, you'll be out in five years. That's five years' free board and lodging that doesn't come out of your pocket, and when you do breathe free air again, there'll be a serious wedge waiting for you. More than you'll ever get in five years' ducking and diving, ten times more than you'll ever earn in five years, even if you could get a job. And all you have to do is let us put your fingerprints on something that we know will be found, or by some other means finger you to the law, and at the trial you say 'not guilty' but go down anyway." In the event he got seven years and if you ask me, the lenient sentence was the judge transmitting a message to you guys, the polis, that you've been offered a patsy and you've fallen for it for the sake of a quick and easy conviction.'

Sensing Montgomerie's discomfort, Mrs Saffa sneered at him. She allowed him to see it, letting it linger deliberately long on her face.

'So boy Ronnie does his time,' Kit Saffa, well into his stride, continued. 'He does four and a bit years, half of which being in an open prison is a pleasant and gentle ride, and then he goes up the West End for purpose or purposes unknown but which we can assume, safely assume, is for the purpose of collecting a large quantity of folding green. But instead of getting what he expects, he gets the Pied Piper treatment. He is offered fifty guilders instead of the promised one thousand. So now boy Ronnie, being totally scunnered at this prospect, does a foolish thing. Ronnie, see, is not known for his foresight and clarity of thought and he throws a blue one, a real wobbly, and instead of walking out when he can and going to the police to make a statement implicating the real culprits, he tells the real culprits what he is going to do unless his one thousand guilders becomes rapidly forthcoming, and so the real culprits say, "Oh no, Ronald, this we truly cannot allow," and the rest is written in this morning's *Daily Record*.'

Montgomerie smiled. He found himself liking Kit Saffa, liking his wit, his style, his patter. 'You and I are on the same wavelength, Mr Saffa. I wouldn't disagree with that as an assumption. It holds water. It hangs together. The question is, who, who, who, who . . . did he go and see in the West End on Sunday evening last? Could you help us there?'

'Made mention of a lassie once. About that time. A name like Cranberrie, except it wasn't Cranberrie, but a name like that. Mary by given name. He seemed taken up by her, but Ronnie did not have a great success with the ladies. Och, he was my pal but he had no success in that area, none at all, even to the point of telling me all about the women he'd pulled at one time or another. He was deluding himself, fantasizing. Tell you the truth, I didn't think he'd got himself off the ground at all. See, wee Ronnie would be quite taken by anyone who cast him a second glance, and so if something other than many shekels was also promised, and which was also not forthcoming, then wee Ronnie would not be a happy chappie.'

'Wouldn't be, would he? And likely to say something he would have cause to regret, if he was allowed to live to regret it.'

Saffa nodded. 'Aye.'

'And the name which is like Cranberrie. Could that perchance be Carberrie? Mary Carberrie?'

Again Saffa nodded. 'Perchance it could. That in fact was it. Mary Carberrie. We talked about her that day he was hopping up and down with excitement, he was like a wean with a new toy to go home to. Aye, Mary Carberrie.'

'Did you meet her at all?'

'I did not. We were drifting apart by this time. He seemed to disappear about that time as well, away for a week or two, I recall. But I didn't take a lot of notice because I was restacking my shelves then. Ronnie belonged to the time gone before and he didn't seem so interested in adult education and opportunities for volunteers as I was. Drifting apart, aye, drifting apart. Still mates. But only just.'

'He was excited by her, though, it would appear? Did he tell you anything about her?'

'Hard to say. I mean you're going back eight years. He was . . .' Saffa seemed to struggle. 'My vocabulary has increased since I started studying, you know, but . . . hey . . . wee Ronnie . . . see, he was excited by this wee Carberrie female . . . but it was like he was more taken by what she did, than what they were to each other . . . see, Ronnie, he had fantasies . . .'

'You said.'

'Aye, but he had fantasies about being a master criminal, in between times he had fantasies about doing one last job and then straightening out but only if he had enough cash. But they were never more than fantasies. He never turned his fantasies into a hard-nosed realistic ambition. They were never more than pleasant thoughts to keep him going through the day, so they were.'

'But then he met Mary Carberrie?'

'Aye, and look what happened to him. You know, I get the impression that it wasn't as though he'd got a relationship for the first time in his life, but it was more like he'd been taken into a club. He started to swagger, like he was really somebody . . . had a kind of gleam in his eye that I hadn't seen before but . . . you know, come to think of it, we were not drifting apart at all, we were racing apart at a rate of knots and we just didn't see it.'

'And this was about eight years ago?'

'Uh huh. It was my fortieth birthday and me and him were going for a bevvy and I called round to his father's flat in Balcurvie Street in Easterhouse and the most I could get out of the wheezing drunken old fool was that Ronnie was north of the city, Kilsyth, Kirkintilloch, some place like that. I remember that because his old dad was leaning in the doorframe in his vest and saying, "Kirk . . . Kirk . . . Kirk . . ." then he changed and said, "Naw Kirk, Kil . . . Kil . . . Kil . . ." trying to get the place name out. Eventually I got the message that wee Ronnie wasn't in, he'd gone to a place called "Kil" or "Kirk" something and he'd forgotten my big four-oh bevvy.'

'Kil or Kirk.'

'Plenty to choose from. Kilsyth, Kilmarnock, Kilkenny.'

112

'That's in Ireland.'

'So it is' – Saffa grinned – 'but you see what I mean. Kilbirnie, Kilbrannen . . . I've heard that name.'

'Well, he won't have gone there, it's a stretch of very deep water between Arran and the Mull of Kintyre . . . but I take your point. I can think of Kilmalcolm, Kilbride . . .'

'Killiecranckie . . .'

'The list can go on a long way. And if he was right the first time and he was in Kirk something, that makes the list even longer. So the where we leave out for the time being . . .'

'Kirkcudbright . . . Kirkcaldy . . . Kirkmichael . . .' Saffa offered, really, thought Montgomerie, less than helpfully.

'Let's look at the why of it. I take it that because you mention him being away, then it was quite unusual for him to be away?'

'Unless he was in the pokey, yes, it was unusual. Ronnie was an Easterhouse guy, never left the scheme, hardly ever, hardly even left Provanhall, that's his part of Easterhouse.'

'I see.'

'So when wee Ronnie Grenn goes to "Kil" or "Kirk" something, well it wouldn't be bigger news if he went to Australia.'

'I see. So what is your birth date?'

'That you could get from CR.'

'We could, I could wait until I got back to the town and ask our collator to put your details on the computer screen, but you wouldn't want me to do that.'

'No?'

'No . . . you see, every time we pull a name out of Criminal Records it's automatically dated. It's a way of being able to tell which particular felon is of interest to various and sundry police officers. So if I was to go back to the town and put your details on the computer screen and find that another officer in another division accessed your file two weeks ago, I would phone him and ask him what interest he had in you. It's a way of finding which felons are still bubbling away and drawing attention to themselves, if not actually being huckled.'

'I didn't know that.'

'It's the way it works. It's in your interest not just to keep out of trouble but also to prevent your file being accessed.'

'First of July.'

'Thanks. So eight years ago on or about the first of July, Ronnie Grenn very uncharacteristically left the city of Glasgow. He was noticed to look pleased with himself and enthusiastic about things in general, again, not being wholly in character. At the same time he is known to start associating with a woman called Mary Carberrie. He was also making noises about going straight after one last job which would give him enough dosh to see him out.'

'Yes.' Saffa nodded. He had been paled by Montgomerie's disclosure of the practice of registering each access to files held by Criminal Records. Montgomerie wondered if Saffa was as clean as he claimed.

'Then three or four years after that, he puts his hand up to a crime, serious in nature, which those who knew him believe he couldn't have committed?'

'That's right.'

'Then four and a half years after *that* he's shot in the head.'

'You think his going away has some connection?'

'Do you?'

'I wouldn't know. Like I said, we were drifting apart by then.'

'Just a couple more questions, Mr Saffa. Firstly, how long was Ronnie away that time?'

'A week or two. I don't know when he went, I don't know when he arrived back in Glasgow but I saw him before he went. We fixed up to have a drink on my fortieth which was a week later . . . then he came back, I saw him . . . I used to live in Easterhouse then myself, saw him in the scheme and he looked pleased with himself and said he'd been in the country. He had a wedge and so we went for a bevvy. I reckon it was about three weeks between the time I saw him before my birthday and the time I saw him in the scheme with a wedge.'

'Did he say how he got the wedge.'

'No. See, that's one thing you could say for Ronnie. He knew how to keep his mouth shut. He knew to do that all right. He knew how to do that.'

'He said he'd been in the country?'

'Aye. That's a wee bit strange too, looking back. He's a city kid. He's scared of the countryside. But he looked pleased with himself. So he hadn't had a hard time wherever he went.'

'Right . . . now, milady Carberrie. How did they meet each other?'

'I really couldn't tell you, Mr Montgomerie. I really don't know.'

Montgomerie sank back in his chair. He looked at the glowering Mrs Saffa and held her gimlet-like stare and then looked back at the smiling Mr Saffa and now saw only false good humour. Saffa had by all indications been fully cooperative with Montgomerie, but he was also scared of something. Probably nothing connected with the murder of Ronald Grenn, but he was frightened of something and Montgomerie raised his eyebrows and said to himself, 'If you're going straight, wee man, then I'm a Dutchman'. He asked, 'What did Ronnie say, if anything, about his future plans when you had that drink?'

'Not in so many words, you know, but the angle was towards getting out of crooking for good.'

'But he'd only do that if he had the dosh to see him out?'

'Aye,' Saffa nodded, 'that was his thinking. He also seemed to be serious. Not having one of his fantasies.'

'Interesting.' Montgomerie nodded. 'Interesting.'

Tony Abernethy walked home. He turned right as he left the police station building, turning his back on the roar of the traffic as it thundered on the sunken motorway at Charing Cross, and walked down Sauchiehall Street, past the Eye Hospital on his left and a gracious curve of Victorian town houses, now offices and basement wine bars, into the area of tenement development as Sauchiehall Street gave way to Argyle Street at the bowling greens of Kelvingrove Park. He continued walking past the imposing edifice of the Art Gallery and Museum, not, he knew, really built back to front as local myth has it, and entered the bustle of Dumbarton Road at Partick Cross, narrow streets, more crowded pavements, more tenements of smaller size than those nearer the city centre, with shops along the pavement length from Partick Cross to Thornwood, one mile distant. If it wasn't a shop front it was a pub. Narrow frontage, long and deep inside.

Abernethy walked on. He had a home to go to at the bottom of Thornwood Drive.

It had not, he thought, been a bad shift. A quiet four hours until he had gone out to Easterhouse to call on the derelict Mrs Grenn, from whom he had received some information, most notably a collection of intriguing press cuttings relating to a kidnap incident of some eight years previously, about which he began to recover memories of media reports. These he had drawn to the attention of Fabian Donoghue who scanned them with a deeply furrowed brow, occasionally muttering, 'Well done, well done, indeed . . . this could very well be highly significant.' It pleased him. He still felt gauche about being seen the day previous misusing office hours. He felt now that he had recovered some credibility in Donoghue's eyes. He lunched rapidly in the too small canteen, then added his recording to the growing Ron Grenn (Code 41) file. He closed the file and handed it to Montgomerie when he came in to start the back shift. Then he decided to walk home. It was a fresh and blustery day, but dry. No rain at all. A good day for a walk from Charing Cross to Thornwood Drive.

He turned up Thornwood Drive and pushed open a street door and entered a 'wally' close of lovingly cleaned and cared-for porcelain tiles, of windows of stained glass, of wrought-iron banisters topped with darkly stained hardwood in which brass studs had been placed at intervals to prevent children sliding down them and perhaps losing their balance and falling anything up to fifty feet. The contrast with the stair at Balcurvie Street was extreme, heightened by the smell. Here was not the place of stairs which hummed of stale urine, but here was the place of stairs swept daily, and cleaned thoroughly with bleach and disinfectant and brass polish. Here was Glasgow Pride.

He walked slowly up the stairs, not rushing at them, but methodically climbing, settling into a rhythm, one step at a time, Alpine guide-like, covering ground with minimal effort, conserving energy. He reached the top landing and opened a heavy pair of storm doors with a huge key and then unlocked a flat door of solid black-painted wood, inset with a pane of decorative glass. He shut the door softly behind him and walked down the threadbare carpet, the carpet he used to run up and down on as a child. He entered the living room. A grey-haired man sat in a chair specifically designed for the frail ambulant; comfortably upholstered in green leather, it was essentially upright with wide, deep arms and a seat which sprang up to an angle of thirty degrees to assist the occupant to his or her feet when vacating the chair.

'Is that you, son?' The occupant of the chair spoke without turning his head.

'Yes, Dad.' Abernethy looked at the dwindling flame in the grate in front of which the elderly man sat. 'I'll build up the fire a wee bit.'

'Aye . . . that you, son?' But Abernethy was already in the kitchen of old, heavy original fittings and fixtures, placing smokeless coke from a bunker under the sink on to a hand-held shovel.

'That you, son?' asked the old man as Abernethy re-entered the room and began to place the lumps of coke on the fire.

'Aye.'

'What time is it, son?'

'Two-thirty, about.'

'What's it like out?'

'Windy, dry though.'

'You in now, son?'

'Aye.'

'Good. Margaret will like that. She doesn't like you out at night.'

Tony Abernethy said nothing. Mrs Margaret Abernethy, who had given birth only once in life, and then very, very late to a husband who was ten years her senior, had died peacefully after a long illness some years earlier.

'What time is it, son?'

'Two-thirty, going on three.'

'You in now, son?'

'Aye . . .' Abernethy stood, brushing coke dust from his hands.

'Good, that'll please Margaret.'

'I'll be going to my bed for a nap now, Dad, I feel a wee bit tired. Do you want anything?'

'No. No, thanks, son. What's it like out?'

'Blustery.'

'Not raining?'

'No. Not raining.'

'Margaret will like that.'

Abernethy crept out of the room and went to the kitchen, made a mug of tea and sat at the table to enjoy it, to savour it before retiring to his room. He had been acutely embarrassed about being the only son of elderly parents and, to his shame in adulthood, had attempted to pass off his real parents as his grandparents and had invented pretend parents who were 'overseas'. Now in his twenties he felt a sense of privilege, his life had been different because of elderly parents, not better or worse, but different, and as such, a world that would otherwise have been closed to him, was opened to him. Before dementia took his father and cancer had taken his mother he could, in conversation with them, reach back further into the history of the city than his peers could with their parents, and his upbringing had, it seemed in retrospect, belonged to an earlier era. It made it all very interesting, as did the knowledge that he would experience the loss of his parents much earlier in his life than would others of his generation. That too, in a way, was interesting. And that also provided a sense of privilege, of being different, not better, nor worse, not greater, nor lesser, in any way, but a life led which is different. He sipped the tea. Very interesting.

'A hunch.'

'That,' Donoghue sniffed, 'is an Americanism.' He rattled the stem of his pipe against his teeth and avoided eye contact with Montgomerie, glancing instead out of his office window at the angular buildings of Sauchiehall Street under a blanket of grey cloud. 'You've had the benefit of at least a part university education, Montgomerie, you could strive for British English. Or do you watch too much television?'

'A notion, intuition . . . I went with it.'

'Better.'

'It seemed to be out of character for him to go anywhere except the gaol, although it was many years ago . . . but the whole point of me talking to Saffa was to get some background information about the deceased and so when Saffa mentioned that Ronnie Grenn had done something wildly unusual for him, really out of character, then I followed a . . .'

'An intuitive notion . . . that's what you followed, Mr Montgomerie, you followed an intuitive notion. We'll leave "hunches" to the cousins. They can have all they want, we, on the other hand, will preserve the queen's English.'

'Yes, sir.'

'Very good. Oh, and that extends to your written work as well. I want no Americanisms or media-speak creeping in there. Good, plain, easy to understand, simple English.'

'Yes, sir.'

'And with your facts presented in logical order.'

'Yes, sir.'

'That reassures me and demonstrates to your colleagues that you possess clarity of thought. I like that in my officers.'

'Very good, sir.' Montgomerie was acutely aware that he was not perhaps DI Donoghue's favourite DC. As a consequence he never relished being in Donoghue's company, but he felt more than usually uncomfortable at the present, as if Donoghue was annoyed or irritated by something.

'I reserve the right to instruct you to rewrite them if necessary.'

'Understood, sir.' My God, the man will not let up. Montgomerie searched his actions over the last few days. He was convinced he had done nothing wrong to merit this assault.

'Mind you, it seems that it was as well that you went with your intuition.' Donoghue paused and relit his pipe with a deft flick of his thumb on the gold-plated lighter. 'You see, Tony Abernethy brought in what appears to be gold dust in the form of these.' Donoghue patted the newspaper cuttings that Abernethy had brought to the police station.

'Clippings?' Montgomerie tried to sound interested and alert.

'Cuttings!' Donoghue put his hand to his brow. 'Clippings, you understand, Montgomerie, belong west, or north, or south of New York City. They don't belong east of that fair place.'

'I see . . . as with . . .'

'Yes, as with . . .' Donoghue drew on his pipe. 'But none-theless the cuttings here relate to the kidnap of the Edinburgh heiress Ann "Annie" Oakley by name. You may remember the press coverage?'

'I do. In fact more than that, I actually saw her once or twice.'

'Oh?'

'She was . . . well . . . this isn't standard English, but she was a rare wee poseur.'

Donoghue smiled gently. 'Tell me about her.'

'I was in Edinburgh at the time, a student feeling very out of place among the smug, self-satisfied types who seemed to make up the Law Faculty. I mean, I remember statements like, "I'm reading law because you never meet a poor lawyer," and another I remember, "You can write meaningless and long-winded letters on your clients' behalf and charge it to them at whatever your hourly rate is." I had enough after one year.'

'Glad you have a conscience, Montgomerie, but tell me about "Annie" Oakley.'

'Well, women can't pose in wine bars like men can, they'll get pestered too much. But what they can do is pose in their cars and Ann Oakley was notorious in Edinburgh for doing that. It seemed the whole town knew who she was . . . she was one of those names and images . . . a bit like the Queen . . . everybody knows her but she knows few.'

'"Annie" Oakley . . . ?'

'Yes, sorry. I just remember her during that first and last summer I spent in the capital . . . roaring up and down Princes Street in a wee Japanese four-wheel drive thing, a white one, blonde hair streaming behind her, one hand on the steering wheel and the other holding a mobile phone to her ear and looking very happy with her lot, and many women would: she had youth, she had beauty, she had money. But that's all she seemed to do . . . apparently if you stood on Princes Street when "Annie" was in posing mood you'd see her roaring down the street towards Haymarket and then a few minutes later you'd see her barrelling back up towards Calton Hill and then a few minutes after that . . .'

'She'd be on her way back to Haymarket . . . I get the

idea. As you say, men do it in wine bars, women do it in open-topped cars.'

'I caught sight of her a couple of times within a day or two of each other and I mention it because that was the summer that she was abducted. That's really the reason why I recall her so clearly driving along Princes Street with a "you can look but you can't touch" air about her. Thank God for her sake that she didn't know what was ahead of her. Her body was never recovered, not that I recall.'

'Not that I recall either. I have made an appointment to speak to the officer of the Lothian and Borders force who was in charge of the case, I won't be in tomorrow morning . . .'

'Very good, sir.'

'The reason I mention "Annie" Oakley is that these cuttings were found in a shoebox in Ronald Grenn's room in his mother's house in Easterhouse.'

'Aha . . .'

'Yes, intriguing, isn't it? And you say that Ronald Grenn went away for two weeks, eight years ago, towards the end of June of that year?'

'Yes, sir. Well, so Kit Saffa informed me.'

'You think he was being honest with you?'

'Yes . . . yes . . . I think he was being fully cooperative with me with respect to Ronald Grenn, but I don't think he was as white as the driven snow, as he claims. His wife was glaring dagger-like at me throughout my visit and his good humour showed signs of cracking under the strain. Perhaps I've been a cop . . . a police officer . . .'

'Thank you.'

'A police officer too long, but I left with the impression that he was up to something, though he had nothing to do with the murder of Ronald Grenn and had nothing to do with Ronald Grenn's criminal activities and so was willing to be truthful and helpful about him at least.'

'I see. You see "Annie" Oakley was reported as having been kidnapped on the twenty-seventh of June, eight years ago.'

'Just when Ronnie disappeared for a fortnight in the country. About.'

'And the ransom was paid ten days later.'

'Just when he returned to Easterhouse. About. Allegedly looking pleased with himself and talking about going straight.'

'Was he now?'

'So sayeth Kit Saffa.'

'You see, Tony Abernethy makes the point, and I go along with him on this, that people may collect newspaper cuttings on a theme if they're interested in that theme, or if it affects their lives in some way, but if someone collects and keeps newspaper cuttings about one incident, and one incident only, then it means that they have some connection with that incident.'

'Or person, or place . . . or thing . . . Yes, I can see that, sir.'

'So Ronald Grenn, who never left Easterhouse unless it was to reside for a brief period of time as a guest of Her Majesty, is revealed to have had some possible involvement with the abduction and possibly murder of an Edinburgh heiress eight years ago. Then, three and a half years later, he pleads guilty to a crime he hasn't got the skill, the expertise, the nerve to commit, but still he seems happy to collect seven years. He's released four and a half years later having been of good behaviour whilst in the pokey and upon release he travels to a place unknown, to call upon a person unknown, and a few hours later his lifeless body is found sans face and brain lying on a grassed area in a part of the city with which he has no known connection. It has a whiff, do you agree, of old fish about it?'

'A can of worms, sir.'

'Did Mr Saffa indicate where in the country Ronald Grenn had his two-week holiday?'

'Not specifically, but he did indicate that it could have been one of many Scottish place names which begin "Kil" or "Kirk", such as Kilmarnock or Kirkcaldy, for example.'

'Did he?' Donoghue reached for a sheet of paper which lay amongst the newspaper cuttings which had been found by Tony Abernethy. 'A place such as Kilsyth, for example?'

'Could well be, sir.'

'This' – Donoghue handed the sheet of paper to Montgomerie – 'as you see, is an Ordnance Survey map of the area to the north and east of Glasgow.'

'The Kilsyth area.'

'Among other places. But you will note that a small circle has been drawn on the map near the town of Kilsyth.'

'Yes, sir. I see it.'

'Now, that very map you're holding was found with news-paper cuttings about the abduction of "Annie" Oakley in the same shoebox in Ronald Grenn's bedroom. What I'd like you to do, if you have sufficient daylight left, and you should if you press on, is to photocopy the map and return the original to me. Draw a camera from stores and drive out to that location which is circled on the map. It seems to encircle a building of some description. I want to find out what the building is, take a photograph of it, just for our records. Don't approach it, don't leave the road, don't hang about. And if you attract attention to yourself, forget about the photograph, we can live without it for the time being. Don't want to tip anybody off.'

'No, sir.'

'Then get back here and if you can, before they close for the evening, contact the Land Registry. We want to know who owns that building now and who owned it eight years ago.'

'Yes, sir.'

'You see, Montgomerie, I have . . .'

'A hunch?' Montgomerie offered. He thought he was being reckless but he offered it anyway.

Donoghue scowled at him but then allowed himself a brief smile. 'Yes, I have a "hunch", a dreadful one at that, that the building in question is a crime scene. I have an even more dreadful "hunch" that that building or the grounds thereof contains the remains of Ann "Annie" Oakley.'

King drained the coffee and replaced the cup on the tray which lay on Pulleyne's desk without taking his eye from the file. Then he looked up at Pulleyne. 'Westwater?'

'Gary,' Pulleyne smiled, 'my half-brother. Different fathers. My father died when I was quite young; after a while my mother remarried and they had Gary together. We're as close as full brothers. He's my wee brother, wee Gary. Well, wee Gary, he grew up to be tall and lanky, like his dad. I take after my own dad, short and stocky. But Gary's dad was a good guy, still is, lives in retirement now, on Arran. Treated me like his own, didn't give Gary preferential treatment, no nonsense like that . . . I had my place in the family as the elder brother, Tom Westwater saw to that, even if that meant me getting the odd wee privilege that his natural son didn't get. That was the right thing to do for Gary as well. Got to be quite close and he was a director here and was the man who took the responsibility for the Bath Street claim, which is why you see his name so often.'

'Perhaps I should be taking up his time?'

'Perhaps you should, but not on these premises, not in his capacity as one of the directors.'

'You haven't fallen out?'

'Bless you, no.' Pulleyne smiled. 'Fall out with Gary, never!'

'Full brothers almost, I recall.'

'Full brothers do fall out. Cain and Abel set the precedent for that, but Gary and I are full brothers in spirit if not by blood. Heavens, we owe the financial health of the company to Gary, perhaps not in the way he intended but the outcome of it is that we do.'

'How so?'

'The Bath Street claim. It was Gary who accepted the proposal on behalf of the company.'

'He did?'

'Oh yes. No other company would accept it, or if they did, their quote was impossible to meet, which amounts to a rejection of a proposal, but Gary clearly felt we ought to accept it.'

Richard King the man returned Pulleyne's beaming smile, but the cop within him began to sit up and growl. But, still smiling warmly, he said, 'Tell me the story.'

'Not a great deal to tell, Mr King. It's going back some years now, but a woman called Carberrie came to the office having made an appointment with Gary.'

'Carberrie?'

'Yes . . . why is there something amiss?'

'It's a name that has cropped up before. It's too early to speculate.'

'I see . . . but you think perhaps . . .'

'Mr Pulleyne, I don't think perhaps anything at the moment. Let's just explore with an open mind and see how far we get.'

Pulleyne extended an open palm towards King. 'I'm in your hands.'

'So the first question is why should the Carberrie woman make an appointment with Gary Westwater, I mean specifically him?'

'No reason, no reason at all, but the policy of the company is that for a proposal of such magnitude, a director would have to vet it and approve it. I could have done it, any of the other three directors could have done it.'

'I see.' King stroked his beard, black, neatly trimmed. 'Fair enough. Now the next question is, would you think it likely that if the Carberrie woman saw yourself or any of the other directors they may well have been able to accept her proposal, but would they have been likely to have done so?'

'No.'

'You seem certain?'

'I remember the ructions in the boardroom when Gary reported what he had done. The other three directors were hostile. I was upset that he'd put so many, in fact all, our eggs in one basket. We pointed out to him that a full claim on that policy could finish us and the other three directors threatened to resign and withdraw their assets from the company. I did what I could to keep the peace, Gary being my brother, but privately I was angry . . . seething, in fact. Talk about going out on a limb . . . he should have consulted the board.'

'I can understand that . . . you see, there are a number of questions spinning round in my mind . . . I'll try and catch them one at a time . . . the first question is why did the Carberrie woman have difficulty obtaining insurance from other companies?'

'I don't know how much difficulty she had, I don't know who she tried . . . in fact, come to think of it, it may not have been said in so many words.'

'May not?'

'We're going back six or more years, Mr King . . . and if you force me to think, I have to confess I had a notion that she had been trying to raise insurance because of something that Hugh said . . .'

'Hugh?'

'Hugh Smeaton, he's one of the directors.'

'I see.'

125

'In the board meeting which nearly became a battleground, Hugh said something like, no wonder she fetched up here, no one else would touch this proposal.'

'So she could have made this company her first call?'

'Well . . . yes . . . she could . . . it was just Hugh's remark that had me thinking all these years that she'd been walking round the central business district of Glasgow trying to find somebody who'd insure her business premises before she came here . . . that and the fact that we're small and not a household name . . . but yes, she could have come here first of all.'

'And got what she wanted?'

'It would seem.' Pulleyne looked as though a seed of doubt and worry had been sown in his mind.

'Tell me what it was about the Carberrie woman's proposal that so upset the other directors?'

'Well . . . in the first place she seemed to have come from nowhere . . . no business history . . . no insurance history . . . she just appeared as the owner, or joint owner, of an antiques business which occupied the whole of a four-storey building in central Glasgow, stocked with valuable antiques, furniture in the main, but oil paintings, and jewellery . . . if you want the catalogue, you write and ask for it and enclose a cheque for the appropriate amount and then view a particular item by appointment. That is top-class, short-league end of the antiques business, no walking in off the street and handling any object that takes your fancy with Cernach Antiques, if you please.'

'So it seems.'

'But Gary went ahead, accepted the proposal, insurance against fire and theft and buildings, three million pounds in all. We stood to lose, and, in fact, did lose that. We made the cheque out to Cernach Antiques. The property in question is being developed, McGuires have it. I walked past it the other day. It had stood a burnt-out shell for years and now McGuire Construction has it. They seem to have built half of Glasgow over the years, they're developing the site. I can only presume that Cernach Antiques have sold up and moved on somewhere.'

King, who was doodling on his pad and had written 'Cernach', and after moving the order of the characters

126

around had come up with the word, beloved of Glasgow-speak, 'Chancer', could only nod and say, 'Yes, I assume they have.' Then: 'Did you make any attempts to validate the proposal?'

'Good heavens, yes . . . buildings and contents. We . . . Gary authorized that, reputable buildings valuer and an auctioneer and valuer, for the contents and as you see, both . . . they're at the front of the file . . .'

'Oh yes . . .' King murmured his thanks as he located the valuers' reports.

'Both reported that the building and contents were as Mrs Carberrie had stated. The building was in good repair. It had the fire alarm and sprinkler system we asked for . . . the burglar alarm was fitted and the contents were validated by Holmes and Lesters, no less. So she was insuring just what she said she had to insure.'

'I see that the last evaluation was done ten months prior to the fire.'

'Yes. The evaluations were redone each time the policy was due for renewal.'

'So, annually?'

'Yes.'

'So you don't know what was destroyed in the fire . . . all you can say you know is what the condition of the building was and what the contents of the building were some ten months prior to the fire?'

'Well . . .' Pulleyne began to look uncomfortable, 'but there was a full investigation . . . one of your chaps from the police station at Charing Cross . . . an elderly man as policemen go . . .'

'Mr Sussock.'

'Was that his name? I can't recall.'

'Well, it's the name written here and he is an officer in P Division which is the Charing Cross police station of which you speak, as you say, just across the road from here.'

'Well, the police and the insurance company investigated and found the incinerated contents appeared to be what was in the insurance manifest.'

'So you paid out in good faith?'

'We had to. The police reported their findings that a felon had broken in, got past the alarms, stolen the jewellery and

127

had set fire to the building, four seats of fire plus liberally splashed petrol to conceal his tracks. The fire got such a hold, as I recall, because the fire brigade were fully committed to a warehouse blaze south of the water at the time and had to summon appliances from an outlying station to attend to the Bath Street fire. By the time they arrived, everything had gone.'

'You don't say?'

'Well, they don't call Glasgow "tinderbox city" for nothing, Mr King.'

King said nothing. He was beginning to find Pulleyne's naivety trying. Two major fires on the same night, in the same city, just don't happen, and if one was clearly a case of wilful fire-raising so might be the other in order to stretch the emergency services. He was also embarrassed for his profession ... Ray Sussock must have wondered ... he couldn't possibly have failed to make a connection ... he just couldn't ...

'So we paid up. We had to.'

'Had to?'

'Gary forced it really, felt obliged ... but he was right ... we have had nothing but a flood of proposals since ... things are becoming fit and healthy again and our name is good. We wouldn't be in this position if it wasn't for Gary.'

'As you have said. Tell me, did you ever meet Mrs Carberrie?'

'Oh, horrible, horrible woman. Truly horrible. Those teeth, that voice ...'

'As a person?'

'Nothing there that I could see, all noise, expensive jewellery and clothing and that was it. An empty vessel making the most sound, if you ask me.'

'I wonder if we know her?'

'You ought not to. Felons don't get insurance. Perhaps not all felons, petty felons probably won't have a problem. But in the event of a claim being made, we do a Criminal Records check and if the check is positive and if it's a serious offence, we deem the proposal invalid and don't pay out. We would refund all payments made to the policy but we won't pay out.'

'It'll still be worth a check.' King scribbled a note on his pad. 'So to recap, the property and all it contained went up in smoke and it was investigated.'

'It was, fully . . . I mean, a claim like that.' Pulleyne reached forward and lifted the silver coffee pot and replenished first King's cup and then his own. 'But as you have said, it was a good-faith payment because we knew what was in the building ten months prior to the fire, not on the night of the fire. I confess I'm beginning to feel a little uncomfortable, Mr King . . . you're implying fraud?'

'I'm really not implying anything, Mr Pulleyne. Not yet.' King laid his pad on his lap and picked up his cup of coffee. 'I'm sure that you are constantly on your guard for insurance fraud . . .'

'Oh, we are.'

'Strikes me it could be a bit like telling a lie . . .'

'Well, it is a lie.'

'In the sense that if it's big enough you'll be believed . . . or a bit like Captain Cook's ship arriving off the north coast of Australia . . .'

'I don't know that anecdote.'

'Apparently when the ship arrived the Aborigines who were fishing in the shallows glanced at it once and carried on fishing . . . just ignored it . . . that something so large could be man made was totally outside their ken. But when the ship, *The Endeavour*, lowered a longboat, they showed the Aborigines something that they could understand and they attacked the longboat. I've heard the story used to illustrate the human being's ability to ignore something very large and obvious if they find it too sinister to take on board, like the dangers of nuclear power and nuclear weapons, for example.'

'And you're saying that the Bath Street claim was a huge fraud, so huge that we just didn't see it as a fraud?'

'I'm floating the possibility.'

Pulleyne rested his head on his left palm and curled his right hand round his cup. 'No . . . no . . . no . . . it can't be . . . Gary would have checked into that . . . their order books . . . I mean business accounts, they were doing good business . . . businesses that start to flounder become victims of insurance fraud, especially if the owner is late middle aged . . . you know the sketch, devoted all his life to building up a business and is banking on selling it as a thriving concern to pay for a comfortable retirement, only to see it begin to fall apart around his sixtieth year . . . people in that situation act out of desperation and do stupid things with petrol. Especially if they try and make it look accidental, but the owner of Cernach Antiques didn't fit that . . . that . . .'

'Profile?'

'That's the word . . . profile, that profile, she didn't fit it. She was still young enough to start over if necessary . . . and she was just at the beginning of her business life, her ambition would be strong . . . and we had access to the accounts. She was doing good business.'

'Perhaps . . . perhaps I'm getting cynical. It's an occupational hazard. Police work makes you cynical. I try to fight it but it gets hold of me from time to time . . . creeps in.' King leafed through the file and came across pages of statements of the Cernach Antiques accounts held at the Clydesdale Bank. 'Money going in, money going out and a healthy bank balance.' King raised his eyebrows.

'You see, that is not the balance sheet of a business that is going to the wall. It just isn't.'

'Perhaps . . .' King studied the account. 'I'm not an accountant, nor a business person, but doesn't something strike you as a little odd about these figures?' He rotated the file and handed it to Pulleyne.

'Odd?' Pulleyne pushed his cup on one side and pulled the file towards him. 'No . . . money going in, money paid out . . . a constant balance with a small variance . . . it's a healthy business. They're trading antiques at the top end of the market, three-, four-figure sums . . . selling at a profit, allowing themselves a personal income and keeping the business in black. Lucky them. Not a candidate for insurance fraud.'

'Again, perhaps.'

'But you find it odd?'

'Probably cynicism again, Mr Pulleyne, but haven't you noticed how the sum of ingoing and outgoing money never exceeds one thousand pounds per month? I mean, if you were to open an account like this, keep a certain sum always in reserve, in this case a few thousand pounds and then rotate another sum of money, in this case one thousand pounds, through the account, but do so on random trading days and for random amounts, a few hundred pounds here, fifty pounds there, but never exceeding the one-thousand-pound figure, or whatever the agreed figure is, would you not achieve a healthy-looking business account?'

'Yes.' Pulleyne nodded. 'Yes, in a word, you would.'

'You see, there just doesn't seem to be a quiet period, that's what I noticed. It's my understanding that businesses have quiet periods and hectic periods, but this account just ticks over quietly, endlessly. It shouldn't do that. Or should it?'

'I don't know . . . perhaps there are no such things as annual fluctuations in the antiques business. The only people who could tell us what happened is the Clydesdale Bank, if they still retained the cheques, which after this length of time, they won't.'

'I really think I'd like to talk to your half-brother.'

'Gary? He doesn't work for us any more. He sold out.'

'Sold out?'

'He stuck it out . . . can't take that from him . . . he got us into the mess with the Bath Street claim but he stuck with us. In fact, he was the first person to put his house up, raised a second mortgage, sold possessions and so led the way out of the mess, enabled us to pay the Bath Street claim and stayed with us until we were almost in the black and with the proposals flooding in. He got us our good name. And then he sold out. I bought his share and I'm now the senior director. Suited both of us. Gary has enough money to see himself out and I've got a major slice of the business.'

'Which you owe to Gary. So where will I find him?'

'Now, he'll be on the rifle range.'

'Oh?'

'He's using the money to indulge in his passion for shooting. He has a rifle and goes into the Highlands and blows the brains out of stags.'

'Stalking.'

'Is the correct term. Gary and I, you know, we may have been close but there were things we did not see eye to eye on and firearms was one of them. But each to his own. He has quite a collection of guns, you know.'

'Really? Where does he live?'

'Busby. Fifty-two, Honeycomb Drive, Busby. He shoots at the Kilmarnock Gun Club. They have a range at the edge of

Fenwick Moor. You'll know instantly whether he's at either place – he has a yellow Jaguar. A Mark II circa 1962. You may have seen it driving about the city. A very distinctive car. Bit loud for my taste, but Gary likes it.'

King thanked Pulleyne for his time. At the door to Pulleyne's office he turned and said, 'Look, we'd be obliged if you didn't mention my visit to anyone. We like to play our cards close to our chest.'

'Understood.'

'And of course there still may have been nothing untoward happened at all.'

Bungalow. Derelict, down-and-outs for the use of. Montgomerie stood by his car and photographed the building which had been circled on the Ordnance Survey map found in Ronnie Grenn's bedroom. It stood set back from the road, remote, on the northern edge of Kilsyth. The nearest neighbour appeared to Montgomerie to be a similar bungalow which stood perhaps four hundred yards away. The town of Kilsyth began about a mile beyond the neighbouring house. Beyond the building was a field in which four or five horses stood contentedly chewing grass. The field was surrounded by black trunks and branches of leafless trees, and beyond the fields lay other fields and woodland, and beyond that the wild, black and green of the Campsie Hills and over all was a complete blanket of low, still, grey cloud. Montgomerie returned his gaze to the building. It would not, he thought, even in its prime, have been a particularly attractive building. It was small, and of unimaginative design. 'Utilitarian' was the word which came to Montgomerie's mind as he considered the bungalow. It had a door set centrally with a window at either side. It was faced with pebble dash and a roof of corrugated iron. The door had been pulled off its hinges and lay beside the house, all the windowpanes had been smashed and half the roof had been removed. It had, thought Montgomerie, by means of compensation, a generous garden of perhaps half an acre. Now overgrown, but with a magnificent oak standing at the bottom of the garden to the rear of the building and doubtless explaining the name of the property, carved in wood and strongly fastened to the gate.

Montgomerie drove back to Glasgow. Oak Cottage was not,

he pondered as he cruised south-westwards on the A803, not his choice of 'des res' and he hoped that he never would come to find Oak Cottage by Kilsyth an attractive place to live, even in retirement. But he had to concede, that if Donoghue's intuition was correct, it would make an ideal place to conceal a kidnap victim, especially in the summer months. No need of light or heating that might attract unwanted attention, for instance.

In P Division, having signed in and taken the steps to the CID corridor two at a time, he peeled off his blue-and-yellow ski jacket and slung it on Abernethy's desk, sank into his chair and picked up the phone. The Land Registry at Kilsyth and Cumbernauld District Council advised him that Oak Cottage of the address given was without certain ownership, all enquiries are to be diverted to Langley, Dells and Langley, Solicitors and Notaries Public, of Kilsyth.

'Langley, Dells and Langley,' said a chirrupy female voice on the other end of the phone line. Happy with her job, mused Montgomerie, even towards the end of the working day. 'How may I help you?'

'Owner died intestate,' the thin voice to whom Montgomerie had been connected dryly told him, 'an elderly lady whose only son is believed to be domiciled in Australia, or New Zealand. All efforts to trace him have thus far failed. There are more distant relatives anxious to assume ownership but all efforts to trace the son and heir cannot yet be said to be reasonably exhausted in the eyes of the law.'

'I see. Can I ask how long has the property been empty? About?'

'Fifteen years. About. It was for sale briefly when the owner was still with us but in hospital.'

'Anybody expressed an interest in buying it at all, or even just viewing the property?'

'Not to my knowledge, but I can check the file.'

'If you would.'

'Phone you back. Glasgow Police, did you say?'

'P Division. Charing Cross.' Montgomerie provided the phone number.

Dryness of tone and thinness of voice, Montgomerie found, did not mean inefficiency. His coffee was still too hot to drink when Hamish Dell returned his call and was able to advise him that a gentleman called Westwater, Gary Westwater of 52, Honeycomb Drive, Busby, had requested keys to the property just over eight years previously. He didn't make an offer to buy and shortly afterwards the owner died a peaceful death at which point the property was taken off the market and attempts to trace her son were put afoot.

'Gary Westwater.' Montgomerie spoke aloud. The name didn't mean anything to him but he noted it, and the address, and he thanked Hamish Dell, solicitor and notary public, for his time, his trouble and his information.

On a whim, Richard King walked into the antique furniture shop on Sauchiehall Street.

'Oh' – the slender assistant in the pinstriped trouser suit looked disappointed – 'we're just closing, sir.'

'Police.' King showed her his ID. 'Won't keep you long. It's a bit of information I need.'

The young assistant suggested that he might like to speak to the owner, Mr Dickson?

Dickson's office was behind a one-way mirror set in the wall of the building, so that he and any other person in his office could look out and see Sauchiehall Street going past, but the people on the pavement would see only their reflection as they passed the window. Some, King noticed as he sat in the chair in front of Dickson's desk, enjoyed their image more than others.

'It's not unusual that people stop and preen themselves at the window.' Dickson took a cigarette from a silver cigarette box on his desk, and, in a movement King had only ever previously seen in old films, tapped the end of the cigarette on the desk top before placing it in his mouth and lighting it with a slim cigarette lighter, also silver. He cupped his free hand round the end of the cigarette as he lit it, as if shielding it from a breeze. He was a small man, King found it difficult to age him, fifty pushing sixty, he thought. Smartly dressed, gold-tinted smile, yellow handkerchief in the breast pocket of his brown jacket. Too much jewellery for a man, in King's view: a ring on each finger, a watch on his left wrist, a broad gold bracelet on his right. 'How can I help you?'

'Picking your brains, really, sir.' King watched a blue-and-yellow Kelvin Scottish double-decker move slowly up

Sauchiehall Street, people rushed past the window, the evening rush hour was just beginning, no time for preening at the moment. People had only one word in mind: home. 'You may remember the fire in Bath Street about four and a half years ago?'

'Cernach's?' Dickson nodded. 'Not many people in the antiques business in Scotland don't know about that fire.'

'They lost a lot of good stuff.'

Dickson remained silent. Then he raised his eyebrows and smiled. 'Are you asking me, or telling me? If I were to ask you to write that sentence down, would there be a question mark at the end of it?'

'Confess I don't know myself.' King returned the smile, and noticed that a sensitive whiff of wood polish in the office emerged from under the odour of cigarette smoke. 'I was hoping you'd tell me.'

'So I take it that the police are renewing their interest in the blaze?'

'Well . . . yes.'

'Good. Look, Mr King, I do so hate beating about the bush. Is the reason that you've walked in off the street to ask me what the scuttlebutt is among the antique-dealing community about the Cernach blaze?'

'I couldn't put it better myself.'

'The scuttlebutt is that the whole affair reeks like putrefaction in a hot airless room, the scuttlebutt is that a king's ransom was paid out by an insurance company for a scam that could be seen with a glass eye. We put our own insurance with Glasgow and Trossachs after that. So did a lot of other firms. An insurance company that pays out like that is a gift horse and you know what you do not do to gift horses?' Dickson raised an eyebrow.

'So put me out of my misery. Tell me what the rumours are?'

'Well, were – rumours have died down now and I also would wish to state that I have no evidence of anything, nothing that I could have come to you about.'

'Accepted.'

'Very well, initially we were saddened . . . they did have some very beautiful stuff in there . . . but after a few months, after a year had elapsed . . . people began to talk and things just didn't add up. You see, the company came from nowhere. Nobody knew them in the antique trade. It was managed by a crone of a woman called Carberrie and she knew very little about what she was selling. Didn't know a thing about antiques. That doesn't happen. It just doesn't happen. You're born into this business, you learn as you grow older, you become known, or you start small and over years you move from your unit in the mews arcades behind Byres Road to a shop in Sauchiehall Street. That progression takes years, during which you become known in the antique-trading community. Mary Carberrie arrived from nowhere and opened the largest antiques-furniture shop in Glasgow. And the classiest. And she had a lot of serious stuff in there.'

'But she knew nothing about it?'

'Not a thing. It was the genuine stuff, all right, the full monty, but she couldn't talk about it.'

'How often did you visit the shop?'

'Three times, and here you have another mystery. I, and other dealers, called to view her stock when she first opened; we call in on each other to see who's got what and where the trends are. This is a consumer-led business, antiques go in and out of fashion, that keeps you on your toes, identifying trends as they start and buying up stuff to satisfy the trend. So we keep an eye on each other, make sure we don't miss out. So I called in on Cernach's and looked round, very impressed with their stock, less than impressed with the Carberrie woman, returned here and carried on, business as usual. I visited six months or so later and nothing seemed to have moved.'

'Moved?'

'In both senses, no item of furniture, or oil painting, or jewellery had moved an inch, that also meant it hadn't been moved in the sense of being sold. Yet they seemed to still be in business. They were still open, view by appointment only.'

'I see.'

'Didn't mention it to anybody but it puzzled me and so I paid my third visit about six months later and I kid you not, having taken more notice of things on my second visit, I came away convinced that they were selling nothing, nothing at all was being moved by that shop. About a year later it all went up in smoke. It just didn't add up. Or perhaps it did.'

'What do other people in the business think?'

136

'As I do, that the whole affair was shot through with criminality. We felt it suspicious that it went up so quickly. Very old hardwood is actually quite difficult to burn, modern stuff no problem, a blaze in a furniture shop selling modern furniture, that gets very hot very quickly and destroys everything equally quickly, but you have to generate an awful lot of heat for a long time before you can reduce oak to a pile of ash, and even more heat to have the same effect on tropical hard-woods, and Cernach's had some mouthwatering mahogany pieces.'

King cleared his throat. For the second time that afternoon he felt embarrassed for his profession. 'I think there's more you want to tell me?'

'It's the fact that there was more than one seat of fire . . . that takes time to organize. The story that it was a burglar starting a fire to cover his tracks isn't credible. Not for us in the trade it isn't. And to start a fire in a shop full of difficult-to-burn furniture you'd need something to help it along. A discarded cigarette on an armchair of modern manufacture is all you need to start an inferno. But if I were to place this cigarette on any piece of furniture in this shop, all I would succeed in doing is causing a superficial burn. I could even play the flame of my lighter against a piece of antique furniture and that would scorch it, but it wouldn't catch fire. To start a blaze like that in Cernach's you'd have to spread petrol liberally, on all three floors. What burglar is going to walk through the centre of Glasgow carrying that amount of petrol?'

King could only shake his head in disbelief. 'I wish you had come to us sooner.'

'Sooner than what? And I haven't come to you, you came to me. Also I have nothing to come with.' Dickson paused. 'Or perhaps, just perhaps, I have.'

King raised his eyebrows.

'Yes. You see, the thing that convinced us that it was a genuine act of vandalism was that if you come into this business, you do so because you love antiques, it is reaching out and touching history. I have in this shop two timepieces which are dated seventeen-thirty. They were in existence when the Young Pretender raised his standard, they were already seventy-five years old in Nelson's day, they were over two hundred years old when the Second World War was being fought and they are here, in this shop. Fine art shops, antique shops and perhaps other ventures I can't think of, don't get burned down for the fire insurance. They just don't, because their owners love their stock. If the business fails you can always sell your stock and move on. So you see, we couldn't believe that anybody would willingly send irreplaceable antiques up in smoke, especially not an antique dealer.'

'But now you think you're wrong? That is what did happen?'

'I don't think I am, Mr King. You see, it's only in talking to you just now that I may be able to suggest a solution. The aforementioned serious stuff didn't go up in flames because it wasn't in the shop.'

'What did go up in flames?'

'Junk.'

A pause. The word seemed to echo round the small room, bouncing off the walls.

Dickson allowed the implication to register and then continued. 'You see, in the antique trade generally there is an awful lot of junk and the antique-furniture trade is no exception. In cheap auctions and charity shops you can buy furniture made of hardwood which has been neglected down the years, deeply scarred by being used as a workbench, broken, repaired with strips of metal, bits missing entirely . . .'

'I get the picture. So, if the good stuff was moved out and sold for what it was worth and the junk put in place of the good stuff, then if the fire was hot and sustained enough, all you'd get would be ash.'

'That's my way of thinking. I'm no scientist but I would have thought that while you might be able to tell from a sample of ash what type of wood had been burnt, pine, oak, teak . . . you couldn't from that sample gauge the value or condition of the piece of furniture before it was consigned to the flames.'

'I wouldn't have thought so either.' King felt weary. He felt he had made progress that afternoon, but it hadn't been a comfortable ride.

'Something I'd like to show you.' Dickson stood, dogging

his cigarette in the ashtray on his desk. He left the room. King followed him.

Montgomerie, having finished his recording of his visit to Kit Saffa in the Ronnie Grenn file, made three further phone calls.

The first was an internal call to the collator. He asked the duty collator to access the file on Kit Saffa, specifically he wanted to know who was the last officer to access the file. The collator said that she would come back to him.

The second call, made whilst sipping a fresh mug of coffee, was to the Female and Child Unit of the Tayside Police at Dundee. Detective Constable Susan Neilson answered the phone.

'. . . guy called Iveson,' said Montgomerie. 'I visited him yesterday, he gave us some useful information about a code four-one we have going on at present, but I felt I ought to phone you about him.'

'Iveson.' Constable Neilson had a pleasant lilting voice. 'I confess that that name rings bells.'

'Surprised you're not deafened by said bells.'

'Oh?'

'He's a paedophile due for release and will be returning to a bail hostel in Dundee and thence into the community.'

'Yes . . . yes, I remember now . . . we received a Scottish Office notice about him . . .'

'I thought I'd phone you just to make said notice come alive as it were. So that he's more real in your minds than might otherwise be the case, sort of lift him off the page, as it were.'

'Appreciated.'

'Prison's done nothing for him.'

'I see.'

'There's two problems with him, first he's so looking forward to coming out that he's already talking with relish about the "Tayside Fairies", as he calls them.'

'Ugh . . .'

'Exactly, and not just to other lags as well, but to prison officers and visiting police officers.

'The second problem is that he's just the most manipulative person I've ever met. It goes beyond manipulation

139

. . . I found myself being sucked in by his mind . . . so far as I can tell it's down to eye contact and a soft voice, but I'm an adult not without life experience and I found myself being sucked in by him and he didn't like it when he didn't get his way with me. I can see how he can make the little people do exactly what he wants them to do.'

'Particularly when two of his known victims were his own daughters. I remember reading his file now.'

'Forewarned is forearmed.'

'And we've been forewarned. Appreciate it.'

The phone rang the instant Montgomerie put it down.

'Collator . . . the information you requested is DC Shirra, Drug Squad. Two weeks ago.'

'Drug Squad?'

'That's what it says here.'

'Thanks.'

Montgomerie put the phone down and made the third call to the Strathclyde Police Drug Squad. He identified himself and asked to speak to DC Shirra.

'He's on leave . . .' Then to one of his colleagues, 'When's Kenny Shirra due back?'

'Next week, Monday, back shift,' called a voice in the background.

'Next week, Monday, back shift,' repeated the voice in Montgomerie's ear. 'Can I help?'

'Dunno, really . . . tell you what it is . . . I had occasion to visit one Kit Saffa this afternoon, he's full of going straight with mended ways but something was missing, it didn't come off somehow and he looked worried when I told him that each access to his file is recorded so we know who is of continuing interest, even though they may not be perpetrating "fellow-nays". I wonder if you could tell me why you're interested, just to set my mind at rest. He gave some useful information, he's a previous known associate of the guy who was found in the West End yesterday morning with his brains blown out.'

'Oh him . . . well, yes, we're interested in Kit, he's a prime target.'

'Not the born-again full-time student wanting to do youth work, then?'

'Well, he's a full-time student and he's interested in youth, but probably not in the way he'd have you believe.'

'Not another sex offender. I've just . . .'

'No, not another sex offender . . . if I were to say that he seems to enjoy great popularity, and is feverish in his activities running up to the weekends in which the cream of Paisley youth have a "rave".'

'Ecstasy?'

'Got it in one. He's thought, known, in fact, for pushing the stuff left, right and centre among the "buddies". He's got Paisley sewn up. Anybody that tries to muscle in on his pitch tends to end up in the Royal Alexandria with broken limbs.'

'Tell me the old, old story.'

'And don't get taken in by the poor-but-honest lifestyle he has in Garthamlock. He needs to retain contact with the East End, that's where the wholesale is to be had. He has a very nice house in Dumbarton, a Porsche in the garage and a gin palace in the marina. Leopards don't change their spots, Malcolm.'

'Poor Ronnie Grenn.'

'Who's he?'

'The guy with no brains. Indications are that he was involved in something that he believed might give him enough folding green to go straight, just like his mentor Kit Saffa. If he'd known the true ID of Kit Saffa, he probably wouldn't have become involved in whatever he was involved in and he'd still be alive right now. Anyway, thanks for the information. I was left wondering, now I'm not. Owe you one.'

'Its a Westmorland dowry chest.' Dickson stood in front of a dark, and even to King's untrained eye, clearly ancient item of furniture. It stood in the corner of Dickson's shop. It was, King estimated, of similar dimensions to the aluminium cabin trunks that university students have delivered to their lodgings at the beginning of each academic year. It was fastened by an ancient lock. 'It's seventeenth century,' Dickson advised him, 'contemporary with William Shakespeare.'

'Blimey.' King found himself becoming fascinated with the

world of antiques, each item around him in this well-lit shop: these tables, these writing desks, these chairs all have a story, all have a place in recorded history. Who sat here, who there, what was written on that surface, what meals taken from that table . . . to say nothing of the craftsmanship of the carpentry. And that was just the furniture. Beyond the wood there are metal and gems, and clockworks, and oil on canvas. This could, King realized, be a dangerous interest if he allowed it to grow, financially speaking.

'As an antique it isn't, despite its age, particularly valuable, it's not in excellent condition and it's of very simple construction. It's just a wooden chest, really, it's the age which makes it interesting. If you want to buy it, it would cost you as much as a weekend break for two in Amsterdam, plus spending money. But the reason that I want to show it to you is this . . .' Dickson paused as if collecting his thoughts. 'The first point to make is that this item of antique furniture is not unique, there are others in circulation but they are few in number. Dowry chests like this would have been owned by daughters of yeomen, in their day they were seen as having little value and so had a high wasteage rate. They were chopped up for firewood or used to keep the coal in, so many were made, but few survived.'

'Understood.'

'Often there's nothing to tell them apart. But if I were a betting man, I'd lay a fiver that this item of furniture was on the second floor of Cernach's on all three occasions when I visited. If I'm right it should be a pile of ash right now, yet here it is.'

'When did you acquire it, sir?'

'Six months ago, or thereabouts, from Fancy's.'

'Fancy's?'

'On the Great Western Road. They're beyond reproach; auctioneers of this city for in excess of two hundred years. They would not touch anything dodgy and it only occurred to me what this chest might signify when I was talking to you, Mr King. You see, I've been walking past this chest for six months, each trading day for six months, and each time I walk past her . . .'

'Her . . . ?'

'Sorry, I can't help but personalize my stock, each one is

a him or a her. Each time I walk past her I find myself thinking, "I know you, I've seen you before . . ." and only now do I realize that it was in Cernach's, as certain as I can be without being certain. And that, you see, is as I said earlier, something else that just slots into place about the Cernach blaze. I mean, look around you, look at this beauty, this craftsmanship, this living history. Only someone with a heart made of Aberdeen granite could pour petrol over this for the fire insurance.' Dickson paused and turned to King and held eye contact. 'They burnt junk. Had to. They stored the good stuff, somewhere there's a barn or a warehouse full of high-value antiques and they're trickling them on to the market, one item at a time, one item every few months.'

'And this being one?'

'This being one.'

Ray Sussock stirred, awoke, for a second he did not know where he was, the double bed in the 'inshot' in the room, the pastel-coloured decoration, the Van Gogh print on the wall. Oh yes . . . yes . . . he'd returned to Langside.

'Afternoon, Old Sussock.' Elka Willems sat in the armchair in the bay window reading the *Glasgow Herald*. She didn't look at him as she spoke.

Sussock groaned. 'What time is it?'

'Five o'clock or thereabouts. You didn't sleep much. You don't sleep enough, really.'

'It'll be enough.' Sussock knuckled his eyes. 'Five o'clock, my poor body thinks it's six o'clock.'

Elka Willems glanced out of the window. Night had fallen over Langside. 'Yes, it does seem strange that it's so dark already. In Holland, you know, my father once . . .' But she fell silent as she realized from a distinct snore that Raymond Sussock had drifted off to sleep. She said to herself, 'I'll wake you at nine, Old Sussock. If you're not awake by then.'

When he returned to P Division Police Station, to the DCs' office on the CID corridor, he peeled off his coat and laid it beside Montgomerie's ski jacket. He said hi to Montgomerie who sat with his feet on his desk reading a two-day-old copy of the *Daily Record*. King sat at his desk and picked up the phone and tapped a two-figure internal number.

'Collator.' A female voice, crisp, efficient-sounding.

'DC King, P Division ... two names for you, can you let me have anything you have on them ... first one is Carberrie, Mary.'

The collator requested clarification. She wanted to know whether it was Mary Carberry or Mary Carberrie. King said he understood it to be Carberrie but would she please try both spellings?

'Do you have her numbers?'

'Don't,' said King, leaning forwards as he spoke, 'but she's believed to be late forties, early fifties.'

'Very good. And the next name?'

'Gary Westwater. Again, no numbers but probably of the same age.'

Montgomerie folded down the pages of his newspaper and looked across the floor at his chubby, bearded colleague. When King had put down the phone he said 'Did you say Gary Westwater? And Mary Carberrie?'

'I did. Why?'

Montgomerie told him.

It was 17.32 hours.

WEDNESDAY

5

Donoghue slept late. He enjoyed the luxury of a slow start to his day, happy to cower under the duvet while his wife chased Timothy and Louisa out of the house and off to school. He rose leisurely and showered and shaved and relaxed once more in his armchair, sipping coffee and reading the *Scotsman*. A long lie is something for him which only happens at weekends, and even then he had to contend with Timothy and Louisa's fights, shouts and tantrums, but to enjoy a long lie without the 'ankle-biters' was an unheard-of luxury. To be at home at nine a.m., still not making a move, on a weekday, when he normally starts his car engine to drive to work at seven-thirty . . . was heaven in his mind, pure heaven. But his wife couldn't relax. She hurried. She scurried. She didn't reply when he spoke to her, not in a huff, but more in the manner of being too busy to reply, as if engaged upon a pressing matter, but for the life of him Donoghue could not identify what that matter of urgency might be. Eventually, but only in his own time, on his own terms, he rose from his favourite chair, the one he always occupied, and put on his jacket and grey woollen coat and homburg and left the house. He was afforded his customary peck on the cheek by Mrs Donoghue, but nonetheless still had the sense that he was being bustled out of the house. The door was shut insensitively the instant he had crossed the threshold out of the house, and the lock turned with a loud click. He got into his Rover and turned the key. The engine roared into life and he backed down the driveway of his bungalow in gentle Craiglockhart. As he drove away he glanced at his house, and saw his wife sitting in her housecoat, looking content, in the chair he had occupied just a few seconds earlier. He drove to central Edinburgh. He had always thought his marriage harmonious and successful. He had never before known his wife behave in such a manner and it had distressed him. He decided not to mention it. Unless it happened again. Unless it seemed to be becoming a pattern. Then it would have to become an issue.

He drove to the headquarters of the Lothian and Borders Police in Fettes Avenue. He approached the reception desk and identified himself. He was ushered courteously into the innards of the building and moments later sat in front of the desk of Detective Inspector Stamp.

'It was,' said Stamp, 'a marriage that shouldn't have worked, everything was against it, but it did. One was Catholic and one a Proddy Dog. I can't remember who was what but one turned and they had a Catholic marriage. They were both just sixteen when they got hitched and they spent their first year in a damp basement where their child was born. Everything was against them, mixed religion, youth, poverty, early pregnancy, but they came through.'

'And how, by all accounts.'

'Yes . . . no education either, no bits of paper that open doors and make vast differences to anybody's life.' Stamp smiled, he was, Donoghue noted, smartly dressed, youthful for his rank. He felt he had much in common with Stamp and warmed to the man, and he felt Stamp warming to him in return. 'When he was eighteen he bought and sold a car. Sold it for quite a mark-up, he told me. He was on his way. These days if you buy a used car in Scotland it has a one-third chance of being bought from an Oakley garage, anywhere from Inverness to Annan.'

'Didn't know he was *that* big.'

'Oh yes, never gives that impression because he uses various different names for his used-car outlets, could be called Bridge Street Motors in one town, McHugh's Motors in another, but really they are all Oakley-owned garages. He said that he thought the punters would be put off if they saw Oakley everywhere, but they'd be more likely to part with their money if they thought they were giving it to a local businessman with only one showroom.'

'Seemed to pay off.'

'I'll say. They own a house on Barnton Avenue. That is where the money is in Edinburgh.'

'I know. I live in this city.'

'Do you? Sorry, I thought you came through from Glasgow.'

'I'm Glaswegian by birth and belonging, but speaking of mixed marriages, my wife is Edinbrovian and will not leave this town. As with the Oakleys, one of us had to turn, and it was me that turned.'

'Very accommodating of you.' Stamp smiled approvingly.

'I was in love. Still am. And as you know, it's a one-hour journey by road or rail. It's not impossible to commute, thousands do so. But I know the Barntons, yes, as you say . . .'

'They moved there when still in their thirties, all the brashness of new money, American cars . . . didn't go down too well with their more reserved neighbours but they had it so they flaunted it. I never knew "Annie" . . . I got to know them after the kidnap, got to know them well, which is how I know about their backgrounds . . . but "Annie" gave me the impression of being an overindulged wee brat, just between you and me, just within these four walls. It's the old story of two people who came from poverty and were determined to compensate by giving their only daughter everything.'

'No other children, despite being Catholic?'

'Puzzled me and I don't know the full reason but they did tell me that they discussed the possibility of more children and decided to ask "Annie" whether she wanted to grow up alone or whether she wanted a wee brother or sister. "Annie" apparently thought about it for a day or two and then told them that she wanted to grow up alone and so on that basis, the Oakleys had no more children. "Annie" was about five at the time.'

'Good Lord.'

'You see what I mean by indulged.'

'Certainly do.'

'I don't know how they got round the birth-control business, being Catholic, but they did. I didn't get that close to them. Shall we have some coffee?'

Sipping coffee, Donoghue remarked on the unfortunate choice of Christian name for young Miss Oakley.

'Was rather, but she didn't seem to mind. Once came across a Mr and Mrs Monroe who had a daughter.'

'They didn't?'

'Oh yes, they did . . . so,' Stamp said, grinning, at his own anecdote, 'the kidnap and disappearance of "Annie" Oakley has come to the attention of the Strathclyde Police?'

'Possibly. The murder victim on Monday morning – you may have read of it?'

'Brains blown out.'

'That's the one. We searched his room at his mother's home and found newspaper cuttings about the kidnap and a building circled on an Ordnance Survey map of the Kilsyth area.'

'Did you now?'

'We did now.' Donoghue put his mug on Stamp's desk. 'I sent one of my team to look at the building, get an impression from the road but not to approach it. I don't know what he found, I've yet to speak to him. I left for home before he had returned. That was yesterday.'

'I see.'

'Of course, it may mean nothing, the building may be totally unconnected with the kidnap but equally, it may be a stone worth turning over.'

'It would be a stone that has to be turned over, sounds like. How can I help you, Fabian?'

'Putting me in the picture about the kidnap, especially anything that wasn't released to the press.'

'I'll let you read the file, I'll draw it from the void for you but I can remember it clearly. It annoys me still that they got away with it, but they were successful kidnappers because, like all successful kidnappers, they'd worked out a way of having the ransom dropped with no possibility of surveillance. There's ways of doing it and they had found one. Essentially they used portable telephones. It's not an original idea. There was a well-publicized case in the States in the nineteen-forties when the kidnappers used ex-military walkie-talkies to communicate with the police. They must have pinched that idea.'

'So what happened?'

'Well, the Oakleys . . . him . . . Hugh Oakley, he wasn't, isn't, the hard-headed realist that you might think. He has a certain flair and instinct and a willingness to take a risk, which is necessary in business, but he has also enjoyed an element of luck. He's ridden from wave crest to wave crest and made a future dealing in used tin. But he retained a certain credulity, a naivety almost. When I first visited them after the kidnap they, he and Mrs Oakley, were full of, "Who'd do this to us? We haven't harmed anybody, we've paid our taxes, why us?" And they didn't let that go. I thought it was a panic reaction but weeks later they still could not believe that they would be victims of crime because they had not committed serious offences. The Almighty wouldn't strike at them.'

Donoghue groaned.

'Painful, isn't it? Anyway, this is all by means of explanation for the reason that they'd left their home wide open, certainly to burglary but also, it transpired, to kidnap. They had two huge stone gateposts at the entrance to their drive but no gates. After the gateposts the drive turned to the left and proceeded for about a hundred yards through thick shrubs and trees, and I mean rhododendrons, twenty feet high, either side of the road and possibly thirty feet deep. And they had to drive through that entering and leaving the house.'

'So once you turned into the driveway you were out of sight from both the road and the house?'

'For about a hundred yards, yes. I mean, you could hide a company of infantry in that lot.'

'No dogs?'

'No. No burglar alarm either.'

'Unbelievable.'

'Well, they paid a terrible price because that's where "Annie" was snatched. Mr Oakley came home and found "Annie's" white off-the-road number blocking the drive. Doors open, engine still idling but no "Annie". Even then he didn't raise the alarm for half an hour or so, spent some time crashing about in the bushes and looking round his house. Then he went back to the car, just to move it, and only then did he see a note trapped under the windscreen-wiper blade: *We've got your daughter*, or words to that effect. The note's in the file.'

'What did you find?'

'Well, he'd probably damaged a lot of trace evidence by crashing about like he did, but there were skid marks where she'd stopped her car. We presume somebody leapt out in her path. Anybody with presence of mind wouldn't have stopped, but she was eighteen years old, bad things only happen to other people, her reaction would have been to do an emergency stop. She was probably pulled out and bundled into another car which had followed her into the driveway. She wasn't a big girl, five feet and a few inches, so far as I can recall. Couldn't have put up much of a struggle. We looked at the ground for spoor and reckoned only about two men, male shoes, anyway, boots, you know, plus whoever else was in the getaway vehicle which left no tracks of any kind. Nothing so convenient as a witness either.'

'Not a lot to go on.'

'Nothing at all, really. The kidnappers didn't leave a trace of themselves in the bushes either, no cigarette stubs, no chocolate wrapping paper, half-eaten fruit. It seemed they were waiting for her only a few moments.'

'Luck or good judgement?' Donoghue ached to smoke his pipe but Stamp, to Donoghue's dismay, had a 'thank you for not smoking' sign on his wall.

'Good judgement, I'd say. They'd done their homework. She was returning from an aerobics session in the gym. Every Tuesday afternoon, always returned home at about the same time.'

'Then what happened?'

'Then it gets frustrating. Just at the time we would expect to be learning about the kidnappers because of their demands, letters they write, paper they use, voice that can be recorded and identified . . . but no, we really lucked out there. They used her Vodaphone and she made the calls. We never heard the voice of one of the kidnappers, nor did we get a description. They allowed her to phone daily, at midday each day for four days, just to say that she was alive. That's all. Nothing else. We weren't given a thing that we could infer anything from . . . you see, when victims are allowed to speak they often give something away like, "they've got me," – or, "he's got me," so the police would know they're looking for a single man or a gang, or, "it's cold and dark in here," in which case the victim may be being held underground.'

'Elimination points.' Donoghue nodded.

'But all we got was, "Hello, Mum, it's 'Annie', I'm still

alive . . ." Then the phone was cut off, as if it was taken from her and switched off. Being a Vodaphone, of course she could have been calling from . . . well, anywhere in the world. By this time we were consulting a lady you probably know, Dr Peta Reid, forensic psychologist at the University of Glasgow.'

'Dr Reid, yes, we've picked her brains before. She's on the ball.'

'I think she was on this occasion. She pointed out that the skill of observing rules is knowing when you've got to break them. In some circumstances the rule book does not apply.'

'Meaning in this case . . . ?'

'Well, the drill with kidnap is to keep the channel of communication open with whoever you can. But in this case there was no communication and we were not able even to pin down the source of the call to a geographical area. So we took the decision to contact Vodaphone and ask them to shut down "Annie" Oakley's unit. They can do that, you know – in the event of theft they can be shut down and taken out of the network.'

'I'm aware of that.'

'So we asked them to do it.'

'Some risk.'

'Aye, and not taken easily nor without top-level consultation. I had to get clearance from on high for that. We wanted to provoke them into wrong-footing themselves. The hope was that without a Vodaphone they'd resort to land lines or the Royal Mail. Then we could begin to trace them.'

Donoghue nodded. 'I can see the logic in that.'

'In the event it didn't help us. There was no contact for a day or two, by which time the Cellnet organization was waiting for the call, so was British Telecom, just in case. She called two days later, by which time she'd been held for about six days. The call came from another Vodaphone and Cellnet was able to give us the number. From the number we could get the name and address of the subscriber. We were elated. But the elation was short-lived.'

'Sorry to hear that.'

'Yes. We discovered the concept of cloned personal phones.' Stamp raised an eyebrow. 'You know, as I am now in my forties, I feel that the world has moved on and I haven't moved with it. I'm just not equipped to deal with hi-tech crime.'

Donoghue said that he knew what he meant, but he had never come across the concept of cloning phones.

'It's apparently quite simple. Each personal phone has a number known by its rentee and the company that owns and operates the phone. With relatively simple and high street-obtainable equipment, it is possible to scan the airwaves and obtain the number of a phone as it is being used.'

'OK.'

'There then follows a conventional theft. The sort of crime that is as old as humanity itself. Say a TDA, and in amongst all the goodies in the car is a personal phone. The owner of the car reports his phone as being stolen and its number is cancelled by the Cellnet organization and you may think that it's a redundant piece of kit. Can't make calls, can't receive them.'

'But not so?'

'No. The phone is not so much deceased as dormant. The phone in its dormant state is sold in the criminal network for the price of a night in the pub for a couple of pals, its purchaser reprogrammes it with the number of a phone obtained by eavesdropping the airwaves and the reactivated phone is then sold for the price of dinner for two in the best restaurant in town. It has now become a "cloned" phone and all the calls made on it are billed to the rentee of the legitimate phone. If you use the cloned phone often enough and for international calls of long duration, you can easily recover the cost of its purchase. The rentee of the legitimate phone won't know anything is amiss until he receives his phone bill.'

'Or until the police chap his door.'

'Which is what happened to a guy in Glamorgan, South Wales. On our request the Glamorgan police pulled him in connection with the kidnap of "Annie" Oakley. By coincidence, he gave his occupation as second-hand car dealer, but he wasn't our boy. He could prove he was overseas at the time of the kidnap, some dreadful resort in Spain, I recall. So we knew we had a cloned phone and were no further forward, but it didn't harm the situation. At least we had that compensation. The experiment didn't work but it didn't cost us anything. We learned, if we learned anything, that they have access to an outlet for these cloned devices and upon enquiries being put afoot, we learned that such outlets are many. Everything from a guy in the pub doing a one-off deal to a "specialist" who makes a living out of it.'

'But at least, as you say, it didn't cost anything.'

'The Glamorgan Police got more than we did, in fact. This guy wasn't known to them, but when they fondled his collar he began to scream his rights, sweat like a pig and demanded his lawyer be present. He had nothing to do with the kidnap but he'd been up to something. So the Welsh boys began to keep an eye on him.'

'But you were no further forward?'

'No, we weren't, though we did get a couple of minor elimination points from the exercise so it wasn't really a waste of time. We asked Dr Reid her opinion of the matter and she said that she felt that the cloned Vodaphone had been purchased as such, rather than cloned by the kidnappers because kidnap as a crime is clumsy, high risk, and definitely for the cerebrally challenged. Cloning phones is low risk and requires hi-tech skill. People who clone phones are just not from the same stable as people who kidnap.'

'I can see that. So if the kidnappers had any track, it was for low-tech, traditional crime?'

'Exactly. And the second thing that she pointed out to us is that we can't look at previously unsolved kidnaps, if any, for pointers about "Annie" Oakley's case because kidnap is not a serial crime. Just isn't. The reason for that is that it's too traumatic for the kidnappers, poor wee things. Killing people you don't know and before you come to know them is relatively easy, pulling bank jobs becomes a way of life. But abducting someone, holding them against their will for an extended period means that a relationship can't help but develop between the kidnapper and victim, so Dr Reid told us. She also pointed out that some kidnap victims have in the past kept their heads and deliberately cultivated a relationship with their captors and so brought about a successful outcome from their point of view. Either they've been released unharmed and the kidnapper has fled without pressing home their demands, or the kidnappers have gone through to the end, but his or her victim has been released with sufficient information to apprehend the kidnapper: or both. Either way, by building a relationship with the kidnapper, victims have often saved their own lives. And in doing so, they've given said poor wee kidnapper an experience they don't want to relive.'

'Poor things, as you say.' Donoghue smiled.

'But it's a valid elimination point. It meant we didn't have to spend time trawling the files of unsolved kidnappings looking for parallels.' Stamp paused. He took a deep breath and glanced out of his office window as a maroon-coloured double-decker of Lothian Transport with a white top, hummed down Newhaven Road towards the red-bricked Ferranti factory. 'Then the situation took a turn for the worse. You see, by using portable phones the kidnappers had solved the problem about being traced to their location.'

'They could have been phoning from New Zealand.'

'Right. But we were to find that they had worked out that personal phones can be used to solve the other major problem kidnappers have, which is how to have the ransom delivered without it being kept under surveillance. We got a call from "Annie", midday to her parents' phone, clear, slow, as if, we thought, reading from a script. The ransom was one million pounds in used notes, in twenty-pound notes. She went on to say that the notes had to be Bank of England notes, Royal Bank of Scotland, Bank of Scotland and Clydesdale Bank notes. So already they had an eye for laundering the money. "Annie" said at the end of her message that we had a week to get the money ready. So we drew from that that the kidnappers felt safe, not at all concerned about being discovered. Their safe house, wherever it was in the world, was a very, very safe house. We took advice, consulted HOLMES, talked to the parents and at the end of the day we decided to collect the money and pay it. We took note of the serial numbers of the notes but otherwise did what they wanted.'

'And waited.'

'Apart from waiting for "Annie"'s daily call to let us know that she was still alive, that's all we did.'

'That's all you could do.'

'Then we got our instructions. The one million pounds was to be placed inside two ex-military canvas kitbags and securely fastened at the opening. The kitbags will be opened immediately and the money transferred into other bags, so do not place tracking devices in the kitbags, nor do anything that may be interpreted as being a means of tracking the money. She said "the drop", she used that term, will take place in two days' time. Then the phone went dead. I should say that she'd been phoning her parents' land line all this time. Then soon after the phone went dead her father's own mobile started to sing. He answered it and it was "Annie", who said that all further contact would be to his mobile so he had to keep it with him at all times. They must have got his number from "Annie"'s filofax.'

'Must have,' Donoghue agreed, but it crossed his mind that torturing the information out of 'Annie' Oakley was not impossible, or even unlikely.

'Then we got a call saying that from ten a.m., Mr Oakley had to start travelling on the slow-stopping train from Glasgow Queen Street to Stirling and then do the return journey. And to keep shuttling backwards and forwards carrying his Vodaphone and wait for instructions. We knew then the reason for the kitbags, he was going to have to toss them and the money they contained from a moving train, and one of my officers said as much. There was a silence, the line was still open and then "Annie" said, "Dad, you're going to have to throw the bags from the train but the train has got to keep going. If the train stops they won't pick up the bags. Don't pull the cord. Throw it from the left side as you face the direction of travel."

'So you had no idea at which point between Stirling and Glasgow the bags were to be jettisoned? That's a lot of square miles to cover.'

'Oh, it gets better, or worse, depending on your point of view. Throwing from the left side as you face the direction of travel makes sense, it means throwing it away from the track whichever way you're going rather than on to the parallel track, so that didn't surprise us. Anyway, we did what we could to cover the area, we had unmarked cars patrolling, either side of the track, we had guys in camouflage observing the track and its environs from a distance using powerful field glasses, we had guys on the train with Mr Oakley, we had our own radio and mobile phones. So we started travelling shortly after ten a.m. That day was a Friday, I remember I had booked it as leave, the following day was our wedding anniversary and me and my wife had planned a long weekend away to celebrate quietly by ourselves. She wasn't pleased when I cancelled but she understood when I explained what was happening and we went away a week or two later. But' – Stamp shrugged his shoulders – 'you marry a cop . . . love me, love my dog.'

'I confess I've encountered the same problem.'

'I'll bet you have; it's the name of the game. Fortunately my wife is an ex-policewoman and so understands what it's like. Other guys on the squad don't have it so easy.'

'But to continue . . .'

'To continue, they must have watched us, because just ten minutes out of Glasgow Queen Street, Oakley's mobile rang. It was "Annie". She said, "Thank you, Dad, I'll phone you later."'

'Somebody watched Mr Oakley get on the Stirling train, made a phone call from a pay phone on or in the vicinity of the station to whoever was holding "Annie" and she then phoned her father using her mobile.'

'So we assumed. Now the cruel bit comes. We started that journey at ten a.m., at eight p.m. we were still shuttling back and forth . . . Mr Oakley was in tears, the tension, the strain, the not knowing, the fear for his daughter . . . no contact . . . that was the hard bit.'

'Oh my . . . I can feel for him. I have two children. One a girl.'

'I've got two boys. The mad fools want to be policemen. Anyway, at eight p.m., we're on one of the homeward legs, we're feeling hungry and weak and dispirited, Scotrail sandwiches and coffee are very good but they can only take you so far, then we got a call on Oakley's mobile . . . we're to leave the train at Queen Street, travel across Glasgow to Central, get the next InterCity to London.'

'So all the surveillance teams were useless.'

'And had been throughout the day, but by that time they were also exhausted, their day's work was out of them. They had no intention of having Oakley chuck the kitbags from the train as it rattled between Glasgow and Stirling. If they had any reason to make him spend a day doing that it was to make ourselves commit men to the ground between those two towns and then having done that, they whisked Oakley and his kitbags away on an express train.'

'Clever.'

'So we were travelling south on the InterCity. The train we were on was the new stock, air-conditioned, can't open the door windows by sliding them down, so we knew Oakley could relax for a while. We knew we would have to change to a suburban line at some point, at least that's what we expected, but we had no idea where we could be sent. They could have been taking us to the south coast of England. At this time dusk was falling and one of the team commented that it was going to be a night drop, and again that made sense, it would make it difficult to fix the exact location of the point that we would be chucking the bags out of the train window.'

'Didn't take chances, did they?'

'You're telling me. Anyway, one guy had the bright idea, which like all bright ideas is simplicity itself, and that was that since it was going to be dark, or at least dusk because this was summer, that we find something small and dark and heavy enough not to be blown away in the wind or the draught from passing trains that Oakley could conceal in his hands and let fall as he let one of the kitbags fall. So we hunted around, couldn't find anything and one of my guys suggested we drop one of our radios, it was small and black, wouldn't travel. There were four of us, we were left with three radios plus a mobile, plus Oakley's mobile, we could afford it. So we decided to do that.'

'Not many radios at the side of a railway line.'

'Not a lot, no.' Stamp paused and scratched the side of his head. 'We crossed the border, that wee stream near Gretna, and then we were called. "Annie" called her dad, told him to get off at Carlisle. Told him to get the next train to Glasgow via Dumfries. You travelled that line?'

'Have not, I confess.'

'Don't unless you have to. It goes through the back of beyond, and does so slowly. I mean, from Carlisle we crawled back to Gretna, tired locomotive, old rolling stock, with windows in the doors at either end of the carriage which could be opened fully by sliding them down. From Gretna we went to Dumfries and by this time it was dark. It was after Dumfries that we got the instructions to drop the kitbags. It was "Annie" again, she phoned her dad on the mobile. She said, "move to the end of the carriage and open the window on the left side of the train facing the direction of travel. In a minute or two you'll be going into a long tunnel, chuck the bags out as soon as you're out of the tunnel."'

'So you didn't need to drop the radio.'

'No. The tunnel fixed the position as accurately as we needed it to be fixed. So we followed instructions. Sure enough we went into a tunnel. Oakley pulled down the window and was ready to heave the bags. As soon as we were out he chucked one bag, then the second, uncontrollable tears as he did so. And the train rattled on. It was all as if someone with a mobile phone was watching the train and just two minutes before the train went into the tunnel, phoned whoever was holding "Annie" and told her to phone Mr Oakley with the instructions. We reported the instructions as soon as we received them, and Dumfries and Galloway Police were at the scene quickly – they had a car shadowing the train. It was all that they could spare at such short notice. We had a look at the times that we were logged as reporting the drop and the time the police car was on the scene and there was only a two-minute delay, and I mean a one-hundred-and-twenty-second time window.'

'Fast.'

'The line's near the main road at that point. The two constables in the car didn't see anybody, they couldn't see the bags, but in fairness didn't look for them. They stayed in the car observing the locus as best they could in the darkness, waiting for a car to start up and headlights to appear.'

'But nothing?'

'Nothing. The tunnel itself is long, about a mile in length. What I now believe happened is that they waited just inside the northern end of the tunnel and picked up the kitbags as they were dropped and then carried them back through the tunnel to a getaway car which was waiting near the southern end. A mile through a railway tunnel is not the sort of journey I'd want to make but if I had a companion, if I had a torch, and if I had the amount of a bottle you could purchase with a million pounds, then I'd do it. If they'd have told us to drop the money at the southern end of the tunnel, they'd have police converging there, if they told us to drop the money in the tunnel, they'd have police at either end of the tunnel.'

'But doing the drop at the northern end of the tunnel had the same effect as having Mr Oakley shuttle backwards and forwards between Edinburgh and Glasgow had had.'

'Exactly my thinking. Lured the police away from the action. These were clever people. Probably still are. Anyway, shortly after the drop "Annie" phoned her father and said, "Thanks, Dad, they've got the money." He burst into tears and said that it was the last time he'd hear his daughter's voice.'

'And he was right.'

'After this amount of time, yes. We kept in contact for a few weeks but with nothing to report, the contact trailed off. Mr Oakley carried on but something had left him. He was just going through the motions of working. Mrs Oakley went into a deep, very black, depression and had to be hospitalized.'

'Outcome of Enquiries?'

'Not a great deal, as you might imagine, we did house-to-house in villages to the north and south of the tunnel, got nothing in Sanquar and New Cumnock, but something in Carronbridge, Thornhill and Dumfries.'

'Oh?'

'We worked out from the time that the money was jettisoned, allowing twenty minutes to walk through the tunnel, possibly half an hour, that any getaway car would be driving through population centres just around the time that the pubs would be turning out, and given the nature of the area, closed rural community, a foreign vehicle . . .'

'Foreign?'

'I mean foreign to the area.'

'Yes.'

'Any foreign car would be noticed, and we got four people who reported an ex-Royal Mail delivery van heading south, quite fast it seemed, but not dangerously so.'

'Ex-Royal Mail?'

'Blood-red Leyland Sherpa with the Post Office logo removed from the side, only one seat in the cab and a wire mesh and wood partition separating the cab from the cargo area. You can pick them up for a song at motor auctions. They're popular with jobbing craftsmen and youngsters who want an inexpensive set of wheels.'

'Ah yes, I know the vehicles.'

'One such vehicle was seen heading south within an hour of the ransom being dropped, four separate sightings. One witness in Dumfries said that he'd not seen the vehicle or the driver before, but the driver seemed familiar with the town, gave the impression she knew where she was going.'

'They'd done a dummy run.'

'That would be my guess, though probably at a busy time when a foreign vehicle would not be noticed so easily, on the basis that the best place to hide a tree is in a forest. But it would seem that the getaway was south, to Dumfries, from there it's a ten-mile dash to Lockerbie and there you join the A74, whereupon ye are lost and gone forever.'

'Oh, we hope not.' Both men grinned. Then Donoghue continued. 'You said "she".'

'One witness described the driver as female with a mane of reddish hair. About forty-five, possibly older, but not younger. No chicken.'

'And what of the money?'

'Laundered over a period of time. And cleverly so. You see, one million pounds in twenty-pound notes amounts to fifty thousand bits of paper. At first nothing happened. Nothing surfaced. Nothing at all.'

'Then?'

'Then came the Glasgow Fair in July. The city shuts down early on Friday and doesn't open again until Tuesday morning, during which hours the good citizens of the dear green place spend like there's no tomorrow.'

'One thousand pounds of ransom money surfaced on the Tuesday the banks opened. All as part of the till receipts of licensed premises, newsagents, food shops, so then we knew that that was how they were going to launder the money. Tediously, but utterly safe. By going into a newsagent's and buying a *Herald* or *Daily Record* and perhaps a packet of cigarettes and tendering a twenty-pound note and saying, sorry, you've nothing smaller; then taking the newspaper into a pub and buying a slimline tonic with ice and lemon and tendering a twenty-pound note and saying, sorry, you've nothing smaller; leaving the newspaper in the bar and then

162

repeating the exercise until you're awash with liquid. Buying a cup of coffee with a twenty-pound note ... buying a handful of groceries ... a couple of gallons of petrol for your car ... each time you make a transaction you launder a twenty-pound note and the change is not traceable. So the one thousand pounds we recovered after the Glasgow Fair amounted to five hundred transactions.'

'Busy squirrels.'

'Divided between three people we thought just over one hundred small purchases each, over the period from Friday at sixteen hundred hours when the banks shut, to Tuesday oh-nine hundred hours, when the traders take their cash to the bank. If you put your mind to it, you can do it. I mean, that is an eighty-nine-hour period, allowing for eight hours' sleep each, twenty-four plus two hours each twenty-four for refreshment, that's still sixty, nearly seventy man-hours, which means an average of one and a bit transactions each hour, three transactions in a two-hour period. The time taken in the transaction is easy. I would think the problem is that you'd run out of premises, can't go to the same shop twice and you'd spend much time walking betwixt and between said minor retail outlets. So perhaps an average of three transactions in two hours amounts to a lot of hard graft.'

'It also amounts to a lot of self-discipline and a lot of planning and does point to kidnappers in their middle years.' Donoghue nodded his head. 'Younger people would be in a hurry to spend all that dosh and so lead a trail to their door.'

'It also points to kidnappers who have no previous connection with the underworld. There are figures in this city and your city, and every major city in the UK, who would trade one million pounds of dirty, traceable money for untraceable money at twenty-five pence off the pound. And do the transaction over a weekend. The fact that they didn't do that was another indication that this team had no track.'

'You mentioned three as being the number of the gang?'

'Nothing firm, but it would make sense, it would add up. The footprints of the two people in the shrubs in the Oakleys' parkland-size garden, who wrested "Annie" out of her vehicle and into the back of the getaway vehicle, which would be driven by a third. Two kitbags for the ransom money, to be carried through the tunnel, one person for each bag, and the getaway vehicle again to be driven by a third person . . .'

'They'd need four.' Donoghue spoke quietly. 'They'd need four.'

Stamp inclined his head.

'Two in the tunnel.'

'Right.'

'They'd have to be dropped off at that locus at least one hour before the train you were travelling in arrived. Couldn't afford to cut it any finer.'

'Agreed.'

'Only one vehicle, possibly an ex-Post Office van plus driver, possibly female.'

'Yes.'

'They would have left Glasgow three hours before you switched from the Stirling train to the InterCity. Two hours to get to the Dumfries area, one hour to take up positions. Two in the tunnel, and the driver tucking the van away out of sight somewhere.'

'Yes.' A puzzled note in Stamp's voice.

'They'd have to have a fourth person watching you to make sure you entrained at Glasgow Central and who phoned the information from a public phone at the station to the person in the van who had a mobile. Who then, armed with a timetable, would know which train you were on, would phone as you approached Carlisle with instructions to change trains and had visual contact with said train as it approached the tunnel, called you up and told you to drop the ransom as you left the tunnel. The person in Glasgow may only have been a gofer, an errand boy, a bagman, junior in the hierarchy, but he or she had to have been there.'

'You're right. It was at least a four-man operation.'

'Not wholly right, Tom, and you're not wholly wrong. The important and dangerous bits could have been done by three – three, incidentally, is the most powerfully loyal of all human groups. Two will fall out, four will split into two groups of two, but three remain constant.'

'I didn't know that.'

'Something I picked up along the way. But it may still be a group of three, the fourth person may have been hired to spy on you without knowing the reason why, maybe told to

164

make a phone call without knowing who it was going to, "Watch for a guy carrying two army kitbags, he should get on the such and such train to London which always leaves from platform one at such and such a time. Watch from a safe distance. When he gets on the train, wait until the train leaves and then phone this number and say, 'He's on his way.' Here's fifty quid. If it all goes all right, there'll be another fifty for you tomorrow, then forget me, forget this, it never happened." It could be like that, so maybe we are looking for a gang of three.'

'Maybe. One a woman with red hair. And being that Scotia is famed the world over for red-haired women . . .'

'What did the prints in the shrubbery tell you?'

'As I recall, one was definitely a man, a tall man, he had huge plates of meat, but was quite light-stepping. The other could have been either man or woman of about nine or ten stones, wearing trainers, so could be either sex.'

'A gang of three, one tall man, one red-haired woman, one who could be either sex. All possibly middle aged. None with previous convictions, at least of an underworld nature. But intelligent, I mean here be planning, here be self-restraint and here be ruthlessness.'

'That chilled me. It appears that once they'd got the money, little Miss Oakley was history.'

'So back to the money.'

'Well, after the Fair holiday . . . oh incidentally, they pursued the spend as much as you can at every outlet policy on the Tuesday after the Fair Monday. I suppose that they reasoned it would take at least one working day for the banks to report the ransom notes had been placed in circulation, but less money was recovered from the Tuesday, so we reckoned that part or all of the gang may have some form of employment. In fact, they could have carried on spending at that rate for another day because it was not until the Thursday after the Fair Monday that we realized how they were laundering the money and only then could we ask publicans and newsagents and the like to take note of people making small purchases with twenty-pound notes, by which time the money had stopped emerging and they seemed to go to ground. Then weeks went by, into August now, and after August Bank Holiday Monday the same thing happened, only this time it was here in Edinburgh and one thousand pounds' worth of ransom money, again as till receipts from small retail outlets or pubs, was recovered. And so the pattern was set, on the Monday after a weekend, or the Tuesday after a holiday weekend the banks in one specific town in Scotland, or the north of England, would recover a four-figure sum of the ransom-money notes. Once the gang appeared to have spent an expensive week in London and the South Coast. In between times, it surfaced midweek in one's and two's and this pattern continued for three years, by which time all fifty thousand bits of paper had been recovered and we were none the wiser about the identity of the kidnappers, and by which time Mrs Oakley had begun her periodic bouts of hospitalization. Mr Oakley had become a hollow man, the Oakley mansion was sliding into ruin and the garden overgrown. Desperately so.'

Donoghue asked: 'Where would you put that money? I mean, allowing for a loss of ten to twenty per cent on each laundering purchase, they'd still have to put upwards of eight hundred thousand pounds somewhere. Can't put that in your Post Office account, not without raising eyebrows, you can't.'

'Careful planning and middle age, Fabian.'

'What do you mean?'

'Well, the hallmark of the kidnap was planning and preparation, people like that wouldn't let themselves be in possession of two kitbags full of cash and say, "Right then, where do we put this lot?" My guess is that bank accounts would have been opened months beforehand, and building society accounts too. Or were already in existence. You see, as the years have gone on – I'm in my forties now . . .'

'So am I, Tom.'

'Perhaps it's the same for them, but I seem to have accumulated building society accounts over the years, there's been a few times when I've been in possession of a cheque on a Saturday morning, all banks shut, wanting to pay it in somewhere and so I walked into a building society, showed some ID and used the cheque to open an account. Just to put the money somewhere safe. Then once I bought a house and the money was advanced by a bank I didn't deal with, my solicitor made all the arrangements, and I remember it was explained to me that "we open an account and then close it again". I didn't fully understand it but I went along with it, as you do in these circumstances, and anyway, when all was done and dusted there was fifty pounds left in the account we'd opened to purchase the house and I was invited to come and collect it so the account could be closed. I asked if it was possible to leave it there and keep the account open. Delighted, they said. So over the years, I've accumulated two bank accounts, one deposit account and four building society accounts, and not much money in any of them, I might add. My wife's been much neater: one current account, one deposit account and one building society account. We have also opened building society accounts for both of our sons. The point I make is that as a family we have twelve separate bank or building society accounts amongst us. If we were the gang and had eight hundred thousand pounds of laundered money to salt away, we'd distribute it amongst these accounts, a little bit at a time over three years. We wouldn't draw suspicion on ourselves, just make the branch managers happy men or women.'

'I see your point. So, months prior to the abduction the gang of three, possibly four, opened as many bank or building society accounts as they could in their own names.'

'It's a way of doing it. So is putting it in a Swiss bank in a single obvious lump sum, but I don't think they did that. Apart from the week they clearly enjoyed on the South Coast, they seemed to be locally orientated.'

'And with no contact with the underworld, as you've pointed out. Yes, I can see that distributing what change they had out of the original million into various accounts would make sense.'

'We were talking about this at the time, and one of the team who has since retired – guy called Petty, Alisdair Petty, nice fella – he picked up the Yellow Pages for the Edinburgh area and he counted in excess of thirty separate financial institutions of the type that a member of the public can walk in off the street, more or less, and open an account. Building societies tend to be easier to open an account with than a bank, banks require written references, but that would not be a problem. If push had come to shove they could have written each other references, I dare say. But I remember we

took thirty as a round figure, and working on the assumption
of three gang members . . .'

'Ninety separate accounts.'

'Right. With, we assume, eight hundred thousand pounds
among them . . .'

Donoghue did some rapid mental arithmetic. 'That's about
twenty-five thousand plus in each account, probably a bit
more. Yes, a bit more, maybe nearer twenty-seven thousand.'

'A figure in that region, but also remember that those
accounts would have inflated by that amount over a period
of three years. It wouldn't really have been noticed as would
a single large deposit.'

'That's the way to do it, if you have to do it.'

'I confess, I have felt awkward about this case. It's the one
I want to crack. What do you think? I mean off the record.
Can I live in hope?'

'Tom . . .' Donoghue shook his head. 'Don't ask me that.
The last thing I want to do is build up your hopes. All I
can say, as I said, is that two days ago a burnt-out ned was
found with his brains blown out and the belongings in his
bedroom in his mother's flat included newspaper cuttings
about "Annie" Oakley's abduction and a map on which was
circled a building. It all may be connected. It all may not.'

'But you'll keep me informed?'

'Of course. Of course.'

Tom Stamp escorted Donoghue not just to the uniform bar
of Fettes Avenue Police Headquarters, but walked outside the
door with him. The two men stood side by side. Donoghue
took the gold hunter from his waistcoat pocket. 'Midday,'
he said.

'Yes. Still has a one p.m. feel to it, doesn't it? Confess it
takes my body a few days to adjust each time the clocks
change, no matter what direction.'

'Aye.' Donoghue repocketed his watch. 'It'll seem late for
the signal gun from the castle right enough. Confess I haven't
heard the one o'clock gun for weeks.'

'You in a hurry to dash back to Glasgow?' Tom Stamp
turned to Donoghue.

Donoghue paused. 'No . . . not especially.'

'I have lunch at midday. A pub ten minutes from here,

excellent menu, generous portions, reasonable prices, they've just started doing bar meals so they're loss-leading at the moment to drum up a regular clientele . . . if you'd care to join me?'

'Love to.'

Tom Stamp gave a single vigorous nod of his head. 'I'll nip back and get my jacket.'

Montgomerie woke at ten a.m. He enjoyed back shifts because of the late start to the day they allowed, without actually turning night into day as the run of night shifts always seemed to demand. The night shifts really were disorientating for Montgomerie, the difficulty of staying awake for that last hour from five to six a.m., difficult for all officers, was for him particularly difficult, when it was compounded by the inevitable experience of going to bed and waking up again in the same day. There was always something he found particularly unnatural about that experience, and something deeply and fundamentally right and proper about waking up, refreshed, with each new day. But the back shifts, 14.00 hours to 22.00 hours, or when the job finished, were tolerable, and later the slumbering in a half sleep, listening to the rush hour thunder down Highburgh Road and knowing that he needn't be part of it, was, he thought, passing acceptable. But going to his bed and then leaving it again on the same day never ceased to feel strange to him.

He rolled from under the duvet and showered as cold as he could thole it and then allowed himself a blast of warm water before stepping out and towelling off. He wrapped himself in his blue dressing gown and walked into his kitchen and sat on a pine bench at the pine table, looking out on to the swing park as he savoured his first coffee of the morning. First coffee, first nail in his smoking days, first drink of a session. Always the best. His attention was drawn to two boys in the swing park, clearly dogging school. They sat on the swings, side by side, smoking cigarettes with manly and accustomed mannerisms. Then one took a packet of crisps and opened them and tipped the contents on the floor. Then he took a tube from his pocket and squirted a substance into the packet. He then put the packet to his face so that it covered his mouth and nose and began to inhale and exhale causing the bag to inflate and deflate, inflate and deflate. Then the boy handed the bag to his mate as he stood up and staggered around the swing park, laughing, swaying, flailing his arms. The second boy also began to inhale the fumes in the bag and he too soon joined his friend, laughing, turning in circles, staggering in the swing park, Highburgh Road on one side, four-storey tenements on the other three sides, at ten a.m. Montgomerie thought them both to be about twelve years of age. But that's the way the city's going, he felt. Once you never saw glue-sniffers, just came across their detritus, rock-hard, screwed-up crisp packets on waste ground, now they do it after breakfast in swing parks. It's also become a rare sight to see smackheads shooting up on street corners: once you never saw it at all. He stood and reached for the telephone where it hung on the wall and reported the incident in the swing park to Partick Marine. It's in their patch, they can send the cops. It then occurred to him that in the 1930s in this city, children and adults alike were escaping by passing coal gas through milk, then drinking the milk, so perhaps nothing is changing after all. Glasgow, like every major city, has its underbelly, always had, always will have. Magnificent place though it be. Live street theatre was Montgomerie's job. He cared not to see it from his window over his breakfast and so he carried the mug of coffee to his living room, padding across the polished, varnished floorboards, on which lay a dead sheep for a rug, and sank into the futon.

His doorbell rang.

He left the living room and walked down his hall to the heavy wooden door, turned the key in the mortise and casually opened the door. Wide.

Their eyes met instantly. She wore the brown-and-yellow-striped rugby shirt. He had once told her that young women in rugby shirts did something for him, speaking as they did of athleticism and health and energy and all things physical. Faded jeans and trainers completed the picture. A dark-blue fleece jacket lay atop a holdall at her side on the concrete landing. In her left hand she held a bottle of white wine. She held up the bottle. 'I know it's a bit early for this, but it needs chilling.' Montgomerie remained silent.

'I've come back.'

'So I see.'

'Well, are you going to invite me in? Or have I been replaced? I mean, ten days is more than ample time for you to find a replacement, big Mal, superstud.'

Montgomerie smiled. 'No,' he said. 'No, you haven't been replaced.' He stood to one side. She, blonde and blue-eyed, picked up her bag and walked across his threshold.

Richard King awoke refreshed at 9.00 a.m. He lay in bed in this house in Bishopbriggs. He had lain awake enjoying the leisurely start to his day which he, like Montgomerie and other officers, had found to be one of the compensations of shift work. He had been awake for ten minutes when Rosemary glided into the room – shoulder-length hair, a long skirt in pastel shades – and placed a steaming mug of tea on the bedside cabinet. They smiled at each other and she left the room, hardly making a sound. King propped himself up in bed and sipped the tea. He remained in bed until he had drained the mug and then rolled out from under the duvet and climbed into his dressing gown. He walked to the bay window of the bedroom and pondered Bishopbriggs on an October morning. Neat semi-detached houses, each with a front garden and a back garden and a drive alongside the house leading to a garage, a small pocket of English-style suburbia in a city of tenements and closes, and gushets and middens. He turned from the window and went into the bathroom and drew a long bath, enjoying the steam as much as the water.

Later, downstairs in the kitchen, he saw Rosemary glancing at the lengths of wood in that quiet Quaker way of hers. The wood stood against the wall where he had placed them upon his return from the DIY store as he murmured something about putting up the shelves 'later'. That had been during the previous November. He padded past her and picked up a length of wood and ran his eye along it, held it up at various heights on the wall where Rosemary had requested her shelves and then, unable to resist the gargling, gurgling squeal being made by Iain, put the length of wood back against the wall and rolled around the floor making eye contact and enjoying quality time with his son.

The message was in Donoghue's pigeonhole when he returned

to P Division Police Station after a relaxed lunch with Tom Stamp in Edinburgh. (Having phoned their respective wives, they had arranged that on the Sunday after next, Mr and Mrs Donoghue and their children would be at home for lunch to Mr and Mrs Stamp and their children; twelve-thirty for one.) Dr Jean Kay from the Forensic Science Laboratory in Pitt Street phoned at 11.00 a.m. Could he phone her back? Once in his office, pipe glowing and smouldering, he did so.

'We were lucky with the carpet, Inspector.' Jean Kay spoke with a certain precision of the type Donoghue often associated with schoolteachers. 'The diameter is unusual, slightly thinner than that adopted by major manufacturers of carpet fibres. We took a single fibre, as agreed, and melted it by placing it on a hot surface . . .'

'Yes?'

'It melted at two hundred and twenty-five degrees centigrade. That means it's a specific type of nylon known as "sixty-six".'

A pause.

'And that's it?' Donoghue couldn't help a note of surprise, if not indignation, creep into his voice.

'That's quite a lot, Inspector,' Jean Kay replied huffily. 'If you did but know how rare "sixty-six" is as a nylon, how rarely it is used in the manufacture of carpets, and how possibly rarer is the sort of blood-red dye clearly used in this case, especially as the strands have a subordinate colour, another lighter shade of red. You need to trace the manufacturer. I'll fax my report as soon as it is typed up.' Then she hung up and Donoghue was left with a phone against his ear which made an angry purring sound.

Israel Fancy was a slender man in King's eyes, sober suit in brown, and ill-matching black tie on a white shirt, as if anticipating attending a funeral later in the day. He was also sombre in a skullcap: black with an embroidered border of silver. He said, 'Westmorland dowry chest?'

'A Westmorland dowry chest,' repeated King. 'It was recently purchased by Dickson's of Sauchiehall Street. They still have it in their shop.'

Fancy leaned forward and pressed a button on an intercom on his desk. 'Judith, can you bring me the manifest of the last auction, please.' He released the button. 'We have auctions of antique furniture once a month, the last one was three weeks ago.' He spoke with Received Pronunciation, like a BBC newscaster; while probably proud to be a Scots Jew, he could easily be taken for an Englishman by his speaking voice. Doubtless, thought King, he was the product of a very expensive education. The two men waited in silence, though the hum of traffic on Great Western Road was distinct and discernible. Judith knocked and entered the room. She proved to be smartly dressed, bespectacled, proudly so, wearing large-lensed metal-framed spectacles. King thought her to be in her early twenties. Fancy, he thought to be about sixty. Judith handed Fancy a thick folder of white paper and then withdrew quietly, efficiently. Fancy began to leaf through the file, slowly, methodically, as if, King felt, unable to scan a page. He settled down for a long wait.

'Westmorland dowry chest,' Fancy said eventually, with no trace of emotion, and King felt the man capable of panning for gold and saying, 'Nugget, as big as a birds egg,' with the same matter-of-factness. 'Yes, sold to Dickson's indeed.'

'From whom did you buy it?'

'A lady called Margaret Mooney. I can tell you that without looking up another file. The auction business is a haven for crooks, Mr King. There are auctioneers and there are auctioneers. Some do not ask too many questions about the origin of the items they place under their hammer. As doubtless you are aware. We, on the other hand, jealously protect our good name. We want to know from whom we buy and to whom we sell. And we keep our records. Our earliest files go back two hundred years.'

King inclined his head. 'I'm impressed.'

'And so you should be. I also want to emphasize that we would not normally give this information out. But you did say it was a murder enquiry.'

'As indeed it is.'

'I really can't imagine Mrs Mooney being involved in anything like that. I've got to know her quite well. We've sold a lot of furniture for her in the last few years.'

'Oh really?'

'Yes . . . every few months, in fact. Some very fine items too, I'll have you know.'

'Really?'

'Yes, really. A pleasant lady. Well kept for her age . . . benefits of an easy life, I assume. She lives in Busby, asks me or one of my valuers to visit her in her home. She's clearing a relative's house, so she told me. Has the item of furniture brought to her home, we value it there and if she asks us to do so, we take it into our storeroom until the next auction.'

'Once every few months?'

'Yes. Nice stuff. Always very good stuff.'

'Nothing that you might have seen before?'

'Probably, but I've been an auctioneer in this city for over forty years, it does happen that items tend to be placed back on the market from time to time.'

'So you wouldn't think it unusual to again sell something that you know that you sold a few years earlier?'

'Not at all.'

'Would you have a note of Mrs Mooney's address?'

'I can tell you, I've been there often enough. It's twenty-three, Muckhart Avenue, Busby.'

King said, 'Thank you.'

On his return to P Division, King phoned the major auctioneers in the west of Scotland. There were just six, including Fancy's. The other five too, he found, knew Mrs Mooney of Busby very well, for had they not been auctioning furniture for her for the last few years, one item every few months? High-quality items too. Again, after each conversation King said, 'Thank you.' He said, 'Thank you, thank you very much indeed.'

Montgomerie too received much useful information by phone. He leaned back in his chair, holding the phone against his left ear with his right hand, his right arm being curled around the back of his head. He held a mug of coffee in his left hand. He spoke to Hamish Dell, solicitor, and notary public of Kilsyth.

'Oak Cottage again?' Dell's voice sounded tetchy to Montgomerie.

'If you don't mind. Sorry to put you to so much trouble, Mr Dell.'

'No trouble. How can I help?'

'Really just to clarify a point. You say the property was

empty and on the market for a period of time some years ago?'

'Yes. How long ago precisely I can't say off hand, but it must be eight or so years. It was summer time, I remember that. As I believe I have already informed you, the situation was that the householder was then elderly and had decided to seek what I believe is to be termed frail ambulant accommodation, and in order to pay for same, she agreed to sell her house. Like many elderly people she was cash-poor, property-wealthy. She did in fact enter a nursing home, with no intention of returning to Oak Cottage. Her house was cleared and her possessions placed in storage. Just one week after she entered the nursing home she was admitted to hospital and became a long-stay patient and her place in the nursing home was given to another elderly person.'

'I see.'

'It was while our client was in hospital that the property was placed on the market, according to her instructions. Her body was failing but her mind was as sharp as a tack.'

'I see.'

'So we followed our instructions. Not many folk were interested in the property, one or two asked for the keys. One guy in particular came back twice.'

'You didn't show people around?'

'No . . . no need, there was nothing in the house. It had been stripped to its floorboards and the fuel supply turned off. We just took proof of identity and handed over the keys. It's the normal practice.'

'I see.'

'In the event, the owner died in hospital before the property was sold. At which point it was taken off the market until her son could be traced. It's remained empty and growing more and more derelict as the years go on.'

'The man who came back to view the property on more than one occasion. That would be Gary Westwater, right?'

'Yes, as I said before: tall guy, middle aged, a bit full of himself as I recall, remember him because of his car, lovely Mark II Jaguar. The colour, yellow, was a bit loud for me. Lovely car though. I see it from time to time around the region.'

Montgomerie sipped the coffee. 'Well, thank you once again for your help, Mr Dell.'

King listening from his desk said: 'Anything new?'

Montgomerie shook his head. 'Not really, but it's all beginning to come together.'

'I think we should go and see Fabian.'

'No.' Montgomerie shook his head. 'I want to check something. I'm going to drive out to Oak Cottage. Coming?'

King stood and reached for his coat.

'There's not a trace.'

'You'd better be right.'

'All the carpets up and away like you said.'

'So I see.'

'Burned like you said. We took it down the East End, some waste ground. Three separate sites. Furniture was given to the charity shops.'

'You've ordered new stuff?'

'Aye.'

'Not the same shops though?'

'No . . . different shop. They're coming tomorrow to measure it up.'

'The gun?'

'It's away, Gary. I told you.'

'Aye . . . did anybody ever tell you that you're one greedy female? You've got pound-note signs for eyeballs, so you have.'

A pause. He glared at her. She blinked timidly at him. Their voices echoed in the room, stripped down to bare plaster and floorboards.

'The police,' he said slowly, 'the police have been asking my half-brother questions.'

'About Ronnie?'

'About Cernach Antiques. Remember them?'

'Oh God.' She gasped the words. 'Already?'

'Aye, that too. See, that's what I came to tell you, Carberrie. That's what's at stake now. They're on to you, on to me, on to all of us. Get this bleached. Get this room bleached down to nothing. Now.'

It rained during Montgomerie and King's outward journey to Oak Cottage, Kilsyth, and it rained during their return journey to Glasgow. But the rain had eased off when they

176

stood speaking to Mrs Test, with grey skirt and black shawl and silver hair and booming voice, and whose cottage was the next cottage along from Oak Cottage, separated by a field in which were horses.

'Didn't care for him. Didn't take to him at all,' she boomed, as if calling children in from across the field rather than speaking to King and Montgomerie who stood at her doorstep, inches from her. '"Laughing Boy", I called him. With his ha ... ha ... ha ... just came to tell you ha ... ha ... ha ... Mind you, he could've left me in the dark, I mind that he could have done that.'

'What did he say to you, Mrs Test?'

'Och ... he was saying he was moving into Oak Cottage and he had a man doing measurements and a bit of work so I wasn't to worry if I saw folk hanging about the place or lights burning at night.'

'And did you?'

'Och aye ... there was a wee guy about the place for a week, driving off in his van.'

'Van?'

'Aye. Ex-Post Office van. My man was a postman, God rest him. It was the sort of van he drove before he died, God rest him. Never lived to get his pension, the poor soul. But I ken the type and the colour, the wee wire-mesh grill behind the driver's seat – ex-Post Office. They sell them off at motor auctions, ye ken. It was one of those.'

'Did you see anybody else?'

'Laughing Boy in his flash yellow motor once or twice, two women, one red-haired and the other dark-haired, and the wee guy supposed to be doing some work on the house. Work? I see him ... I'm an old woman and I do more work in my bed than he ever did. Sunning himself by the side of the house, giving his scrawny wee body a tan. Mind you, he'd nothing else going for him, nothing for it but to tan himself. Oh, but see my Jack, see him, now there *was* a man. Army, that's where we met ... then the Post Office. All his days he worked. Aye ... I've not much in my wee home but I've fine, proud memories.'

Montgomerie smiled. So did King, who then asked, 'And all this was some time ago?'

'Eight years, or thereabouts. See my man Jack, he was still

warm in the clay . . . that's how I noticed the Post Office van because just a week or so earlier my man Jack was driving one. Then he was in the clay and then the same sort of van was at the door of Oak Cottage, so yes, eight years ago this year. Be nine years next summer.'

'They only stayed a week?'

'Or so. Then they just left. Thanks be . . . I mean, who'd want them as neighbours?'

'And the wee guy? He did no work?'

'Not that I saw. Except when he first arrived. He dug up the back garden.'

'Dug it up?'

'Dug a hole, I mean. Right at the bottom of the garden. I was a wee bit curious. Dare say I did a wee nosy out my back window, but then a couple of times I saw him he was after carrying rubbish out and putting it in the hole and burning it. So then it made sense. I thought, well, at least they're keeping their pitch clean. Took no notice after that, except in passing, y'ken.'

Having thanked Mrs Test, King and Montgomerie returned to the road and their car. Neither man could help his gaze being drawn to Oak Cottage, its garden, and especially the bottom of its garden.

'Now,' said Montgomerie, fishing in his ski-jacket pocket for his car keys, 'now we speak to Fabian.'

It was then that the rain came on again.

Upon their return to P Division Police Station, King found a note waiting for him in his pigeonhole. It was from the collator. One Carberrie, Mary, forty-seven years of age, had a conviction for theft ten years earlier and which is now spent.

Fabian Donoghue finished his pipe, placed it in his ashtray and picked up the file and walked to Findlater's office. He tapped on the door of Findlater's office and walked in as custom and practice and personal working relationship allowed. He found Chief Superintendent Findlater standing staring at a huge rubber plant that dominated his office; having been bought as a young plant and repotted twice, now it grew out of a pot the size of a dustbin and spread its tentacles up the walls and along the ceiling. The plant, it seemed, was all and everything to Findlater, and many a CID officer had stepped silently into Findlater's office believing the office to be vacant in order to leave a file on his desk or to perform some other task, only to find Findlater standing stroking the plant and murmuring sweet nothings to the nearest fleshy leaf.

'I've got a problem, Fabian.' Findlater turned as Donoghue entered his office.

'Oh?'

'It's Heathcliff.'

'Heathcliff?'

'My rubber plant.'

'I see.'

'What to do with him when I go.'

'Go, sir?'

'Retire, Fabian. I'm coming up to my retirement in a few months. Thirty years' service. Police Cadet Findlater in Elgin is now CS Findlater in Glasgow. Tell you, I remember the early days better than I do yesterday. Myself and Mrs Findlater are going on preparation for retirement courses. It's apparently a major upheaval in a marriage, especially if the husband is the only breadwinner. The wife is used to having her man out of the house for eight, ten hours at a time, then all of a sudden he's there all the time, in the way, under her feet, she has to start sharing her personal space. Marriages have foundered on retirement. So we are told.'

Donoghue caught his breath.

'Say something to reach you, Fabian?'

'Frankly you did, sir. I think you explained something.'

'Well, that's all to the good, eh?'

'I think it is, I really think it is.'

Findlater nodded and smiled at Donoghue, always dressed in a sombre pinstripe suit with a gold hunter's chain looped across his waistcoat. 'But what do I do about Heathcliff?'

'Prune it, sir.'

'Him. Prune him.'

'Yes, sir.' Donoghue shifted his weight from one leg to the other. 'Prune him.'

'Want to avoid doing that, Fabian.' Findlater turned and considered the plant. 'It can be taken out in a one-er. I know it can. We have a team of willing volunteers, we can get him

179

into the car park. I can hire a lorry . . . a five-tonner. I can get it into my house. It can be done. No, the real problem is with Mrs Findlater. You see, she has brought this up in our pre-retirement discussion groups. It is not that she objects to having to share our home with me on a full-time basis, but she objects to having to share it with Heathcliff as well. Especially since I'm going to put him next to the television. The problem really is how do I stop her poisoning him while I'm at the golf club? A good dose of saline solution and my lovely wee boy's a goner. I can't see the committee allowing him to take up residence in the clubhouse. It's a worry. I fret about it. But you didn't come here to speak to me of plants and things?'

'No, sir.' Donoghue patted the file. 'I'd like to put you in the picture about the murder . . .'

'Fella with no brains that greeted us on the day the clocks went back? Two days ago?'

'That's the one, sir. We've made headway and its shaped up to be more than a petty ned getting filled in by like felons.'

'Really?' Findlater indicated the chair in front of his desk. 'Take a pew and tell me about it.'

Findlater listened intently and without interruption until Donoghue said '. . . and that's about it, sir.'

'Let me see if I've got this right, Fabian.' Findlater leaned back in his chair. Behind him on the wall hung a photograph of the man fly fishing. 'Ronnie Grenn, the deceased, served time for a jewellery robbery and wilful fire-raising which nobody believed he was capable of committing, but he put his hand up for it and collected a lenient seven years. In the pokey he makes noises about having enough dosh waiting for him to come out to enable him to go straight like his mentor, Kit Saffa, who is as bent as a three-pound note, but that is by the by. The point is that Ronnie Grenn is coming out to a wedge so as to go straight. So he says. And in prison he is visited by a woman called Mary Carberrie who apparently reinforces that notion, and also allows him to think that he has got her waiting for him as well. And yet upon his release, he gets his brains blown out.'

'Yes, sir.'

'Investigations into the antecedents of the deceased indicate some possible connection with the abduction and presumed murder of the Edinburgh heiress, Ann "Annie" Oakley, by name. It then transpires that the ownership of Cernach Antiques is registered in the name of Carberrie, Mary. The insurance on Cernach Antiques was arranged with a certain Gary Westwater of the Glasgow and Trossachs Insurance Company. He insisted, during a boardroom battle of El Alamein proportions and intensity, that their insurance company meet the claim even to the point of fellow directors selling their personal belongings and raising second mortgages. As if he was determined that the insurance company should pay up, despite some misgivings about it being an insurance scam of epic dimensions. Anyway, they pay up, and the insurance company, more by accident than design, goes from strength to strength and said Gary Westwater sells his interest and goes into retirement in order to spend his time blasting Monarchs of the Glen to pieces with very powerful rifles. So we have a high-velocity link there, don't we? Gary Westwater's passion is for the type of weapon that extracted Ronnie Grenn's brains. So by this time, if you are right, abduction, murder, insurance scam, we are talking about money having been criminally obtained in the sum of . . . ?'

'Four million pounds minimum.'

'And the premise that the furniture which went up in the Cernach Antiques blaze was junk, hardwood junk, but junk nonetheless, is reinforced by the fact that the items of good furniture known to have been in Cernach's just before the blaze, seem to have trickled back on to the market, one item every few months, for the four something years since the blaze, all being sold on behalf of a woman called Margaret Mooney?'

'Again, sir, correct.'

'And it was the feeling of our colleagues in Edinburgh that the outfit who abducted "Annie" Oakley was a gang of three with a possible gofer?'

'Yes, sir.'

'Right, Fabian, within these four walls, just you, me and Heathcliff, nothing recorded on the file. Stick your neck out. What do you think has happened?'

'Well, I was impressed by Tom Stamp in Edinburgh. He seemed to me to be on the ball and he made a case for the felons being a gang of three plus at least one gofer. I believe the gang of three are Mary Carberrie, Margaret Mooney and Gary Westwater and their gofer was Ronald Grenn. I don't know what relationships exist between them or how they met, but I believe that that is the profile and the identities that we are looking for.'

'All right.' Findlater glanced at Heathcliffe and then back to Donoghue.

'I believe the insurance scam was planned years earlier. I believe Westwater planned to rob his own insurance company. And the method he chose was a fire job, and, being a senior director, he'd be in a position to force the honouring of the insurance policy. If he couldn't push it past the board, then he still had his assets, even if the company had to declare bankruptcy.'

'Nothing to lose.'

'Except the money he put into Cernach's. That in my view was raised by abducting "Annie" Oakley some years earlier.'

'Three or four years?'

'Long-term planning, sir. I believe it took them that long to launder the ransom money and to establish Cernach's as a stable company.'

'A little here, a little there. Yes, that can't be done in a weekend.'

'Then they put the money, drawn from many bank and building society accounts, in Cernach's. Bought the property, fitted it with very nice antiques, and oils and jewellery, but didn't appear to sell a great deal. After allowing it to appear as though it was thriving for a period of a few years, they then removed all the valuables and replaced it with junk, emptied the jewellery from the boxes and the trays. They then set four seats of fire, after first possibly setting fire to a warehouse south of the water to draw off all the fire brigade appliances. So the appliances that did attend the Cernach blaze had to come from outside the area, and by the time they arrived, there was nothing left to save. The building was a burned-out shell. We found jewellery containers in Bath Street with Cernach's name on them covered in Ronnie Grenn's prints. He's well known to us because of a series of petty offences and so we pull him. He doesn't cough to anything so he won't talk about anything. Like he's sticking to a script. He's found guilty of theft and wilful fire-raising and is sent down. And we close the case like we were expected to do.'

Findlater groaned. 'Who was the investigating officer, Fabian?'

'Ray Sussock, sir.' Donoghue paused. 'He's close on his own retirement. I don't think there's anything to be gained . . .'

'Yes . . . yes . . . yes . . .' Findlater rested his forehead in his palms. 'Go on, painful as this is. Go on.'

'Well, at the High Court in Glasgow some weeks later, the Lord whoever clearly believes that Ronnie Grenn is a willing patsy, handed to the police so as to buy off a more thorough investigation and thereby allowing the culprits to go free. And when press and other observers are expecting a sentence of life or detention at Her Majesty's pleasure, such being the gravity attached to wilful fire-raising, especially incidents resulting in huge loss, in the centre of the city, possibly wasting fire brigade time to a huge degree, and most important, alarming the lieges by endangering life and other property, said Lord brings forth gasps of astonishment by handing down a sentence of just seven years. Four years actual with remission. It was a slap on the wrist.'

'A slap on the wrist for Ronnie Grenn, which in fairness was probably no more than he deserved. He probably never set foot inside Cernach's. He would have been given the jewellery containers to handle a day or two before the blaze. But the sentence was a body blow to the police. As you say, the only interpretation there was that His Lordship was passing a comment about the police investigation. Fabian, I want the earth to swallow me up.'

'Yes. It feels like that for me.'

'When Ray Sussock pulled Ronnie Grenn he must have visited his home. Didn't he notice the newspaper cuttings about "Annie" Oakley's abduction?'

'You'll have to put that question to Ray, sir, but in fairness the last thing that would have caught his eye would have been newspaper cuttings.'

'Stop defending him, Fabian. I like to think they would have caught my eye, and I know they would have caught your eye. In a box, all about the same story and no other, a map with a building circled . . . you know, blunder just is not the word here.'

'No, sir.'

'But it would have been too late to help "Annie" Oakley and it looks as though we're closing in on the culprits now anyway. I don't know what to do about Ray Sussock . . . let me sleep on it. So then . . . ?'

'Well, Ronnie Grenn kept his part of the bargain. He served his time, he kept his mouth zipped. He went to collect. They refused to pay, he threatened to squeal, he got his brains blown out.'

'Greed, eh?'

'That's the word, sir.'

'If you're right, and if they had paid him what they agreed to pay him, he'd have gone home happy and spent the rest of his days digging his allotment, we'd have put him down as a burnt-out ned and left him alone, and none of this would have come out. So what's for action?'

'Well, sir, I think we find out if the Mary Carberrie that our collator has dug up for Richard King is the same Mary Carberrie that visited Ronnie Grenn in Traquair Brae, and if so, why did she? What is their relationship? I'll put Richard King on that, I think. I'd like to know more about Mr Westwater. I'd want to know why he pushed through what on the face of it looks like a ruinous decision to settle an insurance claim which clearly stank like two-day-old fish. I'd like to know who Margaret Mooney is, find out where she fits in this equation. That's something for Montgomerie and Abernethy. It's my guess that those three and Ronnie Grenn were the four people seen at Oak Cottage the week that "Annie" Oakley was abducted. And I'd like a look at Oak Cottage.'

'I'd be inclined to make that your priority task, Fabian. You know you're going to find "Annie" Oakley's body there, don't you? In a pit at the bottom of the garden which Ronnie Grenn dug like he was told to dig, and in which he burnt rubbish like he was told to burn rubbish so as to give the impression that the pit had no sinister purpose at all?'

'Yes, sir.' Donoghue stood. 'I know all that. I think you're right. I think Oak Cottage is priority one.'

It was Wednesday, 17.30 hrs.

THURSDAY

6

Montgomerie thought the word for what he was feeling
must be 'poignant'. Poignant, poignancy . . . whatever, here,
standing by this hole in the ground which had been exca-
vated, carefully so, by constables in white coveralls, on this
blustery day when the wind swept off the Campsies, causing
the blue-and-white police tape to flap angrily, causing the
collar of his jacket to tug and strike his cheekbone, causing
the oak in the garden to sway, on this blustery day when grey
clouds scudded southwards, threatening rain any minute, in
this silence borne out of reverence among the police officers
present, the only word was poignant. Or poignancy. For here
in a hole was a human skull, upturned, mockingly grinning.
It was the skull of the young woman whom Montgomerie
had last seen when he was an undergraduate in Edinburgh.
Then, in those heady summer days, the woman was often
to be seen driving her little white Japanese off-the-road,
soft top, up and down Princes Street. Hood down, lemon
hair flowing behind her, one hand on the wheel, the other
invariably holding a mobile phone to her ear. One side were
fine impressive buildings, the Waverley Hotel, Jenner's, on
the other the Scott Monument, Princes Street Gardens, the
Castle. And she, streaming between them, up one side of
Princes Street and down the other, turning at Haymarket
and repeating the journey, eighteen years old and life was
fine and fun and frolicsome.

Then she was murdered. For money.

Chopped in her prime.

Filled in while still on the threshold of life.

Filthy, filthy, filthy lucre.

That, thought Montgomerie was bad enough. Sufficient to

motivate him as a police officer, but it was worse, worse in a way, he felt, for in this hole, skeletal, curled up in a foetal position 'Annie' Oakley seemed to occupy a larger hole than the hole she had been allowed to occupy in life.

Another word was 'menacing'. He had from his vantage point by the hole in the ground that had been 'Annie' Oakley's resting place, been able to ponder the rear aspect of Oak Cottage. Its small windows, its dull grey pebble dash, the meanly narrow door from which many years earlier some panels appeared to have been kicked out to be replaced by a sheet of corrugated iron, now thin and rusty as if, thought Montgomerie, as a result of some incident of domestic violence which had occurred long, long before Ronnie Grenn and his captive took up their incumbency. And what of the previous occupants, the woman and her son, the latter of whom left not just the cottage at Kilsyth and Scotland, but left these shores completely and went as far as he could remove himself on this planet? And once there, had clearly done what he could to remain isolated and uncontactable, caring not for his mother in her decline, nor about any property that might be his to inherit. What had gone on under that roof in that squat little house of unimaginative design all those years ago to make a man do that? Oak Cottage, even from the outside, had a chill about it, it looked menacing, as if it had had a dreadful history. Behind Montgomerie, in the field, a chestnut mare whinnied and reared; the shrill sound pierced the stillness and solemnity of the group of officers in the garden at Oak Cottage.

'Montgomerie!'

'Sir?' Montgomerie turned to Donoghue, over whose shoulder in her cottage in the middle distance he could clearly see Mrs Test and another woman peering keenly at the spectacle he and his colleagues presented.

'I think you and I had better have a shufti inside the house.'

To Montgomerie's relief, they found little of evident relevancy inside Oak Cottage. Anything that 'Annie' Oakley's kidnappers might have left as trace evidence had clearly been smothered by years of occupancy of the building by down-and-outs, who left empty tins which had once contained the brass polish they had turned to when methylated

spirits began to be manufactured in such a way that it was
rendered undrinkable. It was smothered by solidified glue in
screwed-up crisp packets which lay strewn about the floor,
and by empty bottles of 20/20, newly introduced and popular
among the youth of the west of Scotland. The floor contained
a number of used condoms which, Donoghue pondered,
proves if nothing else that people are wrong about kids
today: they *do* listen. Clearly the youth hereabouts, thought
Donoghue, believe that the best way out of Kilsyth is to find
a partner and then claw your brains out with solvents and
very cheap, very fortified wine. The walls contained graffiti,
illustrating the sexual obsession of youth; oddly, observed
Donoghue, the sectarian hatred that motivated graffiti artists
in Glasgow housing schemes was absent in Kilsyth. But he
did learn for possible future reference that Hamill is devoid
of sanity, McCourt a police informer and evil Anne a sexual
walkover, should any lad of the town feel so inclined. That
aside, neither officer could find or was able to observe any
item which linked 'Annie' Oakley or Ronnie Grenn or Gary
Westwater, or Mary Carberrie or Margaret Mooney to Oak
Cottage. Even the charred remains in the fire grate didn't
contain anything more than two years old, going by sell-by
dates and dates of newsprint. In one of the two rooms at the
back of the house, on the far side of the house from Mrs Test's
cottage, Donoghue said, 'She was kept in here.'

Montgomerie glanced out of the window at the back
garden where a screen was being erected around the hole
that had been dug by two officers in white coveralls, and
dug ironically, or perhaps appropriately, Montgomerie had
reflected, as a grave is dug, keeping the sides perfectly vertical
and the floor perfectly level, all the time working down, more
of a layer-by-layer peeling than a dig, not at all like a navvy
might dig a hole. He turned and looked at Donoghue. 'In
here, sir?'

'It's where I would keep her. Back of the house, back
window looks on to the garden and the field and then the
woodland and the hills, the side window, open ground and
more woodland.'

'Couldn't argue with that, sir.'

'But I don't think that there's anything for us here. We're
too late, about eight years too late.' Donoghue turned and

walked towards the front door and the open air. It was then that Montgomerie felt palpable relief. Oak Cottage had an atmosphere that made his scalp crawl, and intuitively, he still felt that it was nothing to do with 'Annie' Oakley very likely having been murdered here, it was older than that somehow, more entrenched, more established.

In the garden, Donoghue turned to Montgomerie and said, 'I'd like you to get back to the city. King's out beavering, Abernethy will have returned and signed off the morning shift by now. We need somebody in the CID corridor.'

'Yes, sir.'

'I'll remain here.'

'Yes, sir.'

Montgomerie drove back to what he always felt to be the welcoming warmth of the city of Glasgow. He entered the city on Springburn Road, Sighthill Cemetery to his right, the old Cowlairs Railway Works buildings to his left, giving to the Galloway Street flats striding across the skyline. He turned on to the M8 and left at the Charing Cross exit. He glanced at his watch. The digital display told him it was 17.17, glowing clear and confident like a year in the history of Western Europe rather than the time of day. It wouldn't be a good time, but no time is a good time. It never is, not for what he had in mind, not for what he had to do. He turned right at the exit to Charing Cross, past the frontage of P Division Police Station, to St George's and turned left up Great Western Road, which drove confidently, strongly, straight as a die, lined with prestigious tenements, trendy shops, solemn churches, it was *the* road to the Western Isles and Montgomerie's most loved thoroughfare of his native city, and he had in the past walked its length from St George's Cross to the Anniesland lights. West of Anniesland lights the road held no fascination for him. But on this day, this windy Thursday afternoon of early gathering dark, of constant threat of rain, he was in no mood to appreciate the ambience of the road and its landmarks, like the second thinnest church steeple in Scotland. He crossed Kelvinbridge and turned right into Hamilton Park Avenue and considered himself lucky to find a parking space. He went to her front door and rang the bell, her bell, topmost bell of four owner-occupied conversions. She had the topmost flat, a kitchen, a bathroom, a bedroom, a living room with a balcony for summer days and a bottle of chilled Frascati, and twee occasional room. It was a starter flat, it changed hands every two or three years, its youthful owners selling up to move one more rung up the housing ladder. He rang the bell again. No response.

He turned from the imposing front door, went down the stone steps and walked to the corner of Great Western Road, turned left by the Homeless Persons' Hostel and walked into the Long Bar. The Long Bar was, as its name implied, a single gantry leading deep into the tenemental building at ninety degrees to the road. It had one entrance/exit at street level, and, at the rear, a fire exit as was dictated by regulations. Being the bohemian West End of Glasgow, the patrons comprised a social mix and it was Montgomerie's constant observation that patrons who were of the unemployed, if not unemployable, the frail of mental health, the drug-addicted, the petty criminal, would, as in all such bars of similar layout in the West End, sit near the door so that upon entering such bars one has often to walk past the hum of unwashed bodies. The patrons of middle-class tastes and conduct, professional people with career aspirations, choose seats deeper in the bar. She sat on a stool towards the end of the bar chatting to a girlfriend. She saw him approach and smiled. He remained stone-faced and her smile turned into a frown. Montgomerie asked if he could have a word outside. She turned to her friend and he heard her say, 'I know what this means.'

Outside on the pavement, in front of a small newsagent owned by an Asian family, he waited until an orange-coloured double-decker bus of the Strathclyde Passenger Transport Executive roared past, just catching the amber lights at the junction, and he said, 'Look, there isn't an easy way to say this, so I'll just say it.'

'It's over.' She held his stare. 'I'll say it for you.'

'Yes,' he nodded. 'Look, the situation is that you caught me on the rebound. The person I was rebounding from has, well, re-rebounded. We're an item again. We did it once, you and me, you didn't damage me, I didn't damage you, but that's it. As you say, it's over.'

She nodded. Black hair, brown eyes, blue jersey, denims. Five foot two. A neat young woman, he thought. 'OK. Thanks for being honest. It's not the end, it's a new beginning. For both of us.'

'That's the right attitude.'

She turned and went back into the Long Bar. He thought that if she was concealing any emotion she was doing it very well. Very well indeed.

At 14.00 Richard King signed in for the back shift. It was to prove to be a very busy shift. Very busy indeed.

He went first to the public library at the Cadder. It was a small branch library, a squat building in a low-rise scheme. People come in to read the newspapers, sit in the warmth with a magazine, escaping the damp at home. Few borrowed books.

'We're not a very busy library, as you can see, Mr King.' The librarian was a small woman, warm, confident, she seemed to enjoy her job. She was a Mrs Smithkey by her name badge. 'Most of our patrons like to come in for a wee warm and a look at the paper. You know, Scotland has a very literate public, that's due to the thorough grounding in numeracy and literacy that Scottish primary education gives to children, but we don't seem to lend many books. But that's all right, a place to come for a wee warm, to read a newspaper, to read the notice board. A library is more than just a place to come and borrow books, so we are still providing a service. But that's not why you're here?'

'No.' King smiled. 'Does the name Carberrie mean anything to you? Mary Carberrie?'

The woman scowled and sighed and said, 'That woman . . .'

'I understand that she was sacked for theft?'

'Yes, some years ago now. We keep a small cache of petty cash, library fines, fees for ordering books, change for the photocopier. Not much, because this isn't a busy library, but it was money nonetheless. Our books just didn't add up, it was obvious someone had their finger in the till so we kept watch and saw her do it. She was so used to doing it by then that she did it without thinking. Our branch manager reported her to the police. She got a wee fine in the Sheriff Court but she was out of a job, pension shot, the lot.'

'I see.' King waited until an elderly man who had shuffled up and laid a three-day-old copy of the *Glasgow Herald* on the counter had once again shuffled out of earshot. 'You see, it may well be that this is not the same Mary Carberrie that we are now interested in, but she's the right age. Some years ago, after she was sacked following the theft that you mention, she visited someone in prison, she was seen to be with a mane of red hair—'

'Greying at the ends,' Mrs Smithkey interrupted, 'wears clothing a size too small because she won't accept how she's ballooned.'

'That wasn't mentioned.' King paused. 'I don't wish to be unkind, but people have mentioned her teeth . . .'

'Oh . . . I think you've got the right woman. I well recall her teeth, black and camel-like. It was remarked behind her back how she would spend money on clothing and other fashion accessories and not have her teeth seen to.'

'She doesn't sound like any librarian I ever met.'

'She wasn't. She was temperamentally unsuited to public service. That's being kind. In fact, it's hard to see what Mary was, or still is, suited to. But whatever she did when she left here, she did well. I saw her a year or two ago driving a flash motor in the town with a personalized numberplate ME 2, as I recall, and I thought, "Well, that's you, Mary."'

King smiled. 'It's the same woman. I wonder, could we go somewhere a little more private? I'd like you to tell me about her. I can tell you that we want to talk to her in connection with one, perhaps two, very serious crimes. But we want to get the measure of the woman before we invite her for a chat about things.'

'Certainly.' Mrs Smithkey turned and addressed a slender young man of hippy appearance. Very non-Cadder. 'Julian, I'll be with this officer in my office if you need me.'

Julian said, 'Fine.' King got the sense that the working relationship between Mrs Smithkey and Julian was strained.

Mrs Smithkey left the 'Returns' desk and led King to a cramped office. Once they were both seated, she said, 'What can I tell you?'

'Well' – King raised his free hand palm upwards – 'whatever . . .'

'I was asking myself, Mr King.'

King opened his notepad, chastened.

'An empty woman,' Mrs Smithkey said after a pause. 'Just

empty, nothing there, really . . . we all knew when she was in the building, forced, deliberately loud laughter . . .'

'In a library?'

'Libraries when open to the public are solemn places, but for a few minutes before the doors open each morning, and for a half-hour period at the end of the opening hours, when only the staff are in the building, they can be a bit noisy, not deliberately so, but there is a sense of reaction to a restriction being lifted at the end of the day especially, staff calling to each other across the length and breadth of the floor area, that sort of thing.'

'I see.'

'It was the beginning and the end of the working day, when she could make a noise, that we all knew Mary Carberrie was in the building, but yet there was no sense of loss when she left the building. We have staff who are quiet, never talk more loudly than they have to, and then only if they have to. Quiet, efficient, modest, yet when they leave the building at the end of a shift – libraries stay open for twelve hours a day, we have a shift system, morning and back, and a day shift for Saturdays.'

'As we do, well, nearly the same . . .'

'You see, when those members of staff are on duty, they make little fuss, but by their efficiency and by their strength of personality, they leave a sense of a gap behind them when they go off duty. They have a "presence". Mary Carberrie let everybody know she was in the building by one means or another, yet when she signed off to go home she didn't leave the sense of a gap, or a sense of loss behind her. She had no presence. She was like a fly buzzing about, you were always thankful when it found the open window.'

Again Mrs Smithkey fell silent as if recalling incidents, as if sorting out memories. 'You see,' she said at length, 'Mary Carberrie wanted, probably still wants, only three things in life: she wanted power, popularity and money, and I have to say it rankles with me that she achieved all three.'

'She doesn't sound like the sort of person who'd enjoy popularity or power.'

'She didn't, yet in another sense she did.'

'I don't follow?'

'What I mean is that she achieved power within the staff

194

group by enlisting herself as a lieutenant to the woman who worked here at the time and who held herself to be the top cat in the alley. If Mary had opposed this woman she would have been left in little pieces and she knew that so she offered herself as a subordinate ally. It really was quite pathetic. The powerful woman, who wasn't really powerful at all, was disciplined by the library service for her attitude to customers; immediately that happened Mary Carberrie brought disciplinary action on herself. In her case it was for poor timekeeping, but by doing so she reinforced her lieutenantship to the first woman.'

'So they could be two bad girls together?'

'Exactly. Talk about juvenile behaviour. The other thing that Mary Carberrie did to enjoy power was to throw her weight about with the younger secretarial staff. I even heard her threatening to kick one secretary.'

'Heavens.'

'That's Mary Carberrie. But she would never oppose anybody who was strong enough to stand up to her. So each working day she had a sense of power. And she was popular because she believed she was popular, just as some people believe the earth to be flat. Her self-assessment was way off . . . totally the opposite of what people felt about her, but did that matter? If she had an unshakeable faith of religious intensity in her own popularity, did it matter that she was in fact universally detested? I would say no. I would say that it didn't matter to her, so she was powerful, and she was popular.'

'The money?'

'I would say that money, acquisition of same was, probably still is, her third motivation in life. I have this image of Mary Carberrie as a wee girl, standing in her bedroom having wrecked all her toys, yelling, "I want to be popular, and I want to be powerful and I want a lot of money and I'm going to scream and scream and scream until I get all three."'

'Funny you should say that.'

'Oh, does the serious crime or two that you mentioned have money as its motivation?'

'Yes, in a word. But beyond that I can't tell you anything.'

'Well, that's Mary, any extra shift going and she wanted

it, not out of dedication to the library service but because of the extra money, and any branch that phoned round for staff because they were short-handed, Mary would want to go because she got a mileage allowance for the car journey between the two workstations. You have seen American cartoons on television where characters sometimes develop US dollar signs for eyes?'

'Yes.'

'That was Mary, except of course she had pound-note signs for eyes. I felt her greed would be her downfall one day. But anyway, she's got the money she wanted, because that flash motor I saw her in, the one with the fancy registration, she didn't get that out of any lucky bag. So she got her power, she got her popularity and she got her money. You see, we've been teaching our children all wrong. If you scream and shout long enough you *can* get what you want.'

King chuckled. He enjoyed Mrs Smithkey's incisiveness. 'What do you know of her home circumstances?'

'Lived alone, I think.'

'Never married?'

Mrs Smithkey raised an eyebrow as if to say, 'Who in their right mind . . . ?' but she said, 'No, I don't think so.'

'The last address we have for her is Partick – Lawrence Street, Partick.'

'That would be the address we would have. You, the police, know her because she stole from the library, at which point she was dismissed. I can't help you with her present address, and, incidentally, all this is off the record. Dare say I feel eager to help because my son has just joined the police.'

'Excellent.'

'Yes, we're very proud. He's with the Met. He wanted to live in London for a year or two. He intends to return to Scotland if he can get a transfer to the Strathclyde Police, once he's ready to settle down and get his feet on the housing ladder.'

'We'll be pleased to have him, I'm sure. But back to the matter in hand. What did Mary Carberrie do in her spare time?'

'She had what in my opinion was a very unhealthy interest in guns. She would defend it by talking about the "sport" of shooting, the precision involved, the patience, the hand-eye coordination, the breathing techniques that need to be mastered. But at the end of the day a gun, especially a handgun, is a tool designed for taking human life and nothing else, and while there may very well be a place for guns in the modern police and obviously in the military, I have to say that we're missing something if we identify them as having sporting potential. That's just my view, you understand. I mean, would we have live hand-grenade throwing as an Olympic Games event? I think not. Then why allow handguns to be used for sport? I'm sorry, but I have a bit of a high horse on this matter, and if I'm honest it's another reason why I found Mary Carberrie a difficult person to like. Her and her gun club. She belonged to one in Ayrshire.'

'That's interesting. Tell me, does the name Westwater mean anything to you?'

'It doesn't.'

'How about Mooney?'

'Again, no. I'm sorry. She didn't mention either of those names to me.'

Ray Sussock steeled himself. He sat in his car and pondered Rutherglen at dusk. No stars yet in the sky, probably too much cloud cover tonight anyway, he thought. All houses burned lights, and the soft yellow streetlamps had been switched on, yet it was still light enough to see a man walking a black dog. He turned his attention to the bungalow, once a proud, well-appointed edifice set in neat gardens, now a building of peeling paint, of loose roof tiles, of overgrown shrubbery and rampant weeds which attracted discarded fish-supper wrapping paper, cigarette packets, empty cans, as overgrown, ill-tended areas of vegetation will. And there they were: him and her. Pulling back the curtain, leaning forward side by side, smiling, grinning as if they felt that they couldn't be seen, as if light travels in one direction only. What was it, he tried to recall it, the term for a jointly shared insanity, folie à deux? Something like that.

He turned away from the bungalow and looked ahead and watched the man and the black dog until they turned a corner and were lost from sight. He was saddened that he'd been seen because his hesitation would be seen as weakness, but he needed this space, he needed to work out the scene in his head.

Eventually he got out of the car and walked up the driveway of the bungalow, feeling his trouser legs being tugged by the brambles. He went to the side door of the bungalow and banged on it three times with the palm of his hand. It was opened, but only after a pointedly long time. Samuel stood there, slicked-back hair, gold earring, smooth hairless hands courtesy of his mother's hair-removing lotion, his black jersey pushed into the waist of his black trousers, his feet wrapped in lightweight black trainers.

'Hello, Daddy.' Samuel smiled, then turned and called out, 'Mummy, Daddy's come to visit us.'

Sussock stormed up the steps and pushed past his son who made a pretence of falling against the refrigerator saying, 'Ooh, Daddy, you hurt me.'

Sussock paced down the narrow corridor as his wife screeched from deep in the front room, 'Get him out, Sammy, get him out. He should be catching robbers, he was never any good to us, was he; was he?'

'No, Mummy.' Samuel sniggered as he lay on the kitchen floor. Sussock wrenched open the door of the boxroom at the bottom of the corridor and began to rummage in cardboard boxes, picking up woollen winter wear, socks, vests, a pullover, and putting them into a plastic bin liner he had brought with him. He walked back down the corridor. His wife yelled, 'Has he gone yet, Samuel?' And Samuel, still prostrate on the yellow lino on the kitchen floor said, 'No, Mummy,' upon which Sussock's wife began to scream. Sussock left the house, left the sniggering and the wailing behind him. The thin October air hurt his lungs and he knew again that winter would be soon in arriving. He drove back to Langside. To Elka Willems's flat, a room and kitchen, warm, loving, just sufficient space for her, and, occasionally, him. It was quite different from the room and kitchen in which he had grown up in the Gorbals of old, of global infamy, the sharing the bed with parents and siblings, the screams in the night, the blood on the common stair the following morning; black, congealing. He pressed the bell, she opened it and smiled warmly, stepping aside as he crossed the threshold. The smell of cooking assailed his nostrils. 'What's that?'

'Spag bol.' She hipped the door shut. 'Bad trip, Old Sussock?' She walked behind him into the kitchen and stirred the spaghetti.

'No worse than usual.' He dropped the bin liner containing his clothing on to the floor and sank into a chair by the table. 'The shrew was there, where else would she be? Sammy . . . oh my . . . did I do *that* to him?'

She lay a mug of tea on the table in front of him. 'I don't think you've got anything to blame yourself for, Ray.'

'It's my investment as well, all my money's in that building and she's letting it go. If it gets any worse we won't be able to give it away once we get the divorce . . .'

'You'll get enough, enough for a two room and kitchen in the South Side, that's what you want, isn't it? Something to see you out, something with a good roof and no subsidence, and far enough away from the Cart so you don't get flooded. Meanwhile you've got a bedsit, and my bed from time to time, so long as you don't move in.'

He reached for her hand. 'Elka . . .'

She pulled her hand away. 'No . . . Ray, don't ask, you know what the answer is. I said "no" and I mean "no". I'm thirty-three years younger than you, and anyway, I don't want to get married, not yet . . .' She kissed his head. 'Look, it's sweet of you, it's a great compliment, but we are leaving things just as they are. And that is it. If you ask again, if you persist, I'll end it, OK?'

Sussock ran his fingers through his hair. 'OK, OK . . . I won't mention it again.'

'Oh, I think you will, Old Sussock.' She squeezed his hand. 'But the answer will remain the same. Are you hungry?'

'Ravenous.'

Montgomerie returned to P Division Police Station. Peeling off his ski jacket as he entered the DCs' room he was not a little surprised to see Abernethy at his desk. 'Still here?' He slung his jacket on to Richard King's desk and strode with long, effortless strides across the room to the table on which stood the mugs, the kettle, the instant coffee underneath a blue-and-white Police Mutual calendar.

'I had a long day at the coast.' Abernethy leaned back in

his chair and let his ballpoint fall on the pad. 'I'm not long back, to tell you the truth.'

'The coast? Coffee?'

'No . . . no, thanks, I'm full of the stuff. Grangemouth, to be exact.'

Montgomerie smiled – chemical works on the windswept Forth estuary was not the image that would come to the mind of most folk when the word coast was mentioned. He enjoyed Abernethy's dry sense of humour.

'Profitable trip?' Montgomerie tipped coffee grounds into a mug.

'Oh, I think so. I think so. Got an address.'

'Useful.'

'Yes, the factory turned out to have produced the carpet fibre, a small batch in flame red, and had made a few hundred square feet of carpet in eye-hurting, brilliant red. They'd sold it to an outlet in Glasgow.'

'Dash here, dash there.' Montgomerie poured boiling water into the mug and added milk.

'With a little help from British Telecom, right enough.' Abernethy leaned forward and picked up his ballpoint. 'Phoned the outlet from the factory, they remembered the batch, said they'd look up their records and find out to whom it was sold. I drove from Grangemouth back to Glasgow and went to the outlet on Queen Street, near the station. The manager recalled the batch, couldn't give it away, except to a soccer club who wanted red carpeting and red paint around their home-team changing and rest rooms. Apparently, they'd talked to a psychologist who said that bright red induces aggression, the theory being that if you expose your players to brilliant red and play stirring martial music to them through the loudspeakers before a match, they'll want to go out and annihilate the opposition. The visiting-team rooms, by contrast, were being painted a soft shade of lilac and decorated with prints of the Impressionists and they were being treated to soft, soothing music before a match so once they got on to the pitch all they'd want to do was pick flowers.'

Montgomerie laughed.

'I kid you not, this soccer team was doing just that. The other purchase was a lady called Carberrie, the manager

200

remembered her because she said the colour would match her hair. The rest of the batch they sent back to the factory. It was such a loud colour that fortunately for them, they'd accepted it on a sale-or-return basis.'

'Carberrie. Now that *is* a name that crops up from time to time.'

'It's more than that now. Fibre from this carpet was found upon the person of the deceased. It means Ronnie Grenn was shot in the changing rooms at Muirhead Athletic or Mary Carberrie's front room.'

'Fabian will be impressed. You may even score a point of approval, not easily given.'

Abernethy couldn't fail to notice the sourness and cynicism underlying Montgomerie's voice, but he didn't comment. Instead he asked Montgomerie if he knew where Fabian Donoghue was and Montgomerie, settling in his chair, told him about Oak Cottage and the garden and the hole in the ground at the bottom of the garden and what lay therein.

'He won't be back for a wee while then?'

'If at all today. He'll be going with the body to the GRI, representing the police at the postmortem. Something he usually delegates but he'll be doing this himself.'

'Shall we pull Mary Carberrie?'

'No.'

'We've got grounds enough, her name keeps cropping up . . . her address, it's just round the corner from where the body was found . . . she visited the deceased in prison . . . what more do you want? I mean, can't see a weedy little guy like Ronnie Grenn setting foot inside a soccer club's changing area, so Athletico Muirhead is out of the game.'

'No.' Montgomerie's jaw set hard. 'I like your enthusiasm, but no. No, no, no, no. Not yet. We don't do anything without clearing it with Fabian. That's the rule. I mean, you're still new, Tony, control your zeal.'

'Softly, softly catchee monkey, is it?'

'In a word, yes. That's how Fabian works. He moves in on his prey by stalking in ever-decreasing circles, never moving until he's sure of his footing. Before they know it, he's standing over them licking his paws. He knows the value of taking his time.'

'I suppose . . .' Abernethy cleaned the end of his ballpoint.

'It's not like she's a multiple murderer that could strike at any time, or has a kidnap victim that puts us under time pressure . . .'

'Now you're thinking like a seasoned cop. I know what it's like . . . when I was new in CID I found the waiting game a bogey too, but then I came to see the sense in it. So where does Mary Carberrie live?'

'Balcarres Avenue. That's less than a hop and a skip from where the body was found, like I said.'

'That's true enough. The other point is that we know other people are involved. If you read the file, three people were seen dumping the body, you remember some confusion over time because the clocks went back an hour this week . . . and Fabian's recording indicates the kidnap of "Annie" Oakley was thought by the Lothian boys to have a feel of three culprits about it. So it's the Carberrie female and two sidekicks. If we pull Carberrie, we could tip the others off. With money on this scale you could be talking false passports and overseas accounts. So we don't want to do that.'

'Softly, softly.'

'Scots Guards.'

'Good enough.' King smiled.

'Fifteen years with the colours, left as a colour sergeant. That was ten years ago, this club had just opened then. They wanted a steward who could run things and also knew a little about guns. I applied, they must have thought I fitted the bill.'

'You like guns?'

'I respect them. There's a difference, and you've actually put your finger on it. Club members have respect for guns. They'll tell you a gun is as safe as the person who's holding it, they'll tell you that more people are killed by cars in a month than are killed in a year by handguns. They'll tell you that if some bampot with murder on his mind can't get hold of a gun he'll use something else.'

'And you, what do you say? Off the record.'

'I've got to work here, Mr King.'

'Off the record. For my interest only.'

'I don't like civilians having hold of guns. Allow the farmer his shotgun, but that's it, that's as far as it goes.

After that, only the military and the special section of the police . . .'

'Tactical Firearms Unit.'

'That's what it's called? Well, only them. You know, there's less control of live rounds in civilian gun clubs than in the army. Did you know that?'

'I didn't.'

'Not so much in total war, but in policing engagements like Northern Ireland, each squaddie has to record every round discharged, what location, what time, what direction. In this club, members buy live rounds on production of a certificate and bang them off here at the club, but who's counting? Nobody. Britain hasn't got a gun culture, yet, and the only reason for that is the continued level of responsible behaviour of gun enthusiasts. But there's no built-in safeguard to protect the public, should the gun enthusiasts turn irresponsible overnight, not necessarily by shooting people but by allowing their guns and ammunition to fall into the wrong hands. Selling them for cash in the car park of a pub one night and reporting the firearm as stolen. The fact that they all say that they wouldn't do that is no safeguard. Not in my book.'

'Not in mine, either, Mr McGuire, not in mine either.'

McGuire, erect even when seated, twirled his moustache and awaited the next question. Behind him on his office wall hung a print of Landseer's 'Monarch of the Glen'.

'So,' King brought the interview back in the tracks, 'Westwater, Mooney and Carberrie . . .'

'All three are members here, as you believed. Long-standing members. Joined at different times, but met each other here, and became a gang of three. I confess I don't care for any of them but like finds like, as they say.'

'Tell me about them.'

'As a group or as individuals?'

King resisted the urge to say 'you choose' because he felt that McGuire, having been drilled to unquestioning obedience in the Scots Guards, would be uncomfortable about making such a decision, that he would rather be told how to address the question. 'As a group, then as individuals.'

'Mr Westwater and Mrs Mooney are partners. They don't live together, not according to the register of members, but they have "a thing" going. Mary Carberrie hangs on to them. I get the impression that she's tolerated by them rather than being welcomed, if you see what I mean.'

'I think I do. It ties in with what else has been said about Mary Carberrie. Not a woman who enjoys universal popularity, it would seem.'

'Aye, well, that's a mild way of putting it. You know, I could never work out the relationship between Margaret Mooney and Mary Carberrie.'

'Oh?'

'Well, they gossiped with each other something dreadful. But the *things* they'd say about each other, even to me who's not supposed to socialize with the members. You see, it was like this, if you'd talk to Margaret Mooney you'd get the impression from her that Mary Carberrie was the lowest of all crawling things, and if you talked to Mary Carberrie you'd get the impression that Margaret Mooney was the lowest of all crawling things, yet if you were to catch sight of them when they were together you'd see them chatting away to each other like a couple of inseparable mates. It's dangerous to be part of that, you know, so when Margaret Mooney came up to me in the refectory with a mug of coffee in her hand and sat down next to me and began complaining about someone who said something and said, "You know who I mean, don't you?" I just hid behind my copy of the *Glasgow Herald* and then she shut up.'

'Sensible of you.'

'The only thing to do, Mr King. Play safe.'

'I, the police, have yet to have the pleasure of meeting them. Over and above the fact that they're coming across as three deeply unpleasant individuals, Carberrie especially, what else explains their friendship, in your view?'

'Money. They are three very greedy individuals, Mr King. Margaret Mooney and Mary Carberrie have a taste for female finery that I can't see how they can afford, and Gary Westwater is always talking very loudly about money-making plans he's got. They're all "self-employed", according to the registry.'

'Which of course covers a multitude of sins.'

'But they're not very employed, self or otherwise. There are self-employed members who rarely get the time to come to the club, but Westwater, Mooney and Carberrie are near-daily visitors; Mary Carberrie in particular, though I confess, having said that, I haven't seen any of them all week, not since last Friday, a week ago tomorrow. Been quite quiet.' McGuire smiled. His eyes, King thought, had a sincerity about them, as if he were a man who was a 'man's man', or a 'good bloke'. 'Aye, we all know when Mary Carberrie's in the club, that voice, can't talk without shouting, you know yon way. Confess I don't think that I have ever met a woman who talked so much but said so little. And that she enjoys small-bore shooting . . . how appropriate.'

'I cared little for him.' Buchanan sat forward at his desk, grey suit, silk shirt. Like Pulleyne, King noted, he was also an ex-rugby player by the photograph on the wall behind him. He had a round face, small mouth, thin lips, white hair, pink eyes, verging on, but not quite, albino. King found him to have an aggressive manner, touchy, ready to explode at the slightest provocation; King found himself to be walking on glass. 'I'm pleased he's gone, left this company in a mess.'

'His brother, half-brother, didn't seem to think so.'

'His brother, half-brother, is the reason why you're in my office talking to me, not him. You want an honest measure of the man. Right?'

'Right.'

'His brother, half-brother, has about him a naivety I find chilling, especially for a businessman. Because of Gary Westwater, we are now suffering from a surfeit of proposals. Which may sound a pleasant state of affairs, but we are underfunded, the premiums are too low and our proposal agreements are far too generous, in the clients' favour, of course.'

'Of course.'

'Otherwise I wouldn't be a worried man. Ultimately the insurance industry is in the hands of the Almighty, and every company depends on not having to have all its customers registering claims at the same time. But even allowing for that, our premiums have been stupidly, criminally low, and our agreements, if we have to meet them, are so stupidly, criminally generous that we couldn't meet ten per cent of our claims in full if we had to do so. What that idiot Westwater

205

did, compounded by the lunacy of his stepbrother in settling the Bath Street claim, was to declare this company as a target for fraudulent claimants. A source of easy money. I bet you haven't been told about all the claims we've been fielding in the last few years, have you?'

'No . . .'

'Well, that's the other side of this coin that John Pulleyne is probably not so keen to talk about. Yes, we've had plenty of proposals, Mr King, but we've had plenty of claims too. You want money for a new motor, no problem, buy a wreck, overinsure it with this company then roll it off a cliff, and we'll pay out. We won't even investigate it. Such is our reputation.'

'You're angry.'

'Oh, I'm pleased it shows. I just wish it would register with that idiot Pulleyne. All he sees is a halo around Westwater's head and nothing else, all he says is, "We've got Gary to thank for all this," and I say to myself, "Yes, I couldn't agree more. We have got Gary to thank for all this." We would disagree about what exactly "all this" is. To Pulleyne it's coffers full of gold and silver, for me it's a financial catastrophe waiting to happen. I can't get out easily, I'm in too deep; as a director, my personal finances are tied up with the company. All I can try to do, me and the other directors, is to turn this ship around before it falls over the edge of the world. And it's all down to that spineless, self-serving, womanizing careerist Westwater.'

'What do you know about him?'

'He pulled this company into a pit it'll probably never get out of and then he got suddenly rich, him and his yellow Jaguar, and sold up and left. We were told that the police had been asking questions, do we assume . . . ?'

King held up his hand. 'Sorry, as I said to Mr Pulleyne on Tuesday, you cannot assume anything.'

'Fair enough.' Buchanan smiled. King found it hard to age him. Fifties, he thought. And that, he also thought, may well explain why the man was remaining with Glasgow and Trossachs Insurance Company, as much as does his personal financial stake in the organization; at his age he had little working-life time left to go elsewhere. Not in these days of downsizing of companies and voluntary downshifting of stressed-out executives moving from the city to the croft.

'But it's worth cooperating, perhaps. What do you know about his personal life?'

'Large house in Busby. Has a thing about a woman, Margaret somebody, who still has traces of Rubensesque beauty, of whom I know little. He's a bachelor, he and Margaret have a relationship but have not merged their houses. It apparently works a lot better if they live separately, but see each other frequently. She's got money by her trappings but I don't know where it comes from, but this is information that's years out of date, you understand. I haven't seen Westwater since he left the company.'

'I appreciate that, Mr Buchanan, but the fact is that any information is good information.'

'He has a strange friend, at least he had when I knew him, a woman, Mary somebody.'

'Carberrie?'

'That' – Buchanan held up a finger – 'was the name. I confess I only met her the once and I do not want to repeat the experience. Odious creature, but she and Gary Westwater knew each other and I suspect may briefly have "known" each other in the biblical sense at some point in their personal histories. She had a house in the West End, a new-build bungalow, well appointed though a trifle garish, brilliant-red carpet in the living room.'

'You don't say?'

'Oh, I do say, the memory of it still hurts my eyes. Gary Westwater and I were on our way back from a business meeting in Perth, my home town, incidentally, and on our return to Glasgow we detoured to the West End so he could drop off a parcel, he intended only to hand it over at the door but we were offered tea and accepted.'

'And you encountered the red carpet?'

'And also the knowing look between the Carberrie female and Westwater, which made me think that there had been something between them, and that there was still a spark, despite the fact that Margaret was on the scene by then. There was also a wee guy in the house who seemed to run around doing Mary Carberrie's least bidding with a twinkle in his eye, though I felt that she was embarrassed by him.'

'Do you remember his name?'

'Short name, three letters, that sort of name, one syllable. Tom . . . Bill . . .'

'Ron?'

'Could be, he was making himself useful, answered the door, made the tea for us. Carberrie never left her seat and really only became animated when she tore open the parcel that Westwater had given her and the money came out.'

'Money?'

'Not a lot, pound coins, loose change, five- and one-pound notes . . . you know, I thought I felt Westwater stiffen with anger as she did that, as if she'd forgotten I was there and couldn't wait to get her paws on the money. Then she tossed the bag to Ron the eager beaver, who trotted out of the room with it. Westwater said, "It's all there, I counted it," but there was tension in the room and the Carberrie woman looked uncomfortable. When we were driving away, Westwater said that was sub money for the gun club.'

'Did you believe him?'

'No. Darts teams in pubs pay their club subscriptions in notes and loose change. Gun enthusiasts pay their subscriptions by cheque. So I thought that there was something that they didn't want me to know about, but in itself it wasn't criminally suspicious. It was a comparatively small amount of money, about one hundred and fifty quid, in the context of the people and setting, it's not a large amount of the folding green stuff. But you know, there was something odd about his behaviour in Perth. It turned out that he had got the time of the meeting wrong, we were over an hour early and that wasn't like him. Stickler for timekeeping, was Westwater. Anyway, he was keen to separate for an hour and rendezvous at the bank, where we were to see the manager, so we did. I walked around the streets, but Perth being such a small place, I saw Westwater scurrying about. I watched him, followed him for a wee while and I kid you not, if he went into one newsagent he went into six. Each time he came out of a newsagent's he was carrying a newspaper and each time he walked out of the shop he walked straight to the nearest wastebin and tossed the paper in the bin and went off at a rate of knots, and dived in and then out of another newsagent's and repeated the sketch. That was about six or seven years ago. Funny though, that behaviour.'

'Probably not as funny as you think, Mr Buchanan.' King stood. 'Thanks for your time.'

The body of Ann 'Annie' Oakley lay on the stainless-steel table in the pathology laboratory in the basement of the Glasgow Royal Infirmary. It lay on its side in a near-foetal position, the soil had been carefully scraped away, a gold bracelet had been removed from her wrist, as had a watch on the reverse of which, after it had been cleansed with industrial alcohol, was the clearly visible inscription, *'To Ann, from her mother on her eighteenth birthday'*.

'I understand that you believe you know the identity of this lady?' Reynolds addressed Donoghue, but did not take his eyes from the skull of the deceased as he slowly sifted through the hair, still identifiable as blonde.

'We do, sir. "Annie" Oakley. You may recall she was abducted about eight years ago?'

'Edinburgh family, used-car dealers.'

'That's the one, sir.'

'Yes, I remember it well. Didn't give the police anything to go on, nothing they could follow up.'

'Again, yes.'

'Well, if you want me to do so, I'm happy to remove the lower jaw so that her lower teeth can be checked against her dental records, because, as always, the mouth is a goldmine of information, but I can confirm that the deceased is human female, natural blonde, as you see. In life she would have stood . . .' Reynolds took a tape measure and measured the length of the spine of the deceased. 'As a rule of thumb, the height of the deceased can be approximated by measuring the spine and other specific long bones, but we must be aware that in death the skeleton can be as much as one inch shorter than the same skeleton in life, due to postmortem shrinkage of the cartilages which tend to pull the bones together.'

'I see.'

'The spine is believed to be thirty-five per cent the length of a person's full height. The spine of the deceased is twenty-two and a half inches in length. How's your arithmetic, Mr Donoghue?'

'Poor.'

'Yours, Mr Millard?'

Millard, the mortuary assistant with slicked-back hair and white smock, shook his head but continued to stare with fascination, which unnerved Donoghue, at the skeletal remains on the stainless-steel table.

'Five feet four inches,' Reynolds announced triumphantly. 'And I did that in my head. The humerus, about twenty per cent of the height in life' – Reynolds stretched the tape measure along the arm of the deceased – 'is twelve, nearly thirteen inches. Going to need a calculator soon . . . twenty per cent . . . sixty-three to four inches, five feet four or five or six . . . long arms are not unknown, and tend to be prized as a sign of grace among women, as are long legs . . . the tibia is twenty-two per cent of the subject's height in life, and here, the tibia I measure at . . . fourteen inches . . . which . . . come on, think, Reynolds, boy . . . five feet five inches . . . perhaps less . . . the femur . . . the thigh bone, is normally twenty-seven per cent of the deceased's total height and here the observed length is . . . seventeen and a half inches . . . You don't mind if I adhere to the imperial measurements, Mr Donoghue?'

'Makes me feel at home, sir.' Donoghue, who had been doing some mental arithmetic, and as such, felt that he had used part of his brain which he hadn't used since primary school in Possilpark, offered, 'Five feet four inches, sir.'

'So, in life the deceased would have been about five feet four or five inches and all in proportion. No overly long arms or very short legs. The leather belt round her waist was looped at twenty-five inches . . . the skull shows no disfigurement, the sutures are not knitted fully so she was a young adult when she died. I don't think that she would have been at all displeased with her appearance. Certainly, her figure would have been the envy of many women. The blonde hair means she was Caucasian.'

'All that fits with the known appearance of Miss Oakley, sir. I can also allow the parents to view the watch and bracelet and the belt, it has a very distinct brass buckle. If they can identify them . . .' Donoghue cleared his throat as the scent of the disinfectant of the pathology laboratory caused him irritation. 'That may be sufficient to determine identification to the satisfaction of the court.'

'I confess I've known the High Court to settle for less. I can also confirm that the rate of decomposition would be appropriate to the length of time that her body had been buried in the damp soil in which it was found. If she was buried at about the time she was abducted. This' – Reynolds extended two open palms towards the corpse – 'is a classic, ten years buried in wet soil, plus or minus three years. She was not kept alive for a long period after she was abducted.'

'That may be of some comfort to her parents, sir.'

'Well, if I can offer more comfort I can note the presence of clothing and the lack of semen deposits, which would be evident . . . semen is very hardy stuff. I once conducted a PM on a young woman who had been raped and strangled and whose body had remained undetected for years, so that it was skeletal when found. The semen was still visible to the naked eye, resting on the bone of the lower vertebrae. You see, the body tissue had decomposed but the semen had retained its chemical integrity, and had fallen slowly due to gravity, until it had come to rest on the bones of the vertebrae. It really is amazing stuff, but I can confirm that it is absent in this case. I would say that the presence of clothing and lack of semen deposits probably indicate that whatever else may have happened to Miss Oakley, sexual violation was not one of them. That may be another crumb of comfort.'

'I'll let the Oakleys know that, sir.'

The tall, silver-haired pathologist nodded and then said, 'As was her cause of death.'

'Oh?'

'If we are satisfied that this is the body of "Annie" Oakley, then it remains only for us, for myself in particular, to identify the cause of death if I can. And I think I can. Would you care to look at this?'

Donoghue padded silently across the thick linoleum and stood next to Reynolds.

'I'll shave the skull. Mr Millard, could you prepare a razor, please . . . Here.' Reynolds parted the remnants of hair just above the left ear.

'Gunshot.'

'Small calibre. I'd say a point-twenty-two. But it's oddly a little elongated. Two bullets, one to do the job and one when she was lying still, probably deceased, fired into the same hole to make sure. That would be my guess. Had we discovered her body shortly after these shots were fired and before she was buried, there would be significant traces of gunpowder around this entrance wound. It's a clean wound, so it's definitely a bullet hole rather than the point of an ice pick, for example . . . and' – Reynolds bent down and looked up at the underside of the skull, parting the hair with his hands encased in surgical gloves – 'no exit wounds. The bullet or bullets are still in there.' Reynolds stood. 'I'll extract the brain, or what remains of it after this length of time, then we'll slice it thinly. At some point we'll come across a bullet or two, or three. I can't do that today, the equipment I need is booked for teaching purposes this afternoon. First thing tomorrow soon enough?'

'I don't think there's any time pressure now; whenever you can do it would suit.' Donoghue held eye contact with Reynolds. 'We've now got enough to start serving a warrant or two, or three.'

'As you wish.'

'Can I sign for the watch, bracelet and belt buckle? I'd like to take them to Edinburgh. I'll do this myself.'

Donoghue left the GRI and drove the short distance to Charing Cross and P Division Police Station, forging his Rover through the beginning of the rush-hour traffic. He went to his office, hung up his hat and coat and went to the DCs' room. There he found Abernethy, King and Montgomerie. Half sitting on a desk, he cradled the offered mug of coffee and listened.

He listened whilst Abernethy told him about the carpet fibres being identical as coming from a batch which was sold to only two customers, one a football club and the other to Mary Carberrie.

He listened whilst King told him about Westwater, Carberrie and Mooney being known to be a group of three by members of the gun club where they met. He listened whilst King told him about Westwater arriving in Perth needlessly early and being seen on what by all accounts was a money-laundering venture, and soon after handing Mary Carberrie a bag full of notes and loose change, and yes, there was a mention of a violently red carpet at Mary Carberrie's house, and a small guy running around for her.

Then Donoghue related the postmortem findings and showed the CID officers the contents of the productions bag he had brought with him from the GRI. 'I'm driving to the Oakleys' house now. I'll show them these. I think they'll ID them. Even if they don't, I think it's time to talk to Mr Westwater and his two lady friends. We'll do that tomorrow morning.'

'A seven o'clock knock, sir?' King asked.

'No, I don't think so. They're apparently very leisured people. They'll still be at home at nine a.m. So we'll do it then. King and Montgomerie, I want you to come in for this. I know you're on the back shift this week, but it's a case of needs must.'

'Very good, sir.' King nodded.

Montgomerie, Donoghue noted, remained mute.

'I'd like warrants drawn up this evening. You can do that, Montgomerie.'

'Sir.'

'So they're in respect of Gary Westwater, Margaret Mooney and Mary Carberrie, addresses in the file, arrest in connection with the murder of Ronnie Grenn on . . . what date was Monday?'

'Twenty-fourth of October, sir.'

'Right, on or about that date . . . don't mention Ann Oakley or the Bath Street insurance scam. We'll add those to the charge sheet in due course. We've got enough forensics to convict, but a cough would be nice. We also want search warrants for the addresses of each arrestee. That's you as well, Montgomerie.'

'Sir.'

'We'll talk about the search tomorrow, but we're looking specifically for a point-twenty-two firearm. With luck, Dr Reynolds may be able to provide bullets with striations to match a barrel signature. So we all know what's happening?'

'Yes, sir.'

'In here at eight-thirty a.m. sharp. Somebody tell the uniformed branch.'

'I'll do that, sir.'

'Good man, King.'

*   *   *

'Latched on to me at the gun club.'

'Latched?'

'Women do, found out who I was, what I was worth and got hold of my shirt-tail.'

'That's what I like about you, modest in the extreme.'

'Thank you.' The man inclined his head and smiled. 'But she was useful. See her, dangle a pound note on a stick in front of her eyes and it's like dangling a carrot in front of a donkey.'

'So I noticed.' The woman paused. 'I want to know . . . before I came on the scene . . . did you and her ever . . .'

'No. She came on really strong, but no . . . I mean, those teeth.'

'She frightened of dentists?'

'I don't think so. She just refuses to see them. She's convinced of her own beauty.'

There was a lull in the conversation. Above the house an aircraft droned in a descent towards the airport.

'Do you think they'll come tonight?'

'Probably. I'm going to stay up. Last night of freedom. I want to savour it.'

'You're calm.'

'Calm and modest.'

'Annoyingly so.'

'What can I do? What can we do? If I could hide I would. But I'm not going to run.'

'You're looking at two life sentences.'

'Don't remind me.'

'A man in his fifties going down for the first time.'

'I don't need reminding.'

'Coming from this lifestyle.'

'I told you.'

'You didn't control her. If you had controlled her . . .'

'If, if, if . . . forget "if".'

'You planned it all, from day one.'

'As soon as I met Oakley. It all came together. I had you, I had her and I had a phase-one victim.'

'A phase-one victim?'

'To take the operation to phase two. Forward planning. The secret of good business.'

'What other direction can you plan in? Can hardly plan backwards.'

But the man just smiled. 'It worked. We cleaned up. Four million pounds. About.'

'There is one thing you could do. I'd do it. If I were you I'd do it. You're too spineless to do it without a stiffener. But given the alternative, if they came tomorrow. I'll stay up with you.'

'What's that?'

'Cried like an infant.' Donoghue gazed into the hissing flames of the gas fire. 'I get the impression that he hadn't done that . . . not ever, not really, it's so important to do that.'

'God help us if we should ever have to go through that.' Mrs Donoghue glanced to the door of the living room, beyond which, down the corridor, their children were sleeping.

'Indeed, but that's probably sufficient for the court to deem positive identification. If not her dental records will be needed for that. Easy enough to get hold of those, though.'

'Poor souls . . . where do they live?'

'Barnton Avenue, rambling mansion of a house, they let it go when their daughter was abducted, it's a bit ramshackle and overgrown now, but it could be rescued.'

'The Barntons . . .'

'Well, you'll not kidnap a lassie from the Pilton and expect her parents to come up with a million pounds.'

'True enough.'

'He's a second-hand car dealer. Not a way I'd like to make a living, even if it does mean a house in Barnton Avenue.'

'Happy in our wee bungalow in Craiglockhart, eh?'

'Aye . . . well, that's something I wanted to talk to you about.'

'Oh . . . Fabian, what's wrong?'

'It's about yesterday morning, you remember when I was late leaving because I had a meeting in Edinburgh . . . I hung around a bit? I don't know if you were aware of it but you were very difficult to be with . . . I found you difficult. Very tetchy. Later I had a chat with Chief Super Findlater and he told me that he and his wife are going on pre-retirement courses . . . apparently a wife who has been used to having the house to herself for the whole working day may find it difficult to suddenly have hubby around the place all the time. I was wondering if that's what annoyed you, I wasn't out of the way quickly enough?' He saw his wife put her hand to her head. He continued, 'I mean, I'm not due to retire, but equally I'm nearer the end of my working life than the beginning and if we've got a problem here . . . and it is my house as well . . .'

'Oh, Fabian.' She crossed the carpet and sat next to him, leaning against him, taking his hand in both of hers. 'That's it . . . that's it. I'm so sorry . . . I knew I was irritated yesterday but I couldn't see why, there seemed to be no reason . . . but that's it.'

He put his arm round her and held her and said that a trouble identified was half solved. That evening they went to their bedroom much, much earlier than was usual and they were as passionate as when they were newly lovers.

FRIDAY

7

Mean spirited.

It was the only way to describe it.

Mean beyond meanness.

Donoghue sat at his desk. His jaw was clenched. He held a pencil in his hands and snapped it in two.

He flung the two bits of pencil into the wastebin beside his chair.

Mean. The meanness of the man. He thought he knew Findlater. He didn't think Findlater would do such a thing.

Just shows, he thought, just shows. Just goes to show how you can work with a guy for years and think you know him and then you find out that you don't. You find out you don't know him at all. A man's personality is a loch, and each man has a kraken hidden in his depths, so Donoghue believed; with some their kraken never surfaces, in others it surfaces rarely and offers a fleeting glimpse of something dark within, in yet others it's always there, on the surface. So now he had seen Findlater's kraken.

Donoghue had arrived at 8.00 a.m. He had signed in after exchanging pleasantries with the uniform-bar duty constable and had then gone up to the CID corridor. He had turned to walk to his office and had seen Ray Sussock walk out of Findlater's office, clearly crestfallen, and walk into his own room.

Donoghue had realized that Findlater must have left a note for Sussock to see him. But Sussock was on the graveyard shift. He is supposed to finish at 06.00. Findlater had asked him to wait on for two hours so he could speak to him. The only thing that Findlater could have to say to Ray Sussock that would make him leave the office looking so crestfallen, was to tell him that he'd fouled up the Bath Street burglary and fire investigation four years ago.

Findlater did that. Not only had he kept Ray Sussock back for two hours to tell him that, but he'd given him that to take into retirement with him. Findlater himself had not long to go before he could devote his days to fly fishing and caring for his giant plant. He, of all people, should be aware that the last thing anybody wants to do is to go into retirement feeling gauche, knowing regret for a monumental error.

So Chief Super Findlater, late of Elgin, now of the city of Glasgow, has a kraken. And what a nasty piece of work it is.

Donoghue stood. He went to Ray Sussock's room and found him clambering into a battered raincoat with a felt trilby resting unevenly on his head. 'Ray.'

'Sir?'

'Ray, I know you're tired, but we're going to arrest Carberrie, Westwater and Mooney this morning. We'll be quizzing them about the abduction and murder of "Annie" Oakley and the insurance claim for the Bath Street fire . . . there's no compulsion, Ray, please feel free to get off if you want, but I thought you might want to be in at the end seeing as you're . . .'

'You're giving me a chance to get it right, are you, sir?'

'Ray, you know I don't mean that, but it would round things off neatly for you. Would it not?'

Ray Sussock smiled. Donoghue knew it was a forced smile. He knew that inside Ray Sussock must be hurting very badly. Very badly indeed.

'Yes.' Sussock peeled off his raincoat and took his hat from his head and Donoghue again saw the tiredness in the man's face and eyes. If ever a man deserved his retirement it was Ray Sussock. 'Yes, thanks, sir. I'd like that.'

'Good. Would you like to come along to the CID room? You can go with young Abernethy to pull Westwater. I think that's the way to play it. Montgomerie can use his charms on Margaret Mooney and Richard King can fondle the collar of the Carberrie woman. Bring them in, put them in separate rooms and quiz them. With any luck they'll cough and implicate each other. Arrest them in connection with the murder of Ronnie Grenn in the first instance, I think, don't you?'

'Whatever you think, sir.'

'No, Ray, it's whatever you think as well. But I think we keep our suspicions about the Bath Street insurance scam and "Annie" Oakley's abduction up our sleeve. We'll do it that way. Pull them for the murder of Ronnie Grenn.'

Montgomerie had it easy that day. Very easy. He drove out to Busby with a police patrol vehicle in which two uniformed officers, one male, one female, followed him. He drove to Muckhart Avenue and to the house of Mooney. The house itself proved to be well set, stone built, well-tended gardens, he thought, he with a 'garden' which comprised a money plant in his kitchen. Before he knocked on the door he knew that there would be no one at home. An empty house is not just silent with no discernible movement, it also has a sense of emptiness. Montgomerie, followed by the two uniformed officers, crunched up the gravel drive and rang the doorbell, which made a loud but conventional 'ding-dong', echoing deeply within the villa. He turned and smiled at the two constables. 'This one's a bum steer.' He turned and rang the bell again for good measure, and then turned and retraced his steps to the car. Such 'visits' suited him: he would return to P Division Police Station and record his entry into the file: *09.15, attended house of Mooney. No response to loud ringing of doorbell.*

The uniformed officers left the locus to attend to normal policing and Montgomerie drove back to the city of Glasgow. He pondered the week. He pondered that, when an undergraduate at Edinburgh, he well recalled seeing 'Annie' Oakley disporting herself up and down Princes Street as if without a care, yet the terror of abduction and certain murder was just weeks, if not days, away. He pondered that he may well have been one of the last people to see her alive, yet he was present when the final film of unconsolidated soil was scraped from her grinning skull. Put that one in your box of coincidences. He pondered the pleasant drive down to the Southern Uplands to Traquair Brae Open Prison, the sights glimpsed from his car window, the tall, thin castle by a river, the large field, the two galloping horses in an autumn landscape. He pondered Jennifer returning. Something there, he thought, something really there. He thought perhaps that

221

Richard King and Fabian Donoghue and others who seemed to enjoy settled marriages may have something after all. He had noticed it, a sense of contentment and a slightly fuller look about the face which comes over a man when he settles with a good woman. He was twenty-seven. High time really. High time.

In Edinburgh. In a house in Barnton Avenue a man and a woman sat and spoke with a priest. When the priest had left the house the man went round the house and opened curtains that had not been opened for eight years. In one room at the rear of the house he and his wife stood arm in arm, pondering their garden.

The man said, 'We really must do something about that garden.'

The woman said 'Aye . . . we'll make a start as soon as she's laid to rest.'

Richard King too had an easy time of it. He too attended a house in the company of two uniformed officers. He went to the house of Carberrie, Balcarres Avenue, G12. It was a new-build bungalow. It had a wrought-iron knocker, old of style but modern of manufacture, and very fashionable. He rapped it twice. He brought forth the response of a figure seen through the opaque glass of the front door bustling down the corridor as if fuming with anger, ready to give a row to whoever was banging on her front door at the unearthly hour of 09.15. The door was flung wide and Mary Carberrie revealed herself to be a squat, overweight woman who had squeezed into a dressing gown about three sizes too small, guessed King, whose faded red hair was everywhere and who paled when she saw the uniformed officers standing behind King. Behind her in the living room, King glimpsed a swathe of blue and as he did so he smelled the unmistakable smell of newly laid carpet. 'Mary Carberrie?'

'Yes.'

'We'd like you to accompany us to the police station. We have to question you about the murder of Ronald Grenn earlier this week.'

Mary Carberrie's jaw dropped, revealing a set of blackened, decaying teeth. 'How did you know it was me?'

'Didn't really,' King spoke softly. 'Not until you said that. But you're now under arrest.'

Ray Sussock and Tony Abernethy also went to Busby, to the house of Westwater on Honeycomb Drive.

The house was a tall, three-storey building of stone which stood in its own grounds and was clearly older than the suburban development which surrounded it. An ancient hunting lodge, thought Sussock, fighting sleep. Abernethy, alert and fresh after a night's rest, saw the date 1740 AD carved in stone above the door and was awed that the building pre-dated the 1745 Rebellion, Culloden and the flight of the Young Pretender to Skye and to the protection of Flora MacDonald. It was stone which pre-dated the legend and the myth of the romance, because there was little romance about starving, shivering Scotsmen being shredded by English grape and run through with English steel. But here was this house, built as a house, used as a house during the period of the Peninsular War and the Napoleonic Wars, the American Wars of 1776 and 1812, the great wars of the twentieth century, through the fight against disease, the development of manned flight, the conquest of space . . . Sussock's sharp rap of the doorbell brought Abernethy's mind sharply back to the matter in hand. As did the yellow Jaguar parked in front of the house.

The door opened silently, swinging smoothly on huge hinges. A woman stood on the threshold. She had dark hair and would, thought Sussock, have been attractive in her youth. She wore a long skirt and a blouse and a cardigan. She looked solemnly at the officers and slowly nodded her head.

'Police,' said Sussock.

'I know,' she said, spoken softly with only the faintest trace of a Scottish accent. 'I've been expecting you. Tell you the truth, I'm really not sorry you've come. I'm Margaret Mooney.'

The officers relaxed. This would not perhaps be so difficult. 'Is Mr Westwater in? We need to talk to both yourself and him.'

'Please step this way.'

Abernethy and Sussock followed the woman into the

gloom of the hallway and paused while she shut the heavy old door. She took the officers into a drawing room, expansive, thought the two men, but oddly low, with a heavily beamed ceiling and small windows. A log fire crackled in the grate and finished the scene. A man sat in a large, high-backed fire chair by the fire. He seemed tall and thin with a craggy face. He looked silently at the officer.

'Mr Westwater?'

'Yes.' He had stubble on his chin.

'Police.'

'Yes?' His eyes were bleary.

'We'd like you to accompany us to the police station in connection with the murder of Ronald Grenn four days ago.'

'I see.' But he made no move to stand. He had a soft, resigned voice.

Margaret Mooney walked silently across the floor and opened a drinks cabinet. 'Would you gentlemen care for a drink? Early, I know, but the circumstances are extenuating.' She poured herself a generous Scotch, swallowed it in one and then poured two more glasses, one of exceptional generosity, in the eye of Sussock, which she handed to Westwater. Abernethy, watching closely, saw an eye contact between them, a knowing look. Then she turned to Sussock and Abernethy. 'Can I offer you gentlemen a drink?' she repeated.

'No, thank you. We would like you to accompany us this instant.'

'It's the price of cooperation.' Margaret Mooney sank on to a leather-covered settee. 'Neither myself or Gary or Mary Carberrie will be having much of this where we're going. We won't wriggle out of it. So you can allow the condemned a last drink, even at' – she glanced at the clock above the fire – 'nine-fifteen in the forenoon.'

Westwater glared at her.

She held his glare and said, 'It's over, Gary, that's why I gave you the drink, such a large one. It's over.'

He nodded. 'Yes.' He drank the whisky. 'Yes . . . yes. Yes, it is.'

'So, do you want to know the story?' Margaret Mooney smiled at the officers. 'Do take a seat.'

'We'd rather stand. And we'll do all the talking at the police station.'

Westwater swallowed the whisky in deep draughts.

'I'd like to tell you.' She reached for a cigarette.

Westwater stood. 'I have to use the bathroom.' He swayed towards the door.

'Sarge' – Abernethy turned to Sussock – 'we shouldn't . . .'

Sussock closed his eyes and opened them. He shook his head. 'He won't be going anywhere.'

'It's not just that . . .'

But Sussock shook his head. Abernethy fell silent.

'So where do we start?' Margaret Mooney smiled. She lit the cigarette.

'At the police station,' growled Sussock, who felt the thin line go across his eyes as he always did when tired.

'Do you want to know only about Ronnie, poor, dear Ronnie, or shall we tell you about other things too?'

'Such as?'

'Insurance fraud, kidnap. How about things like that? The ones we got right, the ones we got wrong?'

Sussock gasped 'There's more . . . ?'

'Than?' Margaret Mooney drew deeply on the cigarette. 'More than what?'

'Sarge . . .' Abernethy appealed to Sussock. 'The guy, one of us had better . . .'

'No. Stay here. I want a witness for this. All right, we know about "Annie" Oakley, we know about the Bath Street insurance job. So what else is there?'

'It was Gary's idea. The whole lot. It started . . . oh, ten years ago. The guy called Oakley came to see Gary about insurance for his business, garages here and there all under different names so they look like one-off family-run businesses, but in fact they were part of a big corporation. Gary realized how wealthy Oakley was, and then he found out he doted on his daughter, the original spoiled little rich kid. Eighteen years old and she had everything she wanted, I mean, money no object. It was Gary's idea. Right from the beginning. His brain work. We abduct the girl, ransom her for a million, which we did, bundled her into a van we'd parked up in her parents' garden. If you ever see the size of the garden, you'd know how we did it. It wasn't a garden, it was the grounds of a palace. Anyway, we did it, took her to a cottage Gary had found in Kilsyth and kept her there, in a cupboard. It was Mary that came up with Ronnie Grenn. I don't know where she found him, but he doted on her. We put him in charge of Ann Oakley in the cottage, but we laid it on the line to him, no funny business. Well, Mary laid it on the line. He did what Mary told him. I mean, you should have seen it, when Mary Carberrie yelled "froggie", Ron Grenn would hop-hoppity-hop round the room.'

'Kind of you to ensure that she wasn't molested, since you murdered her anyway.'

Margaret Mooney paused. 'Gary did that. He didn't tell us he was going to do that but he'd been right so far, the way he got the money delivered so it couldn't be kept under surveillance . . . even if we had to stumble through a railway tunnel for the best part of half an hour. That was a close-run thing, all the police had to do was seal the tunnel, have men at either end and they would have had us cold but they didn't. Gary said that that was a chance we had to take. He'd planned it that the police had been stretched so thinly, that if they had officers available at all they probably only had enough to watch the area where the money had been thrown from the train, but even there they could only arrive after it had been thrown. There was a just sufficient time window to pick up the bags and hot-foot it into the tunnel and hope that they didn't seal the tunnel. That was the plan and it worked. So when he shot the girl . . . we didn't go for that but by then it was too late. But he'd planned that all along, I think, he'd told Mary to tell Ronnie to dig a deep hole in the bottom of the garden and burn refuse in it. The hole was needlessly deep for refuse.'

'We know now what it was for.'

'Aye . . .' She took a deep drag on the nail. 'So we laundered the money. Again, that was Gary's idea, it was tedious but foolproof. He kept the ransom money in a locked filing cabinet in his office at the insurance company. He gave it to us in batches of four hundred pounds. We laundered it by . . .'

'We know how you laundered it. We worked that out.'

'All those newspapers and magazines and cigarettes. Mind you, I read the glossies and smoked the fags. So we got something in return for the tedium.'

'Sarge . . .'

'No.'

'Then we decided to use the money for an insurance scam. Antique furniture and jewellery, we'd insure it in Mary's name with Gary's small insurance company. He'd force the pay-out, but we'd only be burning rubbish anyway, take the valuable stuff out and trickle it on to the market, so we'd get the money for the pay-out, we'd sell the gems and the good furniture, our one million pounds became four. Mind you, a bit better police work at the time of the insurance claim and we could have lost everything.'

Beside him Abernethy felt Sussock jolt, as if struck by a lance.

'But' – Margaret Mooney raised her glass – 'we were very lucky. We lucked in at the tunnel, we lucked in at the insurance scam. We've still got a lot of good furniture in a lock-up in Barrhead. I'll give you the address.'

'Now you've lucked out.'

'Thanks to Carberrie. I knew greed would be the end of her. We got Ronnie Grenn to agree to be implicated in the burglary of the antique furniture shop and let it be claimed that he set fire to it to cover his tracks. We said we'd see him all right when he came out. He was scared. He was in awe of Mary Carberrie and he was scared, he was a petty ned who was in too deep and he just wanted to go straight. We agreed to give him fifty thousand pounds in exchange for his cooperation.'

'Generous of you.'

'Fifty thousand pounds wouldn't keep me for a year, but it would keep Ronnie Grenn in clover for the rest of his life. So he cooperated. Mary visited him in the slammer, just to tell him the plan was still on, "Keep eating your porridge like a good boy and you'll collect."'

'And?'

'He was released, called on the only woman he'd ever loved and, far from keeping her promise, she laughed at him, told him she'd changed her mind, so she admitted to us, told him he wasn't to collect a penny. He threatened to go to the law, and so Carberrie, who fails to see beyond the end of her nose, did the only thing she thought fit and picked up a gun, which she keeps in defiance of the law and gun-club regulations,

227

and sent him to meet his Maker. Then she called Gary and me in a panic and we in a panic carried his body out of her house on to an area of open space and . . .'

'And we stand here.'

'And you stand here.' She poured another glass of whisky.

'That's sufficient, Mrs Mooney, we'd like you to make a statement to that effect, and more.'

'More?'

'You indicated other crimes?'

'Did I? Greed was our crime, greed was our motivation and greed was our undoing. If Carberrie had only given him his fifty thousand all this would never have come out. And you would be none the wiser.'

'So there are no other crimes?'

'Perhaps. I'll not be talking about them if there are.' She drained her glass. 'Well, thank you for listening to me. I should think Gary's finished in the bathroom now.'

'Finish— What do you mean?'

'Oh, I should think he's cut his throat.'

'For God's sake, Donoghue, it's not a mess, it's a complete disaster. What is it?'

'It's a complete disaster, sir.'

'And you of all people . . . what have we got? We've got the Carberrie woman pacing up and down her cage screaming her rights and convincing herself of her whiter-than-the-driven-snow innocence, despite what she said to Richard King; we've got the Mooney woman sleeping off a lot of alcohol, we've got a verbal confession from her which she could have made before a hundred officers and it still wouldn't be admissible because she was in the drink when she made it and she wasn't cautioned. We can link the carpet fibre on Ron Grenn's skull to the Carberrie house only by an invoice from the retail outlet, we can link Carberrie to Ron Grenn because she visited him once in prison, we can link Carberrie and Mooney and Westwater as a social group, we can link Westwater to the insurance scam through his company . . . It's enough, just enough for the Fiscal to proceed, I've known the Fiscal to proceed with less, but it's still not the neat package we'd have had if you had pulled

Westwater, he's the prime mover. Why did you send Ray Sussock? He was tired, he needed his rest, if you're tired you're less strong, you don't have the energy to say no to people . . .'

'I felt he needed it, sir.' Donoghue stood in front of Findlater's desk.

'He needed it like a hole in the head. And you of all people . . . your internal reports always have referred to your "healthy caution", "never moving forward unless you're sure of your footing", "knowing the value of taking your time", because of that observed behaviour you're earmarked for greater things in the police force and now we find that those still waters of caution contain an impetuous spirit which darts about uncontrollably from time to time.' Findlater paused. 'Probably serves to make you human.'

'I wouldn't have sent him out at all if you hadn't done what you did, sir.'

'And what was that?' Findlater's door was open. Both men raised their voices. Both men were aware and unconcerned that their row was echoing down the CID corridor, and courtesy of gossip and scuttlebutt, far beyond, into all corners of the building. Eventually.

'I saw him come out of your office this morning . . . doing what you did was spiteful and unfair, he didn't need to be kept back so you could burn his ear about fouling up the Bath Street fire investigation four years ago. He didn't need to go into his retirement with that, sir!'

'So you sent him out to recover the ground, as it were?'

'Frankly, yes, sir! Somebody had to give him something to make him feel good about himself. He hasn't long to go, he has to go into retirement on a positive note.'

Findlater buried his head in his hands then looked up at Donoghue. 'So not only do you act with the overzealous impulsive stupidity that we see in eighteen-year-old cadets, but you compound the felony by acting on an assumption. You, with your rank, your experience, you shouldering the responsibility that you shoulder . . . Fabian, what's happening, are you losing it?'

'I don't understand.' A slow dread began to dawn on Donoghue.

'You would if you'd have come to me picking a fight. I don't mind people doing that if it prevents catastrophes outside. Fabian, watch my lips . . . I didn't keep him back from going home on time, he was here anyway when I arrived, working over, his shift was running over . . . so I asked him to pop into my office so I could talk to him about the Bath Street fire, to tell him not to worry about it, not to take the guilt of lack of thoroughness about it into his retirement. All right, he could have wrapped it up then, but no harm was done because we're wrapping it up now and because the felons didn't commit any further crimes of a similar nature, that we know of, and that he might have prevented. I said that to him as one soon-to-retire officer to another.'

Fabian Donoghue bent forward as if kicked in the stomach by a mule. 'I didn't know . . .'

'And you also didn't know that he was working late because he'd spent the shift sorting a double murder in Riddrie. Man stabbed his girlfriend or wife or whatever when he found her in bed with another guy. Stabbed the guy too, ordinary kitchen knife, but it is Scotland's number one murder weapon and it was put to good effect in an apartment in Gala Street about four o'clock this morning. We've got the guy. He didn't get far, Ray Sussock saw to that. He made a better job of wrapping up his investigation than you did of yours . . .'

'He . . . he didn't say.'

'Why should he? He was probably too tired to protest, it can get you like that. If you remember the days when you worked shifts, you'll recall the feeling of succumbing to pressure that you would otherwise withstand. And he felt a loyalty to you, he knew that you were short-handed, he may have been receptive to your wanting to do him a favour and didn't want to throw your good intentions in your face, but whatever, he was sent to the house of Westwater with a relatively inexperienced CID officer who looked to him for leadership and he hadn't the energy to control the house, and what happened, happened.'

'I feel sick.'

'And well you might. God knows what Ray Sussock is feeling. If one of us has given him something he'll have to live with in his retirement, it's not me.'

*   *   *

Three weeks later Mary Carberrie occupied a cell in Cornton Vale, having been charged with kidnap, extortion, conspiracy to murder in respect of Ann 'Annie' Oakley and the actual murder of Ronald Grenn. On a daily basis she threw her food about and screamed her innocence. In an adjacent cell Margaret Mooney spent her days reading romance novels, having instructed her solicitor to plea-bargain with the office of the Procurator Fiscal. She would, she said, offer a full and complete confession in which she would fully implicate Mary Carberrie and the deceased Gary Westwater in the abduction and murder of 'Annie' Oakley, and the Bath Street fire insurance fraud and Mary Carberrie in the murder of Ronald Grenn. She would also fully cooperate with the efforts to recover what illegally obtained monies could be recovered.

In return she requested reduced charges and that mention be made of her cooperation in her pre-sentence report. Privately, with some confidence, and with good behaviour, she expected to walk in five years.

Three weeks later Fabian Donoghue called at the offices of the Glasgow and Trossachs Insurance Company. He wanted to interview Mr Pulleyne, just to clarify one or two details for the report he was to send to the Procurator Fiscal. He found the executives excessively drunk in the boardroom. Being overcommitted and underfunded, the company had gone into receivership, the directors were financially ruined. They had thought to a man that the only thing that they could do was to get very, very drunk. The receptionist, whom Donoghue found to be a self-possessed young woman, who was clearly capable of answering a torrent of abusive phone calls whilst simultaneously scanning the situations vacant pages of the *Glasgow Herald*, advised Donoghue that 'something had happened' to Mr Pulleyne. So far as she heard, he had been unable to believe that his half-brother could betray the company like he had done and he had disappeared. He was found wandering along the side of the motorway. He was now in Gartloch Hospital. She believed the diagnosis to be severe clinical depression.

Three weeks later there was still a distance between Donoghue and Ray Sussock, despite a four-cornered full and frank discussion about the matter among Donoghue, Sussock, Abernethy and Findlater, during which Donoghue offered his full and unreserved apology. Three weeks later Donoghue intuitively knew that the distance between himself and Ray Sussock would never properly be bridged.

Something had been lost.